# THE CELTIC CUPID TRILOGY

## IMOGENE NIX

Cover Art by Fantasia Frog

Editing by Sassie's Editing

ISBN: 9780648484141

A long time ago in some distant and dark past, I wrote Blame the Wine for a submission into an anthology. Sadly the house I wrote it for, didn't take the story so... I changed it, polished it and it became the first in a trilogy of fun stories I call the Celtic Cupid Trilogy.

Since first published, it has only ever been available as an ebook, but now I have the rights back and I'm in the position to do something exciting and new.

The books have all be re-worked, re-edited and in the case of Blame The Wine, the name of the hero has changed. Don't get me wrong though, the stories remain at the heart what they were before, only improved and now for the first time available in paperback!

It wouldn't have got to this point if I hadn't had a lot of support and assistance (and some judicious wine and chocolate!) along the way and I must thank my usual gang of Tara, Sassie, Suzi, Keri & Tracey.

Also my family Mark, Charlotte & Beth.

To the world's most awesome MIL June for whom I hope these bring both pleasure and magic.

Thanks also to my Makers & Fakers!

Without everyone this book wouldn't have come back and gone into print.

Imogene Nix
2019

# CONTENTS

Please note:

This book is written in US English with the exception of the word Mum for which I have chosen to use the Australian variation of Mom. *This is not a spelling error.*

*Diocail* is a minor deity of one of the Celtic belief systems and I've taken some liberties showing him as the son of Lugh and a brownie.

*Cailleach* is known as the "Old Hag" of certain pantheons in the Celtic belief systems and has many names, but also often takes on the mantle, "Mother of All". She's also considered to be both an ancestral and weather deity of uncertain temperament.

*Lugh* is a Celtic God of War and considered as an equivalent to the god, Mars. He is also typified as a king and saviour as well as a member of the *Tuatha De Danann* (the *Tribe of the Gods* who dwell in the Otherworld.)

*Senuna* is a little known deity who was worshipped prior to Roman Britain. Very little is known of her place in any of the beliefs systems (which suited the storyline), however a major find in 2002 uncovered a cache of 26 votives in a farm in Hertfordshire at a shrine dedicated to her worship.

While there is no actual Cupid as such in the Celtic belief systems, I've taken a poetic license with this concept, for which I hope you'll forgive me.

*Imogene Nix*
*2019*

# BLAME THE WINE

## CELTIC CUPID BOOK 1

*What will happen when two clueless, wannabe lovers get a little divine intervention?*

Cara is stuck. A job going nowhere and a hankering for the sexy gorgeous boss who doesn't even know she exists. Fate, in the guise of a temp position arrives... Where will it lead?
James is a geek. No other word could possibly describe him. He may be sexy and super brainy, but he's totally clueless with women and especially the sexy plus size Cara. But when his PA takes emergency leave before her wedding, the luscious Cara is the best applicant for the position. It's an opportunity he can't pass up.

# CHAPTER 1

The dusty, dingy little diner was full, even with its current state of cleanliness—or lack thereof. People from the surrounding offices didn't care about anything except the incredible, well-prepared food at a reasonable cost. They flooded in, like waves to the shore. As one tide left, another swept in.

"Honestly, Simone. I'm going to try getting his attention one more time. If that doesn't work, I'm out of there. I mean, how long can I keep trying?" Cara picked at the caramel tart she hadn't been able to resist with the cheap metal fork and flicked the blob of fresh cream that sat on top to the side of the plate.

"You've said that tons of times before. Besides, what are you going to do to get his attention? Hmm? Walk naked through the typing pool?" Simone bobbed the straw in her smoothie as she eyed her friend with a frown. "It's been what? Eighteen months since you saw him, and you've mooned over him from a distance ever since you met him. You need to move on, Cara. That is, unless there's something you haven't shared?"

The query was arch. Cara shivered even as she shook her head. "No."

Simone quirked an eyebrow, obviously unconvinced with the

answer. Cara let out a deep sigh of frustration. "There's a position...it's only temporary, for a PA reporting directly to him." She speared a forkful of tart, chewed quickly and swallowed, before continuing. "In his office, full-time for the period of the engagement. I saw the memo yesterday. I mean, I have the skills, right? I can type, answer phones, make coffee, file, greet people. What's more, I can probably do it better than all those size eights in the typing pool that Ms. Jackman seems to prefer." She nodded thoughtfully. "All I have to do is get past the ogre in Human Resources."

Simone stared at her, disbelief clear on her face. "Girl, I so remember that woman. If you think you can get past her, you're doing better than I ever did. That's why I left Veha Industries, remember? Maybe it's time to haul out your resumé and consider some other options. Look for something better." Simone shook her head and billows of her crimson hair swirled through the still air.

Cara understood Simone only had her best interests at heart. But this time she knew the outcome would be different. Hell, she could feel it in the air. The tingle of expectation.

"Cara, the HR ogre will hang you out for breakfast before she offers you anything like a position in that office. Remember her mantra? Good looks and good work make for a positive workplace!"

Simone didn't sugar-coat anything. It was another great reason for their long- term friendship. Honesty. But Cara didn't want to hear the truth in the statement. Even if it was exactly as her friend said.

Cara nodded quickly. "Yeah, I know, but if I don't try, then I won't know how close I can get to him, right? And the only way to catch his attention is to get past *her* and see him in person." Cara quaked a little at the information she needed to share. The favor she needed to ask. "Anyway, I tidied up my resumé and dropped the application into a memo envelope yesterday, so it's too late to back out now. I mean, fortune favors the brave. Doesn't it? If I don't snag an interview, I'm going to visit the career advisor across the street and register with them." She shrugged. "I'll look for temp work until something more long-term shows up. I can see what they have on offer and well...who knows? Maybe a job with the right boss is just waiting for me. But I'd rather this worked out, to be honest." Her voice trailed off into a whisper. "I really wish he would notice me."

Simone took a long slurp of her banana drink, and Cara noticed her questioning gaze even as she squirmed. Finally, Simone nodded. "It's your funeral. So anyway, you'd better show me this memo if you want me to be a referee for you. I'm guessing that's what you need, right? I'll have to know what I'm supposed to say about you before they ring."

Cara smiled. "Thanks, Simone. I knew I could count on you." She slipped a piece of paper out of her handbag and handed it over. "Sorry it's a bit creased. It was in the bottom of my bag, I stashed it so none of the others from the pool would see. You know how it is."

Simone snorted, accepting the crumpled pages, and nodded. "Yeah, I do. Eat or be eaten."

Simone scanned the sheet while Cara fidgeted, picking at the tart she now regretted ordering while she thought about James Veha. The one man who filled her dreams each night. She'd tried everything else she knew to capture his attention, each action more unsuccessful than the last, including undoing buttons, personally delivering memos. And the most desperate attempt? Offering to deliver the memo to the gym locker room, knowing he was in there.

Now, after eighteen months of listening to her aunt ask her when she was going to bring home a nice boy, and watching her sisters pop out perfect little babies, she conceded that the time had come to move on. With or without James Veha.

If only she could move on with him.

Therein lay the problem with her plan. She needed one last chance to make it work.

Cara twisted her fingers and waited quietly. She turned back to her friend, even as Simone started to mutter. "Yeah, okay. You can do all these things easily. But you're going to need a suit if they ring you for an interview. Something special and professional. Something to knock him dead." Simone snapped her fingers, emphasizing the point. "I have this cool little black number I bought ages ago, just before I lost all those pounds, so it doesn't fit me anymore, but it'll work for you. I reckon you'd look hot in it...in a professional kind of way, of course. Oh and I even have the right shoes and bag." A grin spread over Simone's face. Cara felt a slow increase of her heart rate from thinking about the opportunity which might just present itself.

A phone trilled. "I guess you have to go." Cara said the words sadly, watching Simone fish around in her large black leather bag.

"Yeah, Nathan said they expected the jury to bring down a finding in that murder case he's working on. Give me a call when you finish tonight, and we'll set up in the lounge with clothes and stuff." Simone jumped off the stool. "You'll be fine!" She tossed the words over her shoulder as she galloped out the door of the tiny diner.

Cara watched her retreating back. She looked around, then picked up the tart and took a bite. She tasted the fresh caramel goodness on her tongue and moaned slightly. Good food was something she loved, almost as much as the man she had hardly spoken to.

And besides, she hated to see something so decadent go to waste. On that thought she smeared some fresh whipped cream on to the pastry before taking another bite.

# CHAPTER 2

*J*ake sat looking through the window as the dark sedan pulled up in front the towering office block and a dark-haired man clambered out.

The man across the road, James, was awkward and uncoordinated, nearly dropping his briefcase as he fumbled slightly with the handle of the car. James pushed his glasses up on the bridge of his nose before glancing around. His well-muscled body hidden beneath one of the many ill-fitting suits James habitually wore as camouflage.

People stopped to watch his movements, those who knew him smiled before they continued to wander by.

More than a few women sighed, noting his angel-perfect face. And probably wishing he would notice them.

Jake's quarry, James, awkwardly disentangled himself from briefcase and vehicle. Jake heard the girl, Cara, stifle a gasp unsuccessfully. She was transfixed by James's movements, looking through the plate glass, as she focused on him fumbling and stumbling.

Intrigued, Jake scrutinized Cara's reactions: the tightening of her fingers on the countertop and the way her eyes followed James.

*So. Here might be another opportunity to make good on my debt.* He grinned at the thought of the larger woman and the toned man in the ill-fitting suit. *Why not?* Jake could increase his count of good deeds much faster than he could have hoped for. True, it wasn't quite the pairing he'd been working towards, but there was plenty of time for that later.

He sat quietly, considering this new and interesting game, then lifted the coffee mug to his mouth. Jake scowled as he realized the cup was empty.

He looked for the server, then stopped still in surprise, blinking, watching as his aunt appeared in the seat opposite him. Her long, wavy, chestnut hair glinted in the dim light. She might be Cailleach, the Mother of All, but more importantly, she was still his aunt.

Traditional Scottish mythology always showed her as an old hag, and this was a never- ceasing source of amusement to her. But then, so was his description as a brownie— many associated brownies with short and stocky height, swarthy and thick skin with uneven features. When he assumed his true body, he was tall, redheaded and bearded. Trim and taut, nothing like the visage he'd currently assumed for this "job".

"Ohhh...no. What now?" The words escaped from his mouth before he could control them. He looked around. No one saw anything unusual with the appearance of the perfectly groomed woman now sitting opposite him, her white suit molded around her firm toned body, so unchanging over the years. She looked around twenty-five, but she was older. So much older than her looks would lead anyone to imagine. Ancient might even describe her. He controlled the snicker that rose.

"Is that any way to greet your aunt? Honestly, Diocail, anyone would think you would rather see that floozy Niamh instead of me."

He winced at the use of his Celtic name, hoping no one else had heard her, but he contained his instinctive action to scan around the small but loud diner.

"Your father is still angry you know. He has...intimated...that you need to pick up the pace a little." She looked down at the greasy food on the plate with a grimace of disgust on her face. "You call this edible?"

Diocail opened his mouth to remind her that around here he was known only as Jake, as close to his real name as you could get. The server, an older woman of indeterminate age and parentage with dark skin and even darker eyes, walked up to the table. She smiled broadly and carried a dented metal coffee pot in one hand and he noted whimsically that it matched her dented and battered face. *Only, I know what lies beneath the visage you assumed daily.*

"Excuse me? Would you like a refill? Ma'am, can I get a cup for you too?" Her voice was slightly hoarse, which was probably the result of the years of hard living and a tangible reminder of the equally hard man she'd known. It was a shame, he thought, she'd been his assignment before he got a little sidetracked. Diocail reminded himself there was always time to make her his next project and smiled at the thought.

Then Diocail started in amazement, realizing that she could see his aunt Cailleach sitting opposite him. He looked at the woman who was sister to his father and she winked conspiratorially. He goggled at the action, never having seen this more playful side of her. Well, at least, never up close and it felt more than a little odd. And creepy.

"No thanks. Just a bottle of water, please." Cailleach smiled.

The flash of perfect white teeth and twinkling eyes must have done something magical to the server and she hurried to fulfil Cailleach's order. Meanwhile, Diocail sat there, stunned at Cailleach's appearance in this greasy little diner.

"Won't be a minute, hon." She scurried quickly behind the counter pulled open the fridge with a rattle and clank, grabbed a bottle and efficiently twisted the top with a quick movement of her hands then returned. Other customers tried to catch her eye as she hustled around the counter but she seemed determined to serve his aunt first.

Jake wondered, not for the first time, if this wasn't some god-power-thing he'd never get the hang of, before shrugging the thought away. He wasn't a full god anyway, just the mixed-up offspring of his father's mating with a faerie.

"Thanks so much. Jake"— Cailleach winked at him—"will fix the bill at the end."

The server nodded and smiled before wandering off to another table. Jake waited as she padded off, her pen hovering over the pad in her hand for just a moment, before he turned his attention back to his aunt.

He cleared his throat. "I'm in the planning stages, Aunt, so if you could please leave me to do my job, I can return home sooner. That is, unless you can change Father's mind?"

Cailleach shook her head. He wasn't surprised. Father had made his point, casting him out of his comfortable home in Scotland until he had made some restitutions for the mess he'd made in the past.

He thought fondly of the woman who he had left waiting, naked, ready and willing in his bed. No doubt she'd be long gone, he thought with a weighty exhalation.

He groaned heavily. "Has he given you an idea...?" Before he could finish the question, his aunt disappeared, and he felt yet another layer of frustration at his fate. "I hate it when she does that." With a quick move, he grabbed his fork and toyed with the cooling food on the plate, but his appetite was gone.

*Back to work.* He turned to look at his new target woman, only to find her gone too.

# CHAPTER 3

*J*ames made his way slowly to the elevators, feeling foolish as he usually did. He had nearly fallen climbing out of the car, and today he felt more awkward than usual. The burning sensation of being watched left the back of his neck itching, but he brushed it aside. It was no different to any other time, he reminded himself.

Tuesday morning and he hoped he might get a glance of the bountiful woman he'd lusted after for eighteen months. Well, to be exact, it was seventeen months, three weeks and two days. Hell, he could even count down the time in hours and minutes, he thought, sparing a quick glance at his watch, doing the mental arithmetic.

Not that he was keeping tabs.

James snorted in his head at the foolish lie he kept tell himself, not that he actually ever believed it. He'd hankered after her ever since she'd raced into the gym to deliver the package for his financial controller. Unfortunately—or in his case fortunately—he'd left the shower, and wore a towel slung around his hips. He had wandered into the locker room, ready to pick up the clothes he'd forgotten to take into the shower room with him, when there she'd been. A siren in the misty locker room. Her cherry-red lips so full of promise. Her blouse strained over sensually full breasts while her little skirt had revealed miles of leg. She'd walked forward confidently, and when she turned, that striking gaze had taken in his state of undress.

He remembered the burn of her inspection down his midriff all those months ago.

James had felt a mesmerizing fascination at the pink tide of embarrassment which crested her cheeks, while her lips formed a subtle moue before she turned away.

It had taken him three agonizing months to find out where she worked in his organization. Three months of intense searching in each and every department until he'd reached the typing pool.

Now, he took any opportunity to wander through the cavernous room, looking for her on the street and in the halls of the offices he visited from time to time. He'd always hoped she too felt that spark of awareness which rushed through his body, but then reminded himself it was a vain hope.

He felt that enervating rush of awareness and desire each time his gaze fell upon her, and it continued riding him without surcease.

*I don't even know her name.*

He had never mentioned the incident in the locker room to anyone, at least not in any context that might allude to his awareness of her. No, he'd reasoned, it was better to study her from a distance. After all, he was too much of an uncoordinated geek for any woman of her fine figure to notice him and feel a similar connection.

James was honest with himself, usually. He liked larger women, finding something arousing in the graceful curves of belly and breast. They made him tingle all the way through.

She reminded him of a Rubenesque beauty in modern clothing, so unlike the scrawny chicken-winged versions magazines seemed to prefer these days.

He wasn't game to approach her in case she rejected him. Experience told him rejection was something he could live without.

Even now, a rivulet of sweat trickled down the back of his shirt and desire pooled deep in his belly when he thought of his personal goddess.

The elevator pinged once, loudly. It pierced the cool silence of the marbled lobby while the door slid open with a grind. He stepped in, feeling the slight rock of the small box. When he turned he noted with amazement that she was also at the elevator, and had been waiting patiently behind him.

Today, she wore a bronze-colored blouse of some silky material with intricate cutwork at the top, shadowing her pale skin, and teamed with matching pants. Spiky nude shoes completed the look and her gorgeous black hair was swept back into a ponytail, leaving her swan-like throat bared for his scrutiny.

Her luscious breasts, full and high, filled the fitted top to perfection and he had to control the urge to step forward and kiss her pale, glossy painted lips. He peeked at her fingers, just as he always did. Still bare. He breathed a sigh of relief knowing she remained single, for now, anyway. Or at least her lack of rings showed no visible signs of a relationship. The thought ricocheted through his mind and he had to control himself, otherwise he knew he would have blurted out a question as to her current status.

"Can you press ten, please?" Her voice filled the air, its breathy quality heating him from within. He wanted to close his eyes as the pleasure curled through his gut.

"Sure." He reached over to depress the button, watching her graceful movement towards the back of the car, and he nearly fell over, losing his center of balance with the heavy briefcase in one hand. He was such a klutz.

"Are you okay?"

He shook his head, unable to answer, too distracted by her small hands supporting him. She touched him! It was only a friendly touch but his hormones went into overdrive as little zings of electricity shot from where her hand rested against his arm down to his abdomen, causing the already firm muscles to contract further.

*Oh God!* Here he was with the woman he dreamed about and he still couldn't get it together. His heart thudded. He wanted to close his eyes and cringe in embarrassment.

"Yeah, I just lost my balance a little."

She smiled at his words and stepped back against the wall, her lips curving upwards. He wanted to lean forward and touch them, but couldn't. Wouldn't, really. *What if she thinks I'm a nut?* He was so much better off concentrating on what he knew best. His business. He gave a mental nod, congratulating himself on the cool-headed thoughts. But it didn't ease the ache in his chest. Here lay an opportunity. One he was too craven to accept, he admitted.

The bell rang once more as they reached the tenth floor. The Muzak playing overhead as the opening doorway revealing the typing pool. Cubicle upon cubicle filled the area, silent except for the tap of keyboards and muted phone chatter. It was soulless. Devoid of personality, but effective in ensuring the work was completed with as few distractions as possible. His aunt Horatia made sure of that, watching over the actions of the men and women who worked for him. It was her single mission in life, to ensure Veha Industries thrived from their commitment to the business, instead of being distracted by personal issues.

He watched as the Siren, as he'd dubbed her months ago, stepped out. The gentle sway of her hips enticed him to do something very unbusinesslike and very personal. James released a breath as she reached a small cell straight ahead, then stepped left and out of sight.

As always after one of their encounters, he adjusted his pants, relieving the pressure of his erection, feeling the action as the lift once more continued upwards to the fifteenth floor. He finally stepped out, crashing into the arms of his waiting PA. "Oomph. Sorry, May," he muttered, feeling clumsy once again. A usual state of affairs for him, and one he hated.

May stood waiting patiently as he collected the files he'd knocked to the floor, then accepted them wordlessly, a broad smile on her face. "I have fantastic news. The internal memo worked a trick. Just as I knew it would." Her voice was exultant, and he watched the way her animated movements mirrored her birdlike frame. "There were three internal applicants, but one was a standout candidate. I have her file here, and I think she'll work out. It's clear she's the best choice." May grinned and he grimaced back as she continued blithely. "Oh, and I've arranged for the technician to check your computer this afternoon since you complained it wasn't running so well after you dropped coffee all over it."

He winced again. Yet another clumsy moment. One he would prefer to forget.

Straight after being in an enclosed area with the woman of his dreams, May's jubilant protestation was too much and it battered at his beleaguered senses. He needed a couple of minutes to gather his thoughts. Obviously, that wasn't going to happen now, not with her trailing along behind him up the corridor.

He raised a hand slowly, ceasing her chatter. "Hang on, May. Wait until I get to my office and then you can show me." He walked towards the wooden door of his spacious office.

The office was more like his personal refuge. The paneled walls were dark, rich and welcoming. The light green carpet cushioned his footsteps as he reached the partner desk he'd chosen for himself and the black leather chair gave slightly beneath him as he sat. "Now, what was that about applications?"

"Three came in, but one looks to be the best of the lot. Cara Chamberlain. She works downstairs in the typing pool. I know her slightly. She has a great sense of humor and is excellent at what she does, so she won't frighten any of your clients. She also attended secretary school, so she would be the best bet, in my opinion."

May dropped a pile of folders on the desk. "I moved her to the top, because I know it's the best. Now, the only issue is Horatia may not like her as an option, because she's not... thin. You know how she gets about larger women."

James nodded as she grabbed the seat opposite his desk. She became quiet, as the smile slipped from her face. "Seriously, James. I need to finish early. I have a ton of jobs to complete and...well...I really need to finish up today, or at the latest tomorrow. The flowers haven't been ordered, my dress fitting has been postponed five times and the wedding planner is threatening to cancel if I don't find time early next week for her."

James felt bad for May. Her mother had run away with her father's partner, leaving the other man depressed and May with no one to rely on during this trying situation of planning her wedding. James knew that.

Although he worried about the change in the office, in his heart James knew he needed to ensure May got her special day. She'd been with him since the beginning, had given up so much of her precious time to help him grow his business. It was time to give something back, no matter how personally difficult he would find it.

"Okay," he said with a nod. "Let me look at this and I'll see what we can manage." He picked up the file only to drop it again with an, "Oww." A welling blotch of blood stood crimson on the pale skin of his finger.

"What's wrong?" May sat forward in her chair.

"Got myself with the darned staple." The words were spoken absently. This time he left the file on the desk and opened the buff-colored card cover, gazing in amazement at the picture inside. Heat bloomed within his chest at the thought of being so close to the lush young woman who haunted his dreams.

May's voice startled him. "That dratted guy in postal. He loves staples and sharp things. I don't know. Maybe he thinks he's Cupid?"

Cara worked furiously, typing the letters and memos assigned to her. She could hear the mutter of other women doing the same and felt frustrated, both sexually and career wise. Eighteen months at a secretarial school to end up in the typing pool. Not exactly the outcome she'd imagined. No, she had graduated with high hopes of becoming a personal secretary to someone important. Someone just like James Veha.

She'd also had dreams of romance and love. Babies and white picket fences, nights by candlelight and a puppy had always figured in her plans. So, she had met the perfect man, but he was still unattainable. The other issue which created an insurmountable barrier, in her mind, was a man like him didn't fall for a woman like her—with large breasts, hips and heaven forbid...a stomach—when he could have any model he wanted.

Being in the elevator with him was like a form of sexual torture. All those desires had rushed back at her, overwhelmingly intense. Then she had topped it off with her inane single comment of 'Are you okay?'. She seethed. Surely, she could have come up with something a little more interesting than that? Her mind whirled with the endless possibilities.

The words scrolled across the screen as the insistent buzz of the phone caught her attention. The light at the top flashed and she realized the buzz was definitely meant for her.

"Cara Chamberlain." She answered the phone using what she always thought of as her automatic sunshine voice. The one they had drilled into her at the school for secretaries.

"Ms. Chamberlain? It's May Anderson from Mr. Veha's office. I was wondering if you would be free for an interview tomorrow at around five-thirty."

A hum of excitement welled. He had seen her application and thought her worthy. She grinned even as her mind moved at lightning pace.

"Ms. Anderson, I would love to attend. Where should I go?" She held her excitement growing inside her firmly in check. She needed to prove herself, because realistically, this was her last best chance at Veha. If this didn't work, she needed to move on. Her stomach quivered.

"His office is on the fifteenth floor. If you can be there at five-fifteen, I can take you through the systems I have in place," May Anderson continued in her melodious voice. Cara scribbled a note in her diary with the date and time.

"I'll be there, Ms. Anderson." The line disconnected.

Hot damn! She was in with a chance.

Cara took a furtive look around, no one was in sight. It was against the rules to use your phone at work, but she couldn't help herself. She pulled the slim unit from her pocket, tapped in a quick text message and sent it before slipping the phone back into place and turning back to the screen. Maybe she was breaking a few rules, but she was sure no one had seen her.

Even as Cara put the mobile away, her phone buzzed once more.

"Cara Chamberlain."

"Miss Chamberlain, please come to my office immediately." Cara knew that voice, recognized Horatia Jackman's tight tones, and closed her eyes. Damn, she'd been seen.

Cara stood slowly, then left her cubicle, heading to the small glassed office at the back of the large room. Two quick raps on the wood door earned a brisk "Come."

With a quick intake of breath, Cara opened the door and entered the cold soulless room.

"You wanted to see me, Ms. Jackman?"

"Yes, Miss Chamberlain. I believe you used your phone during working hours?" It might have been a question, Cara thought, but there was also a warning implied in her very correct tones.

"Umm, yes, I did." She waited stock still, feeling like a schoolgirl being hauled over the coals by the principal. Except she wasn't twelve anymore and this wasn't a playground incident. But even so, Cara knew there was nothing to be gained by lying, just as it had been as a child.

"We do not tolerate personal interaction during work time." Ms. Jackman rose from her chair, her action regal and no doubt many people would see it as intimidating. "And your current attire is also inappropriate. Peek-a-boo cut outs…"

Cara wanted to laugh at the look on her face but worked hard to keep her own still. The woman had no dress sense so how could she possibly be expected to know that this was more than acceptable attire?

"…are not acceptable at Veha Industries. You may consider yourself counselled this time and a notation will be made on your personnel file."

Heat flared on her cheeks. *The old bat!* Cara might have flouted the rules with messaging Simone, but she was careful when it came to dressing for work. Nothing could be seen through the intricate cutwork on her blouse.

Swallowing the anger churning in her gut, Cara shrugged inwardly. It wasn't worth upsetting Ms. Jackman if she wanted to keep her job or have a decent reference when she left. She'd already seen what had happened to Simone after a run-in with this woman. Her reference hadn't been worth the paper it was written on. So Cara waited in silence while the woman opposite her ran a scathing glance up and down.

"You may go, Miss Chamberlain."

Cara was left in no doubt that the dismissal meant she would be watched, closely. On her way back to her seat, she heard furious whispers from Jackman's pets.

"I can't believe she'd wear something like that. I mean it's obscene when you're that big."

As always, Cara ignored the snide remarks. *I won't be stuck in the typing pool forever*, Cara told herself, then she grinned, gaining her seat and getting back to work, but it was only half-hearted now. With just half an hour to go before she could finish up for the day, her concentration was minimal, so Cara cleared her trays, returning the completed documents to the central repository, dragging her heels on return to her cubicle where she then cleared off the desk. She kept in mind Ms. Jackman would be watching her every move and she didn't want another opportunity for the woman to take potshots at her. Or worse, dismiss her, now that her goal was closer than ever before.

Five came around and Cara gratefully logged out then rose from her chair, grabbed her bag and identification. She moved hurriedly through the bodies that waited for the elevator.

Cara took one look at the crowd and shook her head. She bent to remove her heels and slipped on the ugly black sandals she drove in. The stairs beckoned. She stepped swiftly. Very few people took this option, normally she avoided it too, but today was different she reflected, descending, puffing and panting while she continued downwards. Her excitement at the possibility of the new job and being close to James Veha drove her to get outside as quickly as possible. Maybe a response from Simone would be waiting.

Outside, she fished in her pocket pulling out her mobile, then checked her messages.

*U got ur in2view? Cool. Share deets.*

Cara grinned, dialing Simone's number.

"Hi! You've reached Simone. Well, Simone's phone. Leave me a message and maybe I'll phone back."

"Simone, I'm heading home to grab some clothes and stuff. I'll swing past at around seven. Lots to tell you then. Oh, and make up the spare bed."

She pocketed the small device once more, heading across the parking lot towards her compact blue car. The new postal guy, Jake, from level two waited beside it, smiling. She smiled back, a feeling of uncertainty flowing through her. The smallish squat man with the bald head seemed somehow odd to her. She dismissed the thought as he turned and walked away.

She stepped up to the car and looked around—*you can't be too careful these days,* she reminded herself—before unlocking and hopping in.

# CHAPTER 4

*C*ara crossed aching feet as she sat in the plush black office chair. She should never have borrowed this suit and the shoes from Simone. She leaned back, enjoying the sound of the argument she could hear from behind the closed door while she waited to be called into the room.

"You can't be serious! She's nowhere near ready for this or in any way suitable for the position. She has no dress sense and she's not what you want clients to see when they arrive. What will they think?" Horatia Jackman's voice was snappy and uptight.

Cara grinned, evilly. Of course she was ready. She had the training and skills to act as a PA. She snorted at what the woman said about her. Well, saying might be an understatement. She was yelling it the top of her lungs.

"It's too late, Horatia. I am committed to following this course of action through." His tone was exasperated.

Cara let a small smirk pass over her face, quickly schooling it back into a calm exterior before they could enter the room where she waited. No way did she want them to realize she'd been eavesdropping. But keeping that calm expression was harder to do than normal because… she had the job!

Excitement zipped through her. Now she had her chance to show him she was the right woman for the position. In more ways than one.

She had spent the previous half hour with May Anderson, learning about the job, and she had known that she could do it. Cara had seen the long list of instructions the Personal Assistant had put together beforehand, the thick folio sat at the end of the desk, ready for May's successor.

That was before the other woman had disappeared inside the office, closeted with James Veha himself.

The quiet discussion had lasted some time while Cara cooled her heels outside the inner office.

Cara remembered that though she had proved herself to May Anderson, she still had to show James Veha that she could do the job. That was when Horatia Jackman from Human Resources had stalked in, straight past the high-backed seat where Cara waited.

The discussions tone had changed then, and Cara had no issues with eavesdropping. After all, she was directly involved in the three-cornered argument. May had squeaked in dismay, telling Ms. Jackman that the decision was already made, before leaving the room, softly closing the door behind her.

May winked as she hurried from the office with the words, "The job is all yours. Just watch out for Ms. Jackman. If James is looking for me, I've gone home. He knows how to contact me." She dashed around the corner, swinging her bag over one shoulder, and was gone.

Cara waited impatiently, wishing she could be in the office watching the argument.

"No." James Veha shouted the final word and her eyes widened in surprise. *So he can shout when need be.* She smiled. She liked a man who could make a point firmly, but still retain a softer side.

The heavy wooden door slammed open, the pictures on the walls shivering in reaction. Ms. Horatia Jackman stalked across the room, grey hair piled into a tight topknot, the head nose in the air.

Cara smothered a laugh. *Gee, if it were any higher it would just about touch the moon.* The woman stopped at the exit to pin her with a furious stare. "You had better do your job properly." Her tone was cold and angry as she whirled on sensible two-and-a-quarter-inch black heels and stormed out the door.

The woman was six feet of skinny attitude, with the salt-and-pepper hair to match her snarly attitude. Frigidly unbending to the last, her piercing blue eyes had always disconcerted Cara. Now they were a source of amusement. With fury bleeding from them anyone would think she had a stake in the outcome of today's meeting.

"Uh? Miss Chamberlain? Please excuse Ms. Jackman. She gets excited easily over HR issues, especially when she thinks we're bypassing her protocols. Now please come through."

James Veha stood in the entrance, looking like an undercover Adonis. His dark ruffled hair highlighted his olive skin. He bit his bottom lip, disguising its sensual fullness. The thick glasses hid his gorgeous grey eyes and the rumpled suit did nothing for a body she knew would inspire erotic dreams in a nun.

Maybe she should describe him as a Geek God?

Cara sighed. Since coming to work for Veha Industries and spying him coming out of the gym locker room in nothing but a towel, her interest had morphed into a fully-fledged lust thing and now used every opportunity to catch his eye. Not that he ever noticed her. Nope, no matter what she did or wore, he never seemed to see her—with or without the glasses.

What did she expect though, with a size eighteen body hidden in a borrowed suit and shoes and her black hair scraped back into a bun?

She stood, the pinprick-thin heels just supporting her weight, smoothed down the short black skirt of the suit and made her way into the office. The door closed with a thud and her heart rate sped up. She had wanted to be in here for some time, to have this opportunity. She swallowed the nerves attacking her. Her stomach jangling as if a million butterflies had taken flight inside it, but she pushed them away, concentrating on the task at hand.

Thirteen weeks working as the temp in James Veha's office and a possibility of further advancement if his PA didn't come back from her honeymoon. Her last chance to show him she could be the woman of his dreams, or at least the best PA possible, she reminded herself.

Successfully graduating from secretary school followed by another year and a half in the typing pool told her she could do the job. After so many months of this self-imposed torture, caused by seeing him in almost all his naked glory, if she didn't grasp this chance, then maybe she should give up and find a job somewhere else. With a boss who would appreciate her skills. Not to mention one who appreciated her too.

Cara pulled a seat forward, making herself comfortable, and waited while he lowered that sexy body into a big black executive chair on the other side of the desk. Damn, it was large enough to support both of them. Erotic thoughts of office sex pulsed through her mind... She pulled the thought up short. She needed to focus if she wanted to make a success of this opportunity, or she should give up on her fantasy and move onto a new job. That thought filled her with cold dread.

Cara struggled to concentrate on him and what he was saying. She couldn't afford to focus on his body or perfect lips as he spoke. Each tumbling word sent shocks of desire rocketing through her system and the fire in her belly burned as bright as ever.

"You will need to answer the phone, open my mail for me, greet clients and keep my date book..." *His date book? No! I can't organize his dates for him!* "...Miss Chamberlain?" He looked at her and she knew she must have squeaked her distress aloud.

"Your date book?" The high-pitched words slipped out from between stiff lips.

"Yes, so I know what engagements and appointments are booked. I like to work from seven-thirty through to about eight-ish. You said that worked for you?"

She nodded furiously. Date book meant appointment diary. Thank heavens. She should have remembered that from secretary school. *Concentrate!*

He shuffled papers on his desk as he continued. "While May, my PA, is on leave, there could be other little things I will need attended to. It could include collecting my dry cleaning, taking calls, making tea and coffee. And there could be other odd tasks as required.

"If this works out well, we may consider giving May a full-time assistant... There is also the possibility that if she chooses not to return to fill the role permanently." He pushed those glasses up his nose, slowly, and she imagined that particular movement somewhere on her body. Oh God, that was such a sexy action. She gulped, catching sight of his soft grey eyes.

The thought aroused her. Her breasts became fuller, and the dampness at the juncture of her thighs made her tingle. She pressed her quivering legs together.

His eyes clouded with what looked like anxiety and Cara wanted to get up and smooth the worries from his face. Clenching her fingers, feeling the grip of pain while maintaining an outer façade of decorum.

"I can do that, Mr. Veha." She nodded, looking down to escape his eyes, and saw that her skirt had ridden up slightly, showing the bottom of one garter clip, black like her outfit and stockings. She hoped he hadn't seen it and got the wrong idea. Gaining advancement based on sex was not her idea of positive promotion.

Cara pushed the skirt hem back down. Sexy underwear was the one thing she would not give up, even if it didn't really go with the rest of her work clothing. It might be a suit kind of job, but her underwear was deliciously scandalous. And who knew, maybe one day she would have a chance to let him see what she wore under her clothes. However, not on work time.

No, she wanted all of him. Forever and in every possible way. In the right setting. She nodded, once more focusing on the discussion. That was a thought for another time.

# CHAPTER 5

*D*ear God, what was she wearing under the tight little short black skirt? A black clip escaped below the hemline and he wanted to explore it. To see what was underneath the tight wool covering. Could it possibly be...? The thought arrested him. *Stocking! She's wearing sexy stockings?* His blood heated.

Cara Chamberlain wasn't one of those bony size eight girls. No, she had thighs, hips and dear heaven...*breasts*. He was sure those beauties would spill over the palms of his hands while she arched backwards in the throes of orgasm. That thought along with one of the silk threads covering her legs, together with the garter belt, captivated his full attention along with other parts of his body.

Her long hair was tied firmly at the back of her head, but small wisps kissed her fine skin, just below the soft jawbone. Her green eyes, rather like a cat's, caught the light and again a vision came, hair wild and free as her body moved over him.

His body tightened in reaction to her nearness, his groin hot and painful making it far more difficult to walk. The burn of hunger that followed him relentlessly gnawed at him, both sexually and physically. James could shift in his seat, but it might embarrass the woman opposite and she might guess what he was doing. It would possibly embarrass and horrify her.

But more importantly than this pulsing need for her was the emotional attachment he already felt. One he desperately wanted to explore. The interlude in the elevator the day before had left him uncomfortable and irritated. He'd remained on edge for hours before he regained his equilibrium.

Then last night's hot dream... Well, it was quite erotic and the memory of it ratcheted up his current state of readiness. Now, here she was in his office. Ready to work for him, near him for the next several weeks. That thought dried his mouth and accelerated his heart rate.

"If something urgent comes up you will be required to work weekends. There could also be the necessity of remaining on call. Your passport is up to date?" He waited for her answer.

"Yes, I live with my parents, so there is no reasons I can't be available when you need me. I also have a car, so I can get here quickly. Depending on traffic, of course. But you already know what Melbourne traffic is like..." Her words trailed away and he saw a pink tinge on her cheekbones. The sight of it intrigued him, and he struggled to focus on the task.

"Good. We may need to head to India to sort out that mess with the Brockman deal next week." She glanced at him, eyes wide as if unaware of the current problem.

"You know the one where they made the parts the wrong size?"

At her nod he continued. "I will need you to accompany me to take notes, organize details and those sorts of things. May usually accompanies me." Truthfully, he wasn't quite sure what May did in the office, just that whatever he needed was always there. But if he hazarded a guess, he would be willing to bet she'd left extensive notes for whoever succeeded her.

He had been watching the gorgeous Miss Chamberlain for well over a year, salacious thoughts filling his nights and days. While he wouldn't have given countenance to her becoming his PA if she couldn't do the job— fifteen years of blood, sweat and brain cells weren't going to be thrown away in a fit of passionate folly because his libido was rampant —he was a man who knew carefully calculated risks made for good returns on investment and he wasn't going to let this opportunity sail by without making the most of every chance to win her heart.

He started calculating the mathematical chances that she would be successful before he pulled himself up. This stroke of luck was a godsend. And May's nod of approval was all he had needed to seal the deal in his mind.

Aunt Horatia might not happy with the promotion of Miss Chamberlain, but then, when was she ever happy? She'd been sour for as long as he knew her. She had fought him toe-to-toe both over the phone and in person. But he wasn't going to give in.

James took a deep breath and watched as she blushed again. The merest crest brightened those cheeks and for an instant, he let himself imagine the rest of her body flushed with desire. She watched him, and he had to force himself to concentrate once more, but when she licked her lips his arousal ratcheted up another notch. That pink tongue peeked out and his thoughts splintering again. *What would it feel like to have her run that tongue over his body?*

"Uh... Miss Chamberlain, given it's so late why don't we grab something to eat and I can update you on the various projects we're overseeing currently?"

He and May usually grabbed a meal at the Viceroy in the evening when they were working late, and tonight looked like it was going to be the same as usual. He nodded to himself. That made sense and didn't make him look over-eager. He had time on his side, true, but he was better to start now and make the most of it.

"My car..." Cara stopped and smiled at him as he held up a hand.

"I'll get you back here in time to pick it up, or alternately, I can have my driver take you home and pick you up in the morning. Whichever suits you best." He sounded considerate and thorough. Nothing out of order, he told himself.

They stood at the same time, and he noticed the skirt had ridden up a little higher and the top of her stocking ended at firm creamy flesh. He swallowed hard, his Adams Apple bobbing painfully in his throat.

"Uh, yeah. Sounds like a fantastic idea, Mr. Veha." Her breathy voice enveloped him like smooth silk sheets. He nearly groaned as his blood surged. He indicated for her to go through the door and watched as she made her way to the large desk. When she leaned over to retrieve a black bag the material of the skirt molded itself to her hips, outlining the twin globes of her perfectly formed bottom, and it took everything he had not to grab her immediately, sling her over the desk and tear that suit off her. James closed his eyes and cursed silently when the scent of her rose in the air.

"Mr. Veha? Are you okay?" Her words were cautious. He realized she must have turned around and seen him.

*Damn.* "Yeah, no, I'm good. Come on, my car will be waiting downstairs."

# CHAPTER 6

Their arrival at the restaurant sent the restaurateur into a spin, Cara noted. As no table was ready, would they care for complimentary drinks? The man had smiled at them both, and James had accepted the offer though Cara wasn't totally sure about the wisdom of his decision.

They were quickly ushered into the wine bar to wait as a table was prepared. The plush seats and dim lighting felt intimate and Cara glanced at James. He was so close and the restaurant dimly lit, with candles flickering on the table between them. Intimate came to mind and flashes of seductive scenes featuring her and James rolled through her brain.

Stop it, she warned her psyche but the images continued. Them. Together in candlelight naked. The dampness between her legs increased and it took every ounce of concentration to focus on the drink menu the waiter handed her after he cleared his throat.

"Oh, sorry." Cara chose a fruity concoction from the drinks menu and waited as the bartender created the beverage. He had seemed vaguely familiar, but she couldn't place where she had seen him before —that bald head and those piercing blue eyes. The willing smile sent up warning signals at the edge of her mind. Cara searched her brain but no previous meeting came to mind. She shrugged away the feeling as the drink was served with a flourish, the small umbrella perched precariously on the side while the bartender found the merlot James—Mr. Veha, she reminded herself—ordered.

The tension between her and James, thick and heavy, almost smothered her. Cara beat a hasty retreat to the ladies room, and after using the toilet, splashed a little water on the inside of her wrists, hoping to cool the fever spreading through her system.

*"Did you see that woman sitting with James Veha? God, she must be a client. He's too cute to take up with such a frumpy cow."* Laughter filled the air on the other side of the stalls.

At hearing the vicious comments the fantasies which had risen in her were crushed. They were right, of course, she told herself. How could she possibly hope to capture the eye of the gorgeous James Veha?

Cara wanted to cry at the unfairness of it all. She had feelings and desires and needs. But now she was cold. So cold and alone, hiding in the restroom, while the man of her dreams waited for her.

Maybe she should leave? That would be the best way out of the situation. After all, he was going to be her boss and with her resistance low, she'd be half as likely to do something foolish after a couple of drinks. The situation could create all sorts of issues for them personally. It could also possibly destroy any future with Veha Industries.

But as the thoughts descended, Cara caught sight of herself in the large mirror, and all she could see was creamy flesh, perfect makeup and eyes that shone brightly. True, they shone with tears, because of the hateful words she'd just overheard, yet there was nothing ugly or obscene in the way she looked. She had waited a long time for this opportunity, and by heavens, she would take it. A quick nod at herself in the mirror was all she needed, even as her lips quivered with the fear of rejection.

Cara squared her shoulders, and reminded herself of her positive traits, while listening for the sound of the door closing and the fading titter of the women as they left.

Cara replayed her mantra in her mind before moving slowly and with determination towards the door. Spying the seat she'd vacated earlier, Cara caught sight of a rail-thin blonde hanging over James's shoulder. She stopped in the shadows, watching. Once more the churning sensation of not belonging washed over her.

He shook his head and removed the blonde's clinging fingers. His face grew dark and something quick was shared. The woman straightened up, flicked her hair over her shoulder and retreated. Waiting an instant longer, dredging up every ounce of self-possession internally, she then calmly moved forward.

"Oh good, you're back." James smiled at her, his eyes bright while indicating to her drink. She lifted the umbrella and took a grateful sip. She was twirling the little stick in her fingers as she looked around… "Oww!"

"What's up?"

"I jabbed myself with the umbrella." Cara's voice was rueful as she smiled at him. Hoping he wouldn't think she was some kind of idiot. She blushed and he smiled, holding out his hand.

"Let me see." His softly spoken demand sent a shiver down her spine and the heat of a blush warmed her cheeks.

"I'll be fine." She mumbled the words.

Large fingers captured her hand, Dillion treated the appendage like spun glass while he checked the wound site. "Thankfully there's no real damage." He hailed the bartender. "Can we get a piece of ice for this?" The barman nodded, fishing a small, cold cube from the tub behind the counter. James wrapped the ice in the handkerchief and applied it to the sore finger, smiling at her.

She melted deep inside.

D iocail congratulated himself. This impromptu coupling was going to plan and he smiled at the almost intimate scene unfolding before his eyes.

"You're doing well, but there is one small problem, Diocail." The voice came from behind him as the silence in the bar grew.

He knew that voice. "Yes, Father?" He turned slowly to see the man seated on a small smooth rock, surrounded by white light. His long white beard fell down over the ceremonial robes he usually chose to wear. His blue eyes glinted in the dark bar. Diocail chanced a quick look around, hoping no one else could see this, but as expected every human present was still as a statue, frozen into the position they had been in when he first heard the voice of his father.

"This couple is moving together very well. I really liked the touch with the staple and the umbrella, so very appropriate to their lifestyles. But of course, you do realize this one coupling won't make up for your failures?" The words were quiet.

Diocail felt a familiar stab of frustration, one that he experienced regularly here on earth. "Why?" Of course, he knew the answer before he asked the question, but he wanted to hear it said.

"They were already halfway to falling for each other. You just offered the final opportunity for them to take the chance. While it is a good deed, it is nowhere near sufficient to make good on your debt. Anyway, they would have eventually have come together, you just gave them a small push, speeding their connection along." He waved an imperious hand in the air.

Diocail watched as Father glanced around. "When can I..." He stopped as his eyes met Father's gaze.

"When I feel you have made adequate restitution for your previous lack of commitment to your role. Cailleach told me you asked her this last time you met." He glanced around once more. "Oh, such little lives, and yet so complicated. I do not regret that my visits here are now limited. Their lives seem so unimportant and pointless with the hurry and scurry of work and traffic...and the food." His words were low and he shuddered before he turned back to Diocail.

"Well, Son, I wish you luck with this pair. You might need to work a small bit of extra magic to allow them to drop the last of their defenses, but then, I am sure I can leave that in your capable hands. And when you are done, there are plenty more out there who need your intervention." His words were jovial as he lifted one hand in farewell.

"Wait!" The words slipped out, but the image of Father and the white light surrounding him faded quickly and finally disappeared.

The music in the bar once more filled the air, soulful and low. The couple before him seemed closer than before, heads bent close together. The woman, Cara, finished her drink and James Veha called for another couple to be prepared.

Diocail released a long breath, making a last single wish for the couple in front of him, feeling the tingle of magic in the air.

# CHAPTER 7

The restaurant was certainly fine and once their table was ready they were quickly ushered to a seat while the owner apologized for the wait. Thankfully nowhere near the trio of blondes who still sent dagger-like looks in her direction. Each time she caught sight of one, her stomach dipped again remembering their harsh words.

The waiters were attentive. James—Mr. Veha, she reminded herself once more—knew his wines. The subtle red he instructed the waiter to pour with its fruity bouquet quenched her dry mouth during the meal. She couldn't have said what she ate, as James ordered from memory in French as she listened, quietly mesmerized.

He talked expansively of the current projects. She watched his hands and face as he spoke. Each move told of his fulfilment both as the CEO of Veha Industries and Research and Development chair. Every time he smiled, a bomb of desire exploded low in her belly. She took another sip of wine, her head feeling a little muzzy. *Maybe I should lay off the wine?* But when he topped up her glass the idea of sobriety skittered away.

"Why are you only just looking for a replacement or temp PA now?" She heard the question escape.

"As you know, May came onboard as my Personal Assistant a when Veha first started to grow. I have to say, when she told me she was marrying Frank I was a little...upset. She has assured me children are not on the cards just yet and when she is ready, she will train my replacement assistant." He said the words self-deprecatingly.

"Anyway, two weeks ago she falls apart. The gown-fitting thing rescheduled for the fifth time, Frank's aunt getting sick and the flower girl had come down with chicken pox. Then it topped off with her mother declaring her undying love for her father's business partner, seeing as she was watching her daughter prepare to marry the man she loved. Then her father's breakdown at his mechanics workshop and a diagnosis of depression, it was all too much for May... What really finished it all was the wedding planner threatening to pull the plug. She just couldn't cope with work and the disaster her wedding was turning into and needed to take immediate leave, opening up the spot for a temporary PA."

Cara's stomach flip-flopped as the sexy man look hit her hard. "No wonder Ms. Jackman was so flustered." It was the only sane thing she could think of to say.

"Yeah, Aunt Horatia gets excited easily."

Aunt? Cara took a great big gulp, the wine hitting her stomach. She was his aunt? Dear God! How many times had she made fun of the woman!

"Try this tequila pecan pie, it's delicious and a specialty of the house." He held his fork out to her. Her resistance to desserts was low at the best of times, so she leaned forward and took a bite. The explosion of flavors hit her tongue.

"Oh my God. That is sinful!" She closed her eyes and savored the taste.

"Yeah, sinful can be good." His words were low and rumbled over her. The waves of desire she had tried to keep at bay lapped at her.

"I don't mind sinful." She grinned. How much more sinful could she get, personally, apart from jumping his bones? Of course, there was the issue of the underwear hidden below the ugly black suit, hiding the tiniest thong she could find in her size and a bra no more than a lacy cups held together with wispy fabric. Thankfully, it was well constructed. Once again she thanked her own aunt, a buyer for a lingerie group. She had introduced her to this particular line. It might've been expensive, but worth every cent Cara paid. The thong and bra were both completely see-through and she shivered. "Too bad he won't see it." The words slipped out of her mouth before she could stop them. She held herself still as a puzzled look spread over his face.

"See what?" His eyes were heavy-lidded, as if he had just crawled out of bed. The throbbing between her legs grew insistent. She was already beyond wet and so ready it wouldn't take too much to push her over the edge.

"Oh, nothing really." *Damn, how can I get out of this?*

"Come on, I have an apartment upstairs, let's go up and we can continue this discussion over coffee."

Something in the back of her mind told her maybe she shouldn't go with him, but inhibition floated out the window when another jolt of desire zinged through her system. The wine was doing its job of masking her normal wariness.

Her stomach quivered with nerves. *Surely he can't mean something more?* Could he really be interested in her? After all, she wasn't skinny or even beautiful. The best compliment she ever got was 'arresting good looks'. But hell, maybe this was the chance she had been waiting for, and she'd be damned if she'd waste it.

Coffee. Her mind cleared for an instant, he was offering coffee. *Get your mind out of the gutter, girl.* But then the moment of common sense evaporated as she agreed, and the surge of dizziness washed over her again. "Sure. Why not?"

He nodded to the owner as they left, surprising her as they headed for the elevators. "You live here?" She watched as he dipped his hand into his coat and pulled out a key card. He slipped it into the reader slot and that reminded her of what she wanted him to do with her. Sexually.

She panted slightly and he turned back to her.

"I thought I just said… Anyway, yep, right in the penthouse. Got the best view of Sydney." He grinned boyishly.

Was he really coming onto her, or was it more because she was there and unmistakably hot for him? The easy girl who was available? Her stomach churned but she pushed the thought away as the elevator arrived and he gestured her to enter. His gaze caught hers as he punched the button for the penthouse.

The movement of the elevator pushed her towards him. He opened his arms to steady her. Enfolding her. Cara closed her eyes as she finally felt him against her body. He was as firm as she had guessed. In more ways than one.

He muttered something unintelligible then leaned in and touched their lips together. Hot and powerful, he pushed his tongue past her lips. Cara moaned and opened to his invasion. He tasted as good as he looked. Intoxicating.

He slipped his hands under her suit, grabbed her bottom and pulled her neatly against him. She felt cradled, while he widened his legs, steadying her against him, and trailed his fingers over the fabric covering her bottom, cradling the twin globes. She felt his erection through his pants and she itched to touch it.

*Ping!* The doors slid open to a tastefully furnished apartment. They drew apart, laughing shakily.

"How about a glass of wine to start with? I have red or white." He walked, a little unsteadily she noticed, towards the kitchen and she followed.

The coffee he'd previously mentioned would be better in her intoxicated state. Save her from an embarrassing mistake. "You know...maybe I should..." The words died on her lips when he turned, his face an expression of loss, which he quickly covered. She made a lightning-fast decision and smiled. "You know what? Maybe a glass of wine would be great. What reds do you have?" She pulled off her jacket, revealing the black camisole beneath, and clicked her way across the tiled floor to see what the choices were.

# CHAPTER 8

*R*ed wine in hand, he watched as Cara made herself comfortable on the chaise, the skirt riding up even further. He could see the tops of the garter, the edge of the black stockings trimmed with lace then a flash of black silk. Swallowed and looked back to her eyes, they shone in the low light.

"So, the woman in the restaurant?" She leaned forward a little, her eyes wide and guileless.

Damn, he'd hoped she hadn't seen that. "Ah, that was Jacinta. I...I went out with her for a while." To be more honest, he'd dated her hoping to catch Cara's eye. Cara obviously had never seen them together though. And in that instant, he was pleased. It had been incredibly shallow behavior on his part. Something he now regretted.

The relationship had ended pretty quickly, once Jacinta got fed up with his refusal to sleep with her. She hadn't been Cara. He couldn't debase himself quite that far to win the heart of the woman who filled his dreams.

"Ahh." Cara nodded.

He cursed under his breath. He'd heard Jacinta and her friends Annabelle and Serena as they exited the bathroom. But Cara had come out looking unconcerned.

Cara placed her wine on the table. "I probably should leave now."

"No! Don't go." The words erupted before he could reconsider. She stopped, already out of her seat.

"Why?"

The quiet word shook him. Nothing but honesty would be fair now. "Because I think there is something special between us."

Cara watched him, as if assessing his words. "Special?" she whispered, dipping back down to the padded surface.

"Yeah. I want to see where it goes."

"Why me?" She closed her eyes. Her face betrayed her uncertainty for the first time. "Because you think I'm easy?"

"What? No. Because you're you. The epitome of everything that excites me. Because you are no hot-to-trot eighteen year old who pushes out her chest at every guy. Because you're bright, interesting. Because I find you sexy. Very very sexy."

"So, you think I'm sexy. Clever. Anything else?"

"Yeah, exceptionally sensual." This time he couldn't contain the longing in his voice. She laughed. Her whole face lightened as she smiled. He held his breath as she turned away, obviously thinking over his words.

The black camisole she wore did little to cover the lush curves he knew were there and his fingers itched to caress them. To uncover them. To savor them.

He shifted slightly in his seat, looking at her lounging in the dim light of the room. When she had watched the twinkling lights of the city for some time, sipping the wine while he enjoyed the view within the room, she sighed. He waited silently for her next move. It had to be her choice, but he still worried that his assurances wouldn't be enough.

Cara shifted and lifted hands to her hair, turning to look at him. "Do you mind if I pull these pins out? My head is hurting." She didn't wait for him to agree. She pulled the ugly pins from the black silk of her hair. He sat, mesmerized, and watched it cascade down, tumbling against her bare shoulders. James gulped. Here sat a real woman. With him. God he hoped she was eager, like him, because...damn it...he was turned on.

Fully on.

James was achingly aware of his level of arousal. Usually his encounters with women were lukewarm. He knew what they wanted and they knew what he wanted. Sex had always felt rather like a business deal. Get it in. Get it on. Get it over.

Not this time. With Cara it felt bigger, deeper and a whole lot more meaningful.

One of the straps of her camisole slipped down over her shoulder, the top gaping slightly and allowing him to spy the lace that lay beneath. A glance assured him it hid nothing at all. This time, when he moved, his erection tented his pants. She smiled as she shifted too, her skirt riding further up, her legs slightly parted and he glimpsed a shadow of black at her crotch.

*Hot damn!*

She was watching him watching her and the thought shocked him, until he realized she was as aroused as he was. The outline of her nipples poked against the lightweight camisole, the puckering points jutting against the thin material. He gulped, leaning forward, and she met him halfway. This time her mouth immediately opened for him. Scalding hot and welcoming his touch.

He moved his hands to her shoulders, feeling the soft skin there. Cara gripped the front of his shirt, pulling on the tie, almost shredding it in her haste and throwing it over her shoulder as she moved against him, her body warmed his. The flare of desire turned white hot. Hunger exploded inside his belly.

She wanted him.

He wanted her.

*By God, they were going to have sex!*

J ames explored her body with shaking hands. They stood up, wobbling slightly in each other's arms. Cara plucked at his shirt, seeking the buttons that kept it closed against her questing fingers, her panties were now soaked and she didn't care. The musky smell filled the air with the hot scent of arousal.

His tongue was warm and smooth in her mouth. He pulled the camisole over her head, tugging at it as it caught on her chin. She pulled away from him enough to let the fabric slide over her flesh. She heard the whoosh as it went flying through the air.

Coolness licked at her skin. She shivered, her nipples puckering harder in the fresh air, while she whimpered at the sensation of plea-sure-pain.

"Oh God, I want you so much." Her words escaped as his lips burned a trail of fire down the side of her neck. She arched into the kisses and caresses as he cupped her breasts through the lacy bra. He stepped back, his eyes widening for just a minute then he smiled. He moved against her once more, enfolding her close against his body. James's warmth made her tingle, shiver and—dear God —shake.

"That's good," he whispered as he pulled her closer, seeking the clasp of her bra. He fumbled slightly but found it. As the lace dropped away, she made to cover her breasts before he could see the sag that came with a size eighteen D-cup body.

"You are sure about this, aren't you, James? I mean, I'm not perfect..." Her stomach wobbled at her question, afraid of his answer. The ugly truth that she feared still sat in the back of her mind. What if —? The thought was cut off, abruptly.

He insistently pulled her hands away. "Don't do that. You have beautiful breasts. I noticed them so long ago. They are so full and womanly. I love the size and shape of them. I dreamt about them. About you." His face was graven in the light as he stared at her.

Cara gazed down to see what he could see. The pink buds were erect. He reached a shaking finger towards one, stroking it lightly and circling the areola. She gasped at the soft touch and wanted to close her eyes, so she could enjoy the sensation, but she fought her body's instinctive action. Her chest shuddering with pleasure.

He smiled. It was wicked and sinful and she basked in the sensations he roused in her. The pull of pleasure filling her body stole her breath away, starting at her drenched, hot and empty core and stretching towards every sensitized spot within her body.

She caught sight of a movement. He reached for the last buttons of his white shirt, and she gloried as inch by delicious inch of his bronzed, hairless chest was slowly revealed. She whimpered, dropped her hand to the button and zip on her skirt.

"Yeah, take it off for me. Slowly." His sexy, throaty words echoed in the quiet room.

She followed his instruction. Her fingers shaking as she found the button of her skirt, releasing it then worked at the zip. Once it gaped open skirt and slip fell to the floor, so that she was almost fully revealed to his hungry gaze. Her sex quivered in anticipation and the skirt brushed against the curls that hid her most intimate flesh.

She hissed with pleasure at the accidental brush of her hands. James moaned.

His eyes turned smoky in the dim light. He shrugged off his shirt, letting it fall to the floor, and reached for her. James pushed the skirt down until she stood before him in nothing but stockings, sodden panties and garter belt.

"My pants. Undo them." The husky instructions along with warm hands directing hers to where they were needed tightened the coil in her belly.

She fumbled, her fingers stumbling against his hard erection marking him as aroused as she was. His body was taut and still as she finally found the zipper. He moaned quietly again as she set about completing the task, until the satin boxers he wore below was revealed. God, she really needed to touch him!

Heat. James emanated heat, and she wanted to bathe in it, in him, with his hands moving over her naked flesh. He toed out of his shoes, kicked them away while he kissed her, ground his lips against hers. His hands framed her body and kneaded the skin of her butt, then traced up to find the back of her garter belt, where she could feel him search for the clasp.

He lifted his head and breathed heavily. "How do I get those panties off you?"

"You could pull them off after the stockings or..."

He grinned wickedly and slipped a hand inside the front of her panties, pulling the lacy black thong away from her skin. He found the thin thatch of hair below and softly caressed her before gripping the material again. One quick jerk and he tore them.

"Miss Chamberlain, I think I like your dress sense." His voice was throaty as he caressed the skin he had found. "And I'll replace them later. But first, you might like to take off your shoes."

Cara quickly stepped out of the spiky black heels which had added four inches to her height, feeling bemused and so ready she panted.

She gripped his boxers, wanting to yank them down to free him in her sensual desperation. It was clear he was as ready as she was. She needed to go all the way now, nothing else could feed the mad beast of desire that clawed at her. The pressure in her chest told her to savor the experience as she pulled the elastic away from his belly, then carefully slid the silk down his legs to pool at his feet. His beautiful shaft stood proudly erect, beaded with fluid at the tip as she moved back into his arms, pulling him closer. The shock of his bare chest against her tightly budded nipples sent a lightning-bolt of pleasure-pain zinging through her system.

He shifted slightly and she stumbled back, surprised as she fell down towards the floor. He followed her and they both lay there, winded and giggling like horny teenagers. Desire washed over her again, as she sat up, her breasts swinging as she turned towards him, still in stockings and garter belt, him with boxers around his ankles and work socks peeking out of the tangle of clothing.

She moved quickly, swooping over him, finding his erection with her mouth, fastening her lips over the engorged flesh, letting her tongue work while she sucked up and down, and grasped him firmly. He groaned and thrashed as she grew hotter, loving that beautiful body. The delicious salty taste of aroused man filled her senses, while the musky scent rising off his skin made her burn. She moaned at the taste of him. "Oh my God. You are so hot," she muttered as she turned to take him once more.

He tugged on her hair softly but insistently. She stopped, looking to his face.

"My turn." His voice was little more than a growl. He pushed her slowly back to the floor, the plush carpeting offering a soft bed to lie upon, as he moved to a kneeling position. Then he rolled her back, spread her legs and lifted her a little so that her knees bent. Cool air hit her sensitive flesh and she cried out at the feeling. Her nipples tightened further, buds of aching desire that she needed him to taste. To lave. She arched upwards inviting him to do just that.

James's body was flushed with desire, his skin glittering with sweat. She panted as he loomed over her, his lips whispering over her skin, barely touching her. He found her neck, loving the skin with dragging kisses before slowly travelling down to find one breast. How she wanted that mouth over her aching skin, but he moved away without making contact.

She whimpered. "No, come back."

"Not yet." He continued kissing her, moving over her belly and lower. Her thoughts splintered. She tried to stop him, but he stilled her actions as he found the line of downy hair. "You shave, you sexy creature. Maybe next time you could get a Brazilian and I can see all of you." His breath caressed her sensitized flesh.

She shook with shock as the air touched her skin.

James slipped his fingers slowly inside her heated core. The pressure was so intense that she exploded in his arms as the orgasm shattered her. Her head whirled and her chest heaved for breath as she arched up once again. He didn't stop though, opening his mouth and descending to cover her flesh. He lapped at her, drinking her essence.

"James, I need you inside me now." The words escaped in a thready whisper.

"Not yet, beautiful Cara. Soon," he crooned as he continued the long slide in and out while she writhed against him, her body still hot, burning beneath his knowing fingers and mouth, even as her body relaxed from the release that had just passed, then started to pulse again.

"Please James. I need you to fill me. Now." Her broken cry into the silent room stopped him. She watched as he lifted his head, the grey eyes intense behind his glasses, his mouth wet, so wet from her release. She shivered as the sensations of pleasure rippled through her body.

"Do you want me now? Do you want me to fill your body?"

She nodded, the movement no more than a jerk of her head. She rose up on her knees as he lay down beside her and pulled her into his arms. "Do you want every inch of me?" His chest rumbled with those deep dark words. She nodded again, wordless with desire.

He tugged her up so that she leaned over him and his jutting erection, which was already weeping and ready. "Then I'm all yours." His grin was wicked. Sexy.

She straddled him, feeling his penis so hot beneath her. She positioned it at her entrance, letting her body slide down to take him inside, feeling the burn as he filled her inch by delicious inch, her canal stretching to accept his engorged flesh. All the way. She knew she was ready for him but the scalding touch of his cock as it entered her was too much.

Cara felt her inner walls beginning to pulse as she rode him, leaning forward so she could enjoy the feeling of him against her. He held a breast with one hand, caressing her tight nipple with his thumb, circling and pressing lightly while he sucked at the other, firm pulls that heightened the sensations. He dropped his other hand, searching for the nub hidden between her legs, fondling it gently. The added sensations pushed her higher as she undulated, faster and faster.

She threw her head back as she experienced a climax like never before, waves of intense pleasure roaring through her. She screamed his name as her body held taut. The continued jerking of muscles radiated throughout her as she gave into the raw sensuality of the moment.

He let go of her for just an instant before once more his brutal grip returned to her hips. He pulled at her harder and faster as he pounded into her from below. One hand released and pulled her face forward, his mouth burning hers as it held her prisoner. Beneath her, he bucked and shattered, his hoarse cry of "Cara!" filled the air even as his release flowed within her. She held him close as her body continued to spasm around him. She gloried in the aftermath of their heated embrace.

Cara lay in his arms, resting after he had stilled her protests and rolled onto his side next to her. She curled into his hot, sweaty chest which heaved from their joint exertions of the last few minutes. She felt both fulfilled and humbled at the experience.

"Well, Miss Cara Chamberlain. I don't think I want you to be my Personal Assistant." His tone carried amusement. She pulled away in shock.

"What? Is that why..." Her heart shriveled in her chest. He'd just used her! Cara pulled away. So he had seen her as the convenient...

"No. I don't want you as my PA. Marry me instead."

She glanced up, shocked as his words broke through her thoughts.

His face was sober in the half-light. "I think I've been in love with you since I first saw you in the gym that day."

Speechless.

She was speechless for about a full minute. He loved her? "But you never..."

"Well, I am the biggest geek in the place. I didn't think you would be interested in me, horn-rimmed glasses and propelled pencil. Besides, you're sexy, all curves and green cat eyes and I wouldn't expect you to notice me." He looked at her and she could detect uncertainty in the depths. The realization shocked her. He had been as uncertain as her.

"About time then that you did. I've had a thing for you since we met in the gym too and was getting quite desperate. So yes. I will, thank you very much." She smiled and leaned in, kissing him on lips that still tasted like her essence. Without thought, she deepened it, moving her mouth against his until they both heaved for breath. He lifted his head.

"Good, then come to bed and we can practice getting even better at love making. We need a quantitative study to work out just what works best for us sexually." He slipped hands beneath her ample curves and lifted her, then strode towards the bedroom they hadn't reached in their haste.

"I love it when you talk dirty." She grinned against his neck.

# CHAPTER 9

*J*ames woke, the black silken sheets beneath his skin cool, his body lethargic and the lack of pajamas making him squint slowly as he thought over the night before. A grin broke over his face as he rolled to find a naked and very sexy Cara sprawled on the silky bedclothes. She was in the bed beside him. It wasn't a dream or a figment of his imagination this time. He smiled.

The familiar morning erection twitched under the covers as he gazed over her body, covered by the light material. Now he knew the dips and swells of her form that he had caressed and kissed the night before. They were no longer a stranger to him. The pink nipples peaked from beneath the sheet calling him to suckle them. He loved how she was curved in all the right places. Her rounded stomach led down to the shadowy curls, tamed into a strip that covered her mound. He itched to slip his fingers inside her, to fill her with his cock and feel the pleasure of their joint release again.

He hoped, one day, they would create a life and he could watch her body blossom and grow large with his child. Her breasts would fill with milk that their baby would take sustenance from. He sucked in a breath as the vision pushed his need higher and he panted slightly. He would share that vision with her soon, and hoped she would feel as excited at the prospect as he did.

James smoothed the sweep of silky hair that spread over the pillow out of the way of her face, smiling as she muttered, and stretched. Cara opened her eyes slowly, taking him in. She smiled. "Tell me this is real. Not another damn dream where I wake up needing something that just doesn't exist."

He moved in slowly. "It's real, sleepy head." James kissed her, the warm give of her lips opening to allow him to slip his tongue into her mouth. He moved closer, feeling the instant warmth of her heating him all the way to his heart. Desire coiled once more low within him. He felt his cock twitch again.

"Oh God! What time is it?" She pulled away, a look of shock on her face as she scrambled for the side of the bed.

"It's about nine a.m.. Why?" He watched her, amused to see the sway of her breasts and finally getting a proper look at the expanse of naked flesh revealed before him in daylight. He rolled back, letting the sheet fall away and watched as she noticed his straining erection. She stopped, sucking in a deep breath, and a rosy flush covered her from head to toe. Her nipples puckered tight.

He patted the bed next to him. "Come back to bed."

"No... She'll sack me for being late."

He noticed she didn't move. Her eyes gleamed in the sunlight as she looked at him.

"Who?" James grinned knowing she was still standing exactly where she had been, before catching sight of his body. She seemed as mesmerized by the sight of him naked as he was by her.

"Jackman. She's an ogre when it comes to being on time." She whispered the words and turned away from his nude body, looking around, as if trying to find her clothes. The ones which were still all over the lounge room floor from the interlude the night before.

"I'll call her. But somehow, I don't think it's going to be an issue for too long. Remember? Personal Assistant? Getting married?"

She froze and turned back to him. Something in her eyes held him still and silent.

"I still want to keep my job for a little while longer though. Just because we're together in a relationship is no reason for you to accept that I am late to work. That would be wrong." She looked at him and the small knot he hadn't realized had lodged in his chest released.

"You are right; that would be wrong." He said the words slowly, carefully, making sure she understood that he knew and accepted her commitment to both Veha Industries and himself. Pleasure filled him that she exhibited such strength of character. But then, it really didn't surprise him. "But I had also told Aunt Horatia that we would likely be late in today." He smiled and saw her look at him with a small grin. "However, I have a proposition for you. Last night I destroyed what could possibly be the most amazing pair of panties ever created by man. We really should do something about replacing them. And I need to find something else. The perfect something else." Her eyes widened as he said the words.

"What would that something else be?" she teased, moving slowly back towards the bed.

He gulped. "An adornment for you. To wear on your hand."

She stopped dead as she looked at him with a question in her eyes. "What?" She placed one hand over her chest.

He smiled, knowing she was still slightly unsure. "A ring for my love. Now, before you get cold, come back to bed." He patted the mattress again and this time she crawled back onto the bed.

"But I didn't think we would rush into a ring. After all, you can't be sure after just one night..." Cara said the words in a rush.

His grin widened, his cheeks tightening as his facial muscles worked. He slipped one hand around her neck, pulling her down toward him. "No. But I know you. Deep inside." The words died away. They kissed once more.

She sighed against his mouth. Finally skin to skin once more, he felt her against him, her damp hot core seated over his erection. He lightly grasped one nipple, flicking it with a tender movement as she hitched a breath. "Hmm...I wonder what would happen if I did this." He arched his back while her knees found purchase either side of his hips.

She moaned and he smiled, pulling her head down to meet his mouth then dropping away to firm around her butt, tugging her closer.

The head of his cock nestled in her entrance, then he felt the movement as the tip moved inside her, filling her.

"More." Her voice was breathy against his lips.

He restrained himself, dipping in then pulling out. He felt the pressure grow in himself, but wanted to make it last for them both. Her nipple was a tight hard bud of pleasure. She panted within his arms.

Her hips moved, but he stilled them. "Not yet."

She didn't listen and this time he felt the slide, unable to stop her before she slid down his shaft until he was fully within her core. Slowly she started to undulate, the pressure and pull of her body sending him white hot.

He thrust.

She moved.

He thrust again and she cried out in pleasure, arching her back, midnight black hair flying as she hurried her movements.

Thoughts fled as he moved faster, plunging within her body, until the milking pulls of her orgasm tore the last shred of control from him and he let go. His seed erupted deep within her and he let loose a hoarse cry of completion.

She slumped forward in his arms. "I love you. You know that, right?" She looked at him with somnolent eyes. "I know it's been fast, but I don't want you to ever regret us being together." Her voice was quiet.

He tightened his arms around her. "I love you too. And I will never regret this." His heart, once empty, now felt full and whole. Now that she was with him.

# CHAPTER 10

The phone beeped as Cara let go of her shirt. It slumped to the floor in a silent puddle.

He groaned at the interruption. "Veha." His voice was tense at the unwelcome break in proceedings.

"James? We need to get a new postal department employee. That latest one didn't turn up for work today. I never really liked him though. Something about that bald head and babyish roundness of his face, as if he fancied himself some kind of overgrown Cupid."

"Aunt Horatia, I did email to say I was going to be tied up for an hour or two. Can this wait?"

"Wait? James, do you have any idea how much productivity we lose being short a postal boy? Our level of efficiency will drop significantly. I'll need to advertise or talk to one of those employment agencies. Such a time-wasting activity." Her peevish voice filled the air. The air that had previously been heated with sexual anticipation.

He sighed. "Yes, Aunt, but..." He watched as Cara waited, nearly naked, looking over at the lounge longingly, the one he had cleared off to make way for their lunchtime conference. Thank heavens she had made sure there were sandwiches in the small bar fridge waiting for afterwards. The glint of the diamond hanging on a chain between her lush breasts winked in the light.

"Really, it is unprofessional. Fancy, just walking out on a job like that..." Horatia Jackman complained through the speaker phone.

He wasn't really in the mood to discuss the man they had hired to work in the postal department right now. He had been enjoying a wonderfully sensual afternoon mutual striptease with Cara.

Afternoon sex was one small indulgence they both allowed in their break since she'd started as his temporary PA two weeks ago. The sex had been hot and frenzied, wherever they managed to find a spot. Whether on his desk, the chair and even against the wooden wall, they had all been well and truly christened now. He grinned at the thought, before making himself concentrate on the discussion.

"Aunt Horatia, I can understand your frustrations..." He winced, wishing he could turn the phone off as the tone of her voice boomed through the quiet office.

"Ever since you promoted that woman..."

He stopped, lifting his head. He had enjoyed the effect tracing his fingers over Cara's belly had wrought. But now stilled, his earlier pleasure seeped away. "No, Aunt Horatia. Stop right there." His voice was firm. Something he would never have been with her previously. For once, his Aunt stopped.

"What do you mean?" Her voice was suspicious.

"No. You won't talk about Cara like that. Never again." The ferocity in his voice caught Cara's attention, no doubt pulling her from the last wisps of the sensual web he had been casting over her. The pink blush in her cheeks leached away. She opened her mouth, but he shook his head.

"James. Dear boy. Your skill lies in making those fabulous ideas come to life. But the interpersonal thing? You really should just leave it to me. After all, that is why I manage your Human Resources department," she wheedled and he steeled himself.

"Aunt Horatia? Cara is the woman I'm going to marry." His voice was flat. He hoped she would just accept his declaration, but the hope was vain.

"*Marry?* You're going to marry the barge-sized...? Why she's too large for anyone to take seriously..."

His body tensed, muscles locked as anger roared through him. No one treated Cara like that. She was more than just her lush body. He clenched his fists.

"Stop. Right. There. Either you accept it or you don't. That is your choice. But you will never discuss her in such terms again. Do you understand me?" His words were firm and the silence on the end of the phone stretched.

"Certainly, Mr. Veha. I wish you well." Horatia's voice was clipped.

He sighed, seeing the concerned frown on Cara's face. "She's amazing. You just need to get to know her." He waited silently for his aunt's reaction.

"For you, James, I will try." Her voice was conciliatory.

He breathed a sigh of relief, feeling the tension in his muscles fade away. His aunt had always been fiery, and he had expected nothing else this time. He knew, some day, she would come around and see the hidden qualities that Cara possessed.

"Okay. Look, I'm in the middle of a conference session, so I'll have to get back to you." The line clicked as the connection ended. "Now, where were we?"

His aunt's words had certainly dampened his mood, but Cara reached out with one hand, firmly grasping his erection. She pumped slowly at first before she pulled back. "I don't want you to fall out with your family...not over me. Honestly."

He stood, erection now jutting proud from his flat belly courtesy of her intimate caress, while she tried to explain and his heart filled again. "You aren't. Aunt Horatia is usually angry like this when she is confronted with something new. For me, in every way, you are perfect. Now stop talking and kiss me, Mrs. Veha-to-be." His lips met hers, as the kiss turned hot and heady. They moaned as they held tightly to each other, the heat of mutual arousal filling the air once more. The delightful feel of her bra and garter belt offered him a sensual combination of skin and lacy roughness, brushing against his nude body.

Cara squirmed against him once more as he slipped his fingers inside her, moving back and forth within her slick entrance. "You know, you should be kind to your aunt. She really does have your best interests and that of Veha Industries in mind." Her voice was absent as she arched more fully into his ministering touch.

"Maybe, but I don't want to discuss that right now. I'd rather do something else with my tongue." He removed his fingers, smiling at her mewl of distress, and slipped his lips down her belly to the curls at the apex of her thighs. They quivered as he moved her into position, fitting his mouth to the folds of flesh that hid her heated core.

"Oh God!" Her voice fractured as he lapped at her. The scent of her arousal drove him mad, the musky scent of sex filled the air. He licked and laved. She moved beneath him while she pulled him closer. One more shuddering lick had her stiffening in his arms.

He stood, moving himself between her legs, reaching behind to free her beautiful breasts from the confines of the pink lace bra, so he could feel the erect nubs rubbing against his chest. He thrust home and Cara moaned.

A flex of his hips and she moaned again, the feel of her surrounding his body, hot and wet, exciting him further. He moved again, feeling the arch of her back while sliding his fingers over her skin. James leaned forward, opening his mouth to one of the pendulous breasts that she offered to him, her hands under the full flesh. He captured her distended nipple in his mouth, suckling as he thrust. The tension grew low and hard and he drove on, feeling her exquisite splintering, the soft milking of her muscles around his engorged flesh.

James gripped her hips firmly with both hands and with one last tremendous thrust, let himself orgasm within her, the jetting spray filling her body, then he held himself against her for long moments. He let his heartbeat settle slowly, shivered as the dampness of their skin cooled, and he reached blindly for his shirt, draping it over her shoulders as she curled into his body.

"Well, we really have something to look forward to now, with working lunches from now on." Her voice was full of humor.

He barked with laughter. "We still have twenty-six minutes before my next appointment. Want to see how quickly we can achieve the same outcome again?"

She giggled, moving back into his arms.

# CHAPTER 11

*D*iocail sat in the same seat he had filled when he had first become aware of Cara Chamberlain. This time he watched the couple, obviously in love, exiting the building. Their hands were entwined as they watched the dark sedan pull up, then climbed in together. No clumsiness about James Veha this time, Diocail thought with a smile. In the few weeks, since they had been together James' clumsiness had disappeared totally. It was also clear in the confident stride of the woman beside him that Cara had finally accepted who and what she was.

"You did good work there." Cailleach sat opposite him once more. Her beautiful chestnut hair was artfully dressed today, and she wore a pale pink sheath. If he didn't know better, he might say it was a vintage Chanel.

"Aunt, I wish you wouldn't just pop in and out like that. It's quite disconcerting." He allowed an edge of frustration to enter his voice and watched her face light up at his tone.

"Yes, I know. You never did like it, that's why I do it. Anyway, your father asked me to tell you he is impressed." His aunt smiled indulgently.

Diocail sat back, a warm glow filling his chest. Perhaps that meant he had finally done enough to be able to go home. "Does that mean...?"

Her smile disappeared. "No. He said to tell you that only counts for a small amount towards your debt, as he has already informed you. But it was a bit." She nodded earnestly. "And just think how happy they will be, with your touch forever in their hearts."

Diocail slumped back in the chair. "I don't suppose—"

"No, he won't tell how much more work you need to do. Just that you need to keep working on it." She smiled broadly, watching beyond his shoulder. "And of course, she is still waiting."

The waitress from before came up to the table. "Hon. I remember you. Water? Bottled?"

"Oh yes! Jake will sort out the bill again."

He sighed. His family did this all the time, leaving him to settle the bill. The server returned with the bottled water, smiling at his aunt. She waited a beat after the older-looking woman left them alone.

"Don't be so down. Think of the experiences you're gaining." With a quick wink she was gone, leaving him alone once more.

He sighed, turning back to consider his next project while poking at the congealed egg on his plate, and he smiled, catching sight of the server. His next project awaited.

# A STRANGER'S EMBRACE

## CELTIC CUPID BOOK 2

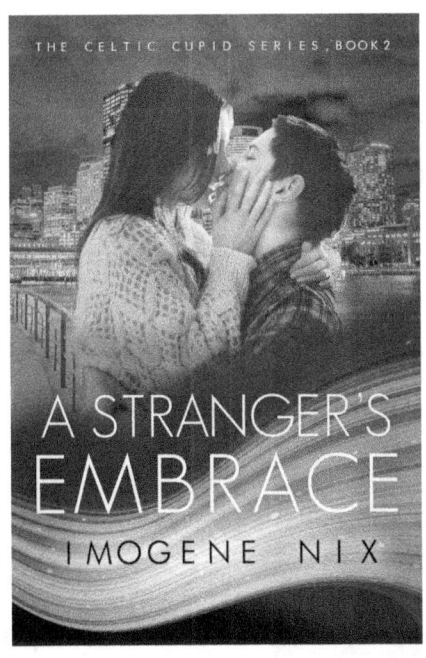

*Cupid is at it again with a little more divine intervention, but can love survive the danger ahead?*

Jane has been living a lie, with her daughter Frannie while on the run from her abusive husband.

Davis Formosa, world famous science fiction author has been intrigued by the quiet and unassuming waitress at the diner he has taken to frequenting.

But Cupid in the guise of Jake has his work cut out helping these two to find their happy ending, especially in the face of increasing danger.

# CHAPTER 1

*J*ane disliked the necessity of working in the small diner across the road from Veha Industries, but it paid the bills and kept her under the radar. It also ensured that no one looking would find her easily. *Especially him.* She wasn't superstitious, but even the thought of him still had her glancing around carefully, hoping he wouldn't magically turn up outside the door to haul her away.

People came in and out, ordering their drinks and food. They rarely paid attention to the woman serving them—the one who hid who and what she really was. She read the body language of the patrons and adjusted her behavior accordingly. She did it with every ounce of her hard-won knowledge and experience of human nature.

Jane wiped her hand on the towel and pushed aside the limp strand of hair that had escaped the scrappy bun. She was already longing for the brief break she could expect to take within the next hour, once her fellow waitress arrived. Mary had rung in late; apparently the doctor's appointment for her three-year-old's injections had taken significantly longer than planned.

"Coffee—flat white, for table ten." Les pushed the tray into her hands. Jane moved quickly, dodging and weaving as people filed out of the eatery, drifting off to work. She made her way towards the table in the corner. At nine a.m. she could expect things to begin slowing down, something the ache of her feet reminded her of. The man sitting there smiled at her as she carefully placed the cup on the scratched tabletop in front of him.

"Thanks."

The man had been coming in for weeks, always picking the same booth, while he did whatever he did on his small tablet device. She'd been drawn to him from the first. It wasn't his rugged good looks or the leather clothing he wore like a glove over a muscular body. She doubted it was the piercing green eyes or the mobile mouth. Jane also refused to believe it could be the chiseled jaw and defined cheeks. No, it was the air of serenity he radiated. Here sat a man comfortable in himself and his chosen profession.

That very first day as she delivered his coffee—flat white, no sugar—she'd caught sight of his work, the lines of red and blue writing meaningless to her, but he'd quickly turned it over, hiding it from sight. She'd scurried away, feeling an embarrassed blush burning her cheeks at being caught looking.

Today he held nothing in his hands except his coffee. She surveyed his blunt fingers for a moment, before turning away with a faint wistful sigh.

He put out his hand, stopping her, and she sucked in her breath at the zing of awareness that speared her. "I wanted to…" He blushed as she turned. "I wanted to thank you for looking after me these last few weeks."

Jane smiled, knowing that answering him would reveal part of the reason she remained in hiding. But he looked at her, as if expecting an answer, and the knowledge that he waited bothered her. It filled her with a vague sense of dissatisfaction. "That's okay." She rasped the words, the sound one she'd practiced for a long time to perfect. It usually kept the men away.

He narrowed his eyes and his face, beautifully formed as it was, hardened. Jane backed away, unable to help herself. That kind of searching look in the past had always resulted in a painful reaction, and she gulped for air.

"Jane? Next order's waiting!" Les called out from behind the counter. Without a word, Jane turned, thankful for Les' gruff intervention, even if it had been accidental.

Les had taken her in the day she'd arrived on the doorstop, little more than a bedraggled rat dragging her barely-teen daughter behind her. He'd never asked why or how and she remained thankful for that small mercy. *There was no way I could even begin to explain how my situation came about. Not easily and certainly not without risk to Frannie. Or me.*

Instead of judging them both for the bruises on their skin and the wild look in their eyes, he'd seen something that she hadn't. That, deep down, she was a fighter. A survivor. He'd offered her a job waiting tables and the small apartment above where she and Frannie now lived. It wasn't the comfortable existence they'd enjoyed previously, but it was safe. *More importantly, it was anonymous.*

The bacon and egg burger with black coffee was a regular order and she knew where it was going before Les even opened his mouth. "Yeah, table five. Got it." He smiled.

"Everything okay?" He searched her face and Jane felt the uncomfortable sensation of awareness. He knew just how flustered she was after that short encounter with the man on table ten.

"Yeah, I'm fine. He's just being friendly."

For a moment Les peered at her, then he shrugged. "You know what you're doing!"

Turning on squeaking feet, Jane made her way over to the table with the food and drink. She remembered his name was Jake; the small squat man with the bald head smiled at her. He may have been working at Veha in the past, but these days he seemed more interested in spending his time in the Wait-A-While Diner.

Something about his eyes reminded her of the pictures she had seen in an art gallery—the distance I sense of whimsy. It wasn't her problem to muse over.

"Thank you, Jane." He smiled.

# CHAPTER 2

*J*ake watched the woman, Jane, hurrying about her business, efficient and personable yet careful to always remain in the background. The diner was emptying out and he was thankful as he pondered how to give her a push in the right direction. It was something he'd been wondering about for weeks.

Lifting the cup to his mouth he took a sip of the scalding drink. The diner wasn't a piece of modern art; it was old and down-at-heel, yet it remained busy in spite of its unassuming decor. The linoleum on the floor was scarred and worn, the tables faded from a mixture of too much light and constant cleaning. Even the seats had lost their springiness from years of constant use. But it was friendly, welcoming and, more importantly, cheap. That alone drew lots of patrons from the nearby buildings.

He sighed, taking a bite of the egg. He'd been watching the byplay between Jane and Davis for the last couple of weeks. Davis an author of some renown though e just looked like a particularly well-groomed biker, with his leathers and helmet. Jane, even though she hid who and what she was: the wife of Carstairs Church. Church owned the biggest motor dealership chain in Australia and was a well-known egotistical over-achiever.

He was also an abusive husband.

One who had gone too far the night he'd lifted his hand to his daughter Francesca.

Jake knew Carstairs Church was looking for his wife and daughter, angry and bitter still because they had continued to elude him for five long years.

For months Jake had been tossing over the best way to help her escape from the man's clutches and the ghosts of her past. How to arrange her freedom, so he could complete the job he had set himself: To hook Jane up with Davis, who was truly her soulmate.

Then Jake could hopefully find his own way home.

"Bit of a cold comfort now." Niamh had grown weary of waiting for him and he thought wistfully of her delicious curves that were now denied him. Jake reminded himself that he needed to stay on task.

He watched the woman as she hurried to serve the customers. She looked older than her age with her carefully streaked grey-black hair, and cleverly applied makeup that accentuated every line on her face. Jane also hid her blue eyes behind colored contact lenses and habitually wore an ugly ill-fitting uniform that detracted from her comfortable size fourteen frame. It was a disguise from the world as much as from her past.

"You know, Diocail, she could look so much better than she does now. Just needs to maybe lose some weight, have a facelift and visit a decent hairdresser."

*Great, Aunt Cailleach comes to stick her nose in.* Jake turned to look at her. "I've asked you not to sneak up on me before."

She grinned broadly, patting him on the cheek, and he growled. "But, honestly, where is the fun in that? Besides, your father sent me with a message."

Jane bustled up to the table before he could ask his question. She grinned at the woman beside him. "I remember you. Water, isn't it?"

Not for the first time, Jake marveled at Jane's ability to remember the regular customers and handle their orders with aplomb.

"That's right, dear." Cailleach lounged in the chair. Today she wore a simple black pantsuit teamed with a white camisole beneath the gaping jacket. Her only adornment was the slender gold chain at her throat, but her mane of chestnut hair was carefully pulled back and up, with small teasing wisps escaping to frame her perfect face. Cailleach always liked to present well.

Jane placed the water on the table she turned to Cailleach. "I know. Jake will fix the bill." She smiled at his aunt and retreated. Jake turned back to Cailleach.

"So, why are you here, again?" He watched her face intently, searching for a hint of what was to come.

"Well, I was speaking to your father earlier. We were talking about the effort you put in with that other couple. He seemed…impressed. In fact…" She stopped and took a sip of her water.

A strange sensation of frustration filled him.

James and Cara didn't need his intervention anymore, now that he had engineered the opportunity to progress their relationship to the next level.

"Yes… Go on…" He waited as she dried her lips and smiled.

"Oh, what was that? Hmm?" Her eyes narrowed slightly. "Diocail, you really should learn patience. Maybe I should…" She rose slightly, as if to leave, and he instinctively reached for her hand.

Then he saw the teasing glint in her eye and swore under his breath. "So help you, Cailleach, if you go without passing on his message…"

She blinked, little more than an artless movement of eyelids while he seethed with both curiosity and anger.

"Oh, all right then." Her petulant voice was totally at odds with her smile. "He says if you can get this mess sorted out, he's willing to allow you to come home."

Jake smiled. Finally, the end was in sight. A bubble of laughter filled him, until he watched her movements.

She pointed a perfectly manicured finger at his chest. "On one proviso."

Jake looked at his aunt, wondering just what scheme his father had cooked up now. "And what would that be?"

"That you find a wife of your own. No more floozies and century-long flings." Her eyes hardened, and she dropped the façade of a careless young woman, becoming the implacable goddess he knew. Cailleach may have looked twenty-five, but she was eons old and known as the mother of their Celtic pantheon, something she had reminded him of over and over again through the centuries. Mother of All accurately described her position of authority. "So, Diocail, if you want that, then you'd better start sorting this pair out and find a woman of your own." This time when she smiled, it was devoid of mirth. "And yes, I know, call you Jake here. But that wouldn't be half as much fun."

A frisson of magic filled the air and she was gone again, leaving him speechless at the table.

# CHAPTER 3

*D*avis watched as the woman, Jane, carried heavy trays filled with food or dirty dishes. He should've been working on his latest manuscript. His editor had been reminding him about it for weeks, but his mind kept turning over that there was something about that woman. She was obviously older than he.

Sometimes, when the diner was only half full, she'd dance a little to a tune, her actions catching his eye, and he would be sure she was much younger than the late forties he'd thought. *Older than me*, he reminded himself again, just like the last time he'd entertained the same idea.

The beeping of his phone called him from his introspection and he lifted it to his ear. "Davis speaking."

"It's Deanna," his agent answered. "So, your speech for tonight? You *are* ready, aren't you? I mean I went to a lot of trouble to arrange…"

Rolling his eyes, he hauled the tablet from inside his helmet, where he'd stashed it. "Hang onto your knickers, Dee." He scrolled through the documents, picked one and emailed it. "There. Check your inbox now."

She thanked him once she confirmed that she'd received the document and hung up. He sat back, letting his gaze roam around the diner.

*What the hell am I going to do about my irrational interest in Jane?*

If only it was as easy as sending an email. He'd taken to coming here every day around nine-ish, not that he was currently achieving much. It was a difficult and laborious way to work, and he would head back to his place after his appointed couple of hours.

He stood slowly, gathering his helmet and tablet, before sliding his legs out of the booth, knocking the coffee cup to the floor in the process. It crashed, sending shards scattering, and he cursed his own clumsiness.

"Oh, don't move." Jane's voice rang out as she hurried in his direction.

His eyes met hers and he read concern in their depths.

"You'll step on a piece of china and cut yourself." For a moment amusement welled, but it subsided quickly as she scurried away. Against his better judgement he waited, seeing her return with a broom and dustpan.

Her movements mesmerized him as she swept with an economy of motion, making a neat pile before dropping to her knees and sweeping it into the dustpan. "Ow!" Her quiet comment startled him.

"Have you hurt yourself?" He bent down beside her and she looked up, a red flush tinged her cheeks.

"It was a splinter, that's all." She muttered and pulled her hand away from his clasp. He felt the loss of her touch deep down in his belly. She pushed away and stood with a small wince. "I'd better go..." She waved a hand towards the staff area. He watched her take the cleaning supplies and retreat.

"Well damn." He picked up the items he'd placed on the side of the table and headed for the door, but as he reached for the cold metal bar he looked back, needing one last glimpse. She wasn't there. The only other person in the diner was the funny little squat man sitting at a booth in the corner, where he always seemed to be. The man gave him a curt nod that Davis reciprocated before he completed his turn and pushed through to the outside. But even as he left he was sure he knew the man from somewhere else.

The familiarity played on his mind before he dismissed it.

# CHAPTER 4

*J*ane hid in the staff room, calling herself nine shades of foolish. "How the hell could you cut yourself on a damned shard?" But even as she wailed, the truth was there. Because she'd been far too busy concentrating on the way he made her feel. Hot and...*hungry* for his touch!

Damning herself for being every kind of idiot, she dumped the pieces of cup into the bin with a savage thrust. But she couldn't push away her body's reaction to his obvious interest. The way her breasts felt warm and heavy. The way the secret recess between her legs had swollen and grown damp. She heaved the lid onto the bin, taking out the sexual frustration she hadn't felt in a long time on the plastic receptacle.

Each day he was here. Each day she'd feel that forbidden thrill of awareness that seemed to hit harder and last for longer with every passing day.

The nights had become a form of sensual torture too, as she dreamed about him. Each morning she woke horribly aroused. Thank heavens the small flat had a second bedroom so she didn't have to share with Frannie.

"Stupid woman. Haven't you already learned your lesson? Men only want what they can get and then use you as a punching bag." She ground out the words as she thrust her finger under the running water. She hissed as she dribbled the antiseptic wash over the injury then wrapped a bandage around her finger. Satisfied that she'd washed away any blood.

It ached unmercifully, but she accepted it, glad the sting pulled her thoughts from focusing on the man who intrigued her.

Now that her injury had been taken care of, she left the staff area, the man on table ten had finally left. Only one customer remained, the little squat man who was finishing his breakfast. He, too, had become a regular and from time to time he was joined by an odd but strikingly beautiful woman.

He waved her over and she snatched up the coffee pot as she headed in his direction. "Want a top up, hon?" Once more she affected the throaty voice that made her seem more anonymous.

He shook his head. "No. But I would like to pay my compliments for another great breakfast." He smiled and she saw a flash of something deep within his eyes, then she mentally called herself a fool, again. The second glance in his direction reinforced the knowledge.

"I'll let Les know."

He smiled as he slid out of the seat, and she started gathering up his plate and cup. Jane heard the squeak of the door as she wiped the table, with quick, efficient swishes of her cloth.

On the surface lay the latest newspaper and she snatched it up. It had been folded over and she glanced briefly to see a story about a gala function, with a famous author presiding. She checked the photo again and shock ricocheted through her system. There was her Mr. Table Ten. *Davis Formosa.* She'd seen his books in the supermarket and each time she'd itched to buy them. They were great science fiction tales, with strong women and well-written fight scenes. She was a huge fan of the Time Warrior series, borrowing them from the library as soon as they came in.

A quick thought flitted through her head about the first editions she'd had to leave behind. Then she snorted. No doubt Carstairs got rid of them in a fit of drunken anger. She shivered, thankful that he didn't know where to find her. She gave the table one last swipe.

# CHAPTER 5

*D*avis tugged at his tie. He hated them. Deanna clutched his arm painfully, and he winced for what felt like the fiftieth time of the evening. "Err, don't suppose you could let go a little, could you?"

"What?" Her breathless voice amused him.

For a woman in her position, she still got jumpy at this kind of affair.

"Your nails are about to slice me through."

She let go and he muffled a laugh as she pinned him with a glare. "Come on. I guess we need to be seen looking at the artwork." Davis wasn't really interested in swanning around, but the first edition copies of his books had been donated by Carstairs Church. Those, along with the jewelry donated by the women of the upper echelons of local society, and the artworks, should fetch a good sum to help with the recent drought crises in the farming sector of Australia.

He sighed, knowing that the night was likely to be long and tedious. Instead he could be working on his latest novel, or reading a book. Either was preferable to the uncomfortable suit he was wearing. He ran a finger along the neckline of his shirt, feeling it constrict his breathing.

"Relax, Davis. We should grab some champagne and act like we're comfortable." Deanna steered him towards a waiter standing in front of a painting. It caught his eye, and he studied it, feeling the cool glass pressed into his hands.

A sense of déjà vu filled him. "I know this woman." He muttered the words, moving his head from side to side, taking in the pale blue eyes and the midnight black hair. If he changed the eye color and removed the grey hairs and wrinkles, well she was almost the spitting image of... Jane! From the diner!

"What did you say, Davis?" He turned to see the shock on Deanna's face. "You think you know her?"

A man beyond her turned and stalked his way over. "Well, she looks familiar," he muttered.

A greasy knot at the base of Davis' belly roiled. He watched as the man peered at him intently before thrusting out a hand. He had cold, bleary eyes. Alarm bells jangled in his mind. The way he carried himself with an air of self-interest made Davis' more than a little uncomfortable. Then the man grinned and introduced himself, slurring slightly. "Carstairs Church."

Davis shook the hand, mentally sizing him up and tagging him as someone to keep an eye on.

"Davis Formosa." The man inclined his head, but the smile on his face didn't make it to his eyes.

"So, you think you've seen her?" Davis waited, interested to see how the guy would spin the story. "That is my wife. She disappeared five years ago and I've been searching for her ever since. She took my daughter, Francesca." As Carstairs leant forward, Davis caught a whiff of whisky on his breath. His stomach twisted further. "Tell me where and I'll..."

Without a thought, Davis shook his head. "I don't think it's her. She looks much older than your wife would be." He trusted his instincts, which had always led him right. This time they screamed to keep her location a secret.

"Well, you lose nothing by telling me where." The man watched him, and Davis could read the implicit threat in his actions.

"I don't want to waste your time. Mr. Church, if you'll excuse us." With a small movement he pulled Deanna away. She squeaked a little but he squeezed her hand and tugged her to the other side of the room.

"What the hell…?" Her voice was sharp. "Who, or, more importantly, what are you talking about?"

"Just someone I know."

"And?"

"I don't know. Something tells me she's trying to stay hidden…" He gulped, knowing she would goggle at his next request. "Bid on the painting for me. Whatever it takes. I want it."

"You *are* kidding, right?" She gazed at him.

He shook his head. If that wasn't Jane from the diner, he'd eat his hat. The picture drew him the same way the woman did. The sadness in her eyes notwithstanding, the woman was a beauty. Then he turned away, pulling out his phone. He had some favors to call in.

# CHAPTER 6

The roar of engines woke her. Jane crawled out of the bed, before dragging herself to the windows, peering out into the cool night air. Her breath frosted the glass and she shivered. Men on big black motorbikes had drawn up outside the diner.

Jane glanced back, checking the small clock radio beside the bed. Three a.m.. Who would be outside the diner at three in the morning? She stepped back slightly as she watched one man climb off his bike and pull off his helmet. The man from table ten! Davis Formosa? What would he be doing here at this time? The chill raised goosebumps on her arms and she rubbed them absentmindedly.

Car lights cut through the gloom. Les' car pulled up. Without a thought, Jane scooped up her threadbare flannel dressing gown and headed for the door just in time to hear a thud.

"Hang on." She muttered the words and moved swiftly in the darkness, flicking the safety locks on it. When she swung the door open she leant forward. "Les? What the hell is going on?" She peered over his shoulder to catch sight of the man behind him.

"Let us in, Jane, and I'll explain." His words were harsh and for the first time since ending up here, living above the diner, she felt vulnerable.

They pushed into the small room and she flicked on the lights. The naked bulb cast a yellow warmth within the kitchen/dining area. The room shrunk under the influence of the two large men, and the small square table and vinyl-covered chairs looked even shabbier than usual. She grimaced but they didn't seem to notice.

Both men sat down at the table and she automatically closed the door, shooting the locks. "So, what's this all about?" She moved to the aluminum kettle, filled it from the sink and popped it on the stove. Bad news required tea.

"Jane, I've never inquired what brought you here. Never really wanted to know. But Davis here…" Les stopped, looking uncomfortable with what he was about to say and a premonition speared her.

"He's found us?" She whispered the words and Les looked sorrowful and nodded.

She jerked over to the table and sank onto the seat. If he'd found them then there was nothing to do… Nowhere else to run.

"It's my fault. I spoke at a gala tonight and he was there. There was a painting. Of you. He heard my comment." The words intruded into her haze of fear.

"What?" She lifted her head and saw the look of concern on his face.

"At the gala dinner for the drought, there was a painting of you. I commented to my agent that I thought I had seen you."

"Well… I guess he's probably on his way." She rose wearily, raising a trembling hand to her brow.

"Mum?" Francesca's voice called from her room.

"Honey, you need to come here." Thoughts and plans filtered through her mind. She had money. Not a lot, but enough to make do until they could find somewhere else. They'd have to leave immediately. She turned towards the darkened bedroom beyond.

"Wait. Davis has an idea." Les interrupted and she whirled back towards the men, forgotten at the table.

"What?" Her mind shifted gears. "And since when did you call him Davis?" Suspicion colored her voice but she needed to know. Surely this wasn't some elaborate joke? But as quickly as the thought came, she discarded it. Les wasn't that kind of guy and she doubted Davis was either... But how had they come to know each other?

"He looked me up. Told me he called in some favors to get my phone number. Made Bernice very unhappy, being woken at one a.m., I can tell you." Les looked earnestly at her, as if willing her to accept what he said.

Her gut churned. *Can I trust Les?* But perhaps now was the opportunity to break free from her husband, to stop hiding in the shadows. Ensure Francesca had the opportunity to enjoy her birthright. *Should I take a chance?*

She glanced quickly at her daughter, only half awake, her hair mussed but with the knowledge there in her eyes. Something no child should ever see. In that instant she made her decision.

"Okay then, so, Mr. Davis Formosa, what's your plan?" She cocked an eyebrow at him and he grinned.

"I get to take you home with me."

"What...?"

# CHAPTER 7

The two females entered his apartment, one craning her neck around, her eyes darting to and fro. "You know this is seriously cool!" Francesca cooed.

He nearly laughed at the expression on her face. *You'd hardly tell that she had been born into this level of comfort*, he thought.

The other—Jane—watched him with turbulent eyes. "Frannie needs to go to bed. She's got school community service tomorrow."

"I don't think that's wise—"

She glared at Davis who closed his mouth instantly.

"I don't really need you to suggest whether she should or shouldn't. She has to go do this. It's mandatory." She didn't look very happy with the situation and he couldn't blame her. Her eyes flashed pale blue fire and she glowed. Jane looked like a dark-haired Valkyrie. A delicious heat filled him and fascination curled in the deepest recesses of his being.

"Frannie needs to go to bed, Mr. Formosa. If you would be so kind as to show us the bedroom?"

He'd been staring at Jane. *Damn.* "Yeah. Come this way to the guest room." He heard a snicker when he picked up the bags and turned. Jane's daughter, a miniature version of her mother, but with softer features, winked at him, then smiled. Taken aback, he led the way through to the bedroom, before settling her bag on the bed. "I hope you'll be comfortable. You have your own bathroom."

"Yup." She grabbed the bag from the bed. "Where's mum sleeping?"

He started at her question and she grinned. "That's okay, she's been talking about you in her sleep."

*Frannie's sizing me up.* It was a discomforting feeling until he realized what she had just blurted out.

"Go to bed, Francesca." There was embarrassment in Jane's voice and she winced as he turned to look at her.

Davis grinned. Her skin shone a delicious shade of ruby. She had dreamed of him? Priceless. But his reaction stopped cold. Holy hell... Did that mean she was interested in him? He gulped down the words he wanted to say. She was in trouble and so was her daughter. Now certainly wasn't the time to think of moonbeams and starlight. Not to mention hot sweaty sex with an older woman.

"I'm sorry about Frannie's little outburst." She spoke clearly, though he could still hear the distress in her voice.

"That's okay. I hear teenage daughters can be like that. My sister's girls are always making comments too." He led her back to the lounge. "Sit down and I'll get you a coffee, or wine or something stronger."

She turned and for the first time he was up close to her. "Look, Mr. Formosa—"

He shook his head. "Mr. Formosa is my dad. And to be honest, it's way too formal." He caught her gaze, holding it. An urgent current of awareness danced between them. "And I'd rather you called me Davis." He swayed just a little before giving in and settled his mouth against hers.

She held herself rigid and he raised his hands to her shoulders, feeling the stiffness in her body. He rubbed gently, she sighed, then her lips opened, just a bit. Triumph roared through him as he hauled her closer, her hands barely touching him.

*She's amazing!*

The lap of her tongue against his pushed him on, his heart rate increasing, and he felt a tightness in his groin. He lifted his lips from hers, as reality crashed down on them, the knock on the door behind him intruding into the sensual web she had woven around him.

"Umm, Mum?" *Frannie.* Hell, he'd forgotten her teenage daughter was there. He took a look at the dark red tide on Jane's cheeks and the glitter in her eyes. No doubt she had, too.

"Coming, Fran."

Davis watched her move away quickly and damned himself. She was scared, tired and on the run. She didn't need him doing the horny hermit thing on her. He sighed and hoped to dispel the need that still coursed through his system.

# CHAPTER 8

*W*hat the hell are you doing, Jane? Her internal voice chastised and she squeezed her legs together hoping desperately to stop the throb that continued hours after that scorching kiss Frannie interrupted.

The situation was dire. *I'm on the run from my husband with a teenage daughter, yet I still couldn't ignore my libido? Since when was that acceptable?* She sighed. The heavy sound threaded through the air. She turned in the bed and a hint of his subtle essence wafted over her. Her stomach clenched as the need warmed her once more.

A hint of pink lightened the sky outside the big window. The apartment block was a converted warehouse from the late nineteenth century and retained many original features, including the large windows.

When she'd entered the room, Davis had closed the drapes, but after he'd left she'd pulled them back open. Now she was pleased that she had. She watched the sun as it banished the darkness and wondered what the hell to do about her situation.

"You know what, Jane? This needs to end." Her words echoed in the room. She acknowledged that they were indeed the truth. She sat up and threw the covers aside as the door to the bedroom opened and in walked Davis.

"Sorry, I heard you were up." He stopped.

She watched him. Amazement filled her as he narrowed his eyes. His gaze dropped to her chest. She looked down and saw the pink tinge of nipple outlined beneath the threadbare white nightgown. He was blushing! And that probably wasn't all he had got a view of. She wanted to moan but clamped her teeth hard, strangling the sound before it escaped.

Heat filled her face as she whirled around, snatching up her light robe, then thrusting her arms into the sleeves.

"Umm. Okay. I brought you coffee." He held a pottery mug toward her and she smiled. *No one has ever done that for me. Well, not since childhood anyway.* She felt tears burn under her eyelids.

He jerked toward her, spilling a drop across his hand. A quiet curse slipped past his lips.

Jane moved and accepted the hot drink, her fingers brushing against his in the process. Awareness filled her again. She glanced away quickly. "Thanks."

"When you're ready, maybe we should talk. Er... Out in the lounge?"

She was about to answer as her daughter's voice echoed through the apartment. "Muummm? I'm gonna be late, Mum!"

"Oh darn. Frannie! I gotta get going." She lurched forward, then snatched up her bag.

"Uh, Jane?" His voice cut through the fog in her mind.

She stopped and turned. "What?"

"You need to get dressed and it's a bit far to walk."

*What?* Then she looked down and saw she still wore her night things. Thoughts of him had stripped her of any of the sanity she'd carefully knitted together over the years.

"Tell me where and I'll take her."

Even as her mouth opened to ask how, he smiled. "I'll take the car."

She breathed out. The pressure that had built in her head seeped away.

"When I get back, we need to talk."

She nodded dazedly. They sure did.

A packet of pastries dangled from his hand. He hoped she had a sweet tooth. They needed to talk, but they also needed to eat and he hoped sugar would help break the ice. He trudged up the old metal stairs, his boots thunking as he went. He could have taken the elevator, but hell, he was in his mid-forties and needed the exercise to ward off the middle-aged spread.

And Jane? Without the crazy makeup, she looked much younger than the late forties he'd thought her to be. In fact, if he didn't know better, he'd say there was a chance she was actually younger than him.

He grew hard beneath the confining denim, as memories of her outline through the thin nightgown came back to him. "Damn." He reached the door and pulled out his keys. "Jane?"

"I'm in the kitchen," She called out, and for a moment fantasy wove around him. Visions of coming home to Jane, maybe a glass of red wine waiting and a sexy smile on her face, played with his sanity. *Wearing nothing but that smile. Naked.*

His mouth dried. A groan of discomfort escaped.

*I can do this.* He took a glance, adjusted his clothing slightly and headed for the doorway. There she was, bustling around his kitchen. The one he didn't ever use.

"There you are." She smiled at him. This time she was fully dressed in a light cotton T-shirt and caramel drill pants. Barefoot. He felt a moment of regret. Damn, he'd enjoyed the view earlier, seeing her pink nipples hidden only by the light cotton of her nightie. And he'd caught sight of the thatch of hair at the juncture of her legs... A twitch below the denim reminded him he didn't need anything else to keep his body interested in her.

He pulled out a chair as she popped a coffee in front of him. "Just the way you like it."

He blinked.

He picked it up and took a cautious sip. The rich strong brew filled his mind and he closed his eyes for just a moment. "Okay. What the hell are we going to do about this?"

"Well, I was thinking this, to start with." A blush stained her cheeks as she moved closer. His heart thudded in his chest and his blood pumped slowly. Surely she couldn't... Didn't mean...

Jane leaned in, and he stared into her blue eyes, wishing he could drown in her. She touched her lips to his.

His mind exploded. Fire could have burnt the apartment down for all he cared. He moved swiftly, their lips still locked together as he rose, pulling her body against him. He didn't really care what had brought this on. He just wanted it to continue.

Davis gripped her, moving his hands up and down her back while she held on to his shoulders, little pricks of pleasure-pain detonated where her fingers dug in. Her mouth tasted so sweet. Intoxicating.

With careful movements, he trailed his fingers down to her butt, feeling the twin globes. They were firm under his touch and he propelled her body hard against him as he tore his mouth away from hers, gasping for oxygen.

She mewled at his movement, but they needed to stop. Slow down. Breathe!

She found his buttons, tugging at them, and he moved her hands away. Who cared about slowing down? Grabbing both sides of his shirt, Davis simply tore the fabric from his chest. The buttons flew everywhere but he didn't care. He needed the feel of her touching his skin. Then they were there. "Kiss me, Davis." Her husky words washed over him, and he gave in to her demand, once more fitting his mouth to hers.

The kiss scorched while he hauled at the band of her pants, lowering the material so he could find the cotton panties hidden below.

He hustled her to the counter and she pushed back against it with an "Oomph". He raised his head, taking in the sheen of desire in her eyes. "Jane, I..." He sucked in a deep breath that expanded his chest while his heart beat a rapid tattoo. "We shouldn't..."

She stilled in his arms, going stiff as if she finally heard his words.

*Shit*! Now he'd upset her. She pushed away but he held on. "I'm so sorry..." she muttered.

He pulled her close. But this time, she didn't respond. "Don't be sorry. But I don't intend using you. I'm a long-term kind of guy. If we get into this... Well, I don't want a quick bang and thanks. Get what I mean?"

She didn't look at him.

He huffed, lifting her chin with a determined move. "Jane? If we do this, it means something."

Tears shone in her eyes and a punch of emotion hit him. He couldn't hurt this woman. Not ever. She was special. He didn't know how or why. Just that she was.

"What do you mean?" she whispered so quietly he had to strain to hear.

"Exactly what I said. If we sleep together, then there is a commitment from both of us." He waited. What would she say next? He refused to push her, but in that instant he knew he wanted so much more than sex with this woman—he wanted a commitment. So, the next step had to be hers.

Jane couldn't believe what she was hearing. Davis. Sexy, super-smart Davis, the one with a chest to die for, needed her as much as she wanted him? *He expects me to make the next move?* She couldn't think of anything that would turn her on more, except maybe seeing him buck naked—a thought that had played on her mind for weeks and invaded her dreams. She shifted position, feeling the dampness of her knickers.

*How?* How did she tell him she wanted what he was offering? *And how the hell did this go from the possibility of a single lustful encounter to something with a degree of permanence. Hell, I could still be married for all I know!*

"Oh God, Davis. You're killing me here." She sucked in a deep breath. "I'm still married, though." She shook her head. "Or, at least, I think I am," she muttered, dropping her head into her hands.

He stilled. "What?" His words echoed through the silence. "Excuse me?"

She reared back, seeing the horror on his face.

"Well…" She spread her hands, agitation flowing through her veins. She took a deep and calming breath.

"You'd better explain that." He stomped back to the table, pulled out a seat and indicated that she should sit down.

She slumped from the counter into the comfortably padded chair and sighed. Yes, maybe she should explain.

He sat and gazed at her, the burning sensation uncomfortable. "So, start at the beginning."

"Well, my…" She grimaced, feeling the twist of her lips. "My husband was abusive, but I was young when I married him. Barely twenty. We married because I was pregnant with Frannie. She was…" Her stomach jittered wildly. She remembered the sensation of fear and excitement she had experienced all those years ago. "She was a surprise. The result of one not drunk, but slightly intoxicated encounter."

He narrowed his eyes as he nodded.

"We were young and well… You know." She stopped, feeling the heat on her cheeks. "Anyway, we married. Things were good for a while. He took over his father's business and money seemed to flow in. Then he changed. Started to hit the bottle. Wanted to party and pretty much told me it was my fault he was stuck at home with a squalling brat."

"Go on."

She shivered at the memory of waves of anger that lapped at her consciousness. "Anyway, one night he'd had too much to drink; he'd taken to partying without me. I really didn't mind by then. He came home. Angry. That was the first time he hit me." The memory of the scene curdled her stomach, but Jane knew she had to press on. Tell him everything.

"He was sorry the next day. Said he wouldn't do it again. But he did." She bowed her head, running her trembling fingers over the fine wood grain of the table. Anything to avoid looking at the dark emotion she saw in his eyes. "It happened again and again. More often the longer we were together. One night he hit Frannie. It wasn't hard, but enough to wake me up. It wasn't just me in danger from his anger. That's when I knew we couldn't stay."

She trembled and Davis folded his large hand around hers. She focused on that small contact. "I ran. We had what was left of my trust fund—most of it was used to fund the expansion of the business, but I still had some left. We headed to a unit a friend rented for me on the edge of town. I hired a lawyer and told him to get me a divorce and custody of Frannie. Carstairs found us one night... It was... I was so scared he was going to kill us both, so we moved. This time I was a little smarter and hired a mail box. I was able to send and receive the documents. I honestly thought we'd got away."

She sniffled as tears trembled on her eyelashes and she pulled away from his touch, dashing at the droplets. "Then a week before the Decree Absolute was due, he found us. Beat me and tried to start on Frannie. We got away with what we had."

"Bastard! I'll kill him—"

"No, Davis! I was weak and scared back then. What I should have done was make sure everything was finalized. But I was terrified. I didn't contact the lawyer, fearing Carstairs would somehow track us down, so I just left it."

"You did nothing wrong." His voice broke through the haze of remembered pain.

"But I did. I let him take control of my money, my life and my child. I should have followed through but I was so afraid. It's time I sorted this mess out. For Frannie and for me." Even as she spoke, the jumble in her stomach turned and tossed. Everything she said was true. She had been weak. Spineless, as her husband had always hurled at her. The time had come to be decisive.

"First thing Monday I'm going to contact my lawyer. See what happened. And I'll find somewhere—"

Davis shoved away from the table at those words, stalking around to her. She jerked upright at his actions. "No. You'll stay here until I'm sure you're safe."

"You know I can't. I mean, where the hell are you going to sleep? On the sofa? It's nowhere big enough for you. Be realistic."

He jerked her up into his arms. "You're staying here. With me." Then he kissed her, stealing her senses as he slid that delicious warm tongue into her mouth and moved his hands over her trembling body.

When he pulled away, she was ready to sag into a boneless puddle on the floor and she panted heavily. "I won't take no for an answer."

# CHAPTER 9

*R*age.

Sheer and unadulterated fury scorched his mind. Jane had been subjected to fear, anguish and privations no one should experience. All because she had a husband who wasn't a real man. It pushed his rage to incandescent heights. No man should treat the woman he married, who had given birth to his child, like that.

Davis wished he could grab the creep and squeeze him until the bloated bastard felt even a percentage of what she'd experienced. Between that and the hard kiss he'd experienced his mind whirled and he lurched away from her.

"Stay here. I'll be back soon."

He needed air. *Fresh air. A ride.* The bike always cleared his mind and right now he needed every speck of clarity his body could muster.

"Davis?" There was fear in her words.

He chanced a look. "I just need to clear my head. I'll be back in time to collect Frannie. She told me the time, and I promised I'd meet her."

Some of the starch holding her upright receded and she slumped down into the seat. "Okay." Her words were quiet and she looked away.

He stepped back, squatted beside her. "I just… I need to burn off some of my reaction to his actions. Not yours." He fought the need to comfort her and the tension that quivered on a cellular level. "I just need some time. You'll be okay here. No one knows where you are."

A jerky nod was her answer and he sighed. His head told him she needed more, but right now he couldn't give it to her. He clenched his fists. "If I stay, I'll need to hold you. To kiss you." He sucked in a deep and shuddering lungful of air. "I'll need to make love to you. So, I gotta go clear my head."

She jerked up. "Make love to me?" she whispered faintly, her eyes now wide with shock.

"Yeah." He turned, headed out of the door then across to the front entrance. His boots clattered loudly as he hurried down the steps.

The garage was below the repurposed building. He hurried towards his bike as he entered the parking area. His steps squeaked on the rubber-covered surface. In the corner sat his Ducati—sleek and powerful. Most people associated style and biking with the Harley Davidson, but for his money, the sensual lines and beauty of his Diavel Dark called to him.

The engine roared to life and the throb between his legs nearly stole his breath. He exhaled, then cursed at the fogging of the visor of his helmet. The road was empty and he accelerated, the wind rushing over him as he leaned into it, moving as one with the bike.

In the back of his mind, that last look Jane had given him continued to bother him.

He rode out of town, seeking the outer suburbs, knowing exactly where he was headed—to a small secluded area where he could open the machine and ride away the anger that threatened to steal his willpower.

H e stopped the bike, then stood, both legs astride and waited for the physical reaction in his body to calm. He laughed slightly, seeing several other bikes at the end of the track. Engaging the kickstand with the heel of one boot, he climbed off the bike. His mind felt much clearer for the ride. He strode over to the other men.

"Nice ride."

He knew two of them. Another looked vaguely familiar—small and rounded, but the man stayed still, his hands on an ancient Royal Enfield Bullet. It was only partially restored, with flaking paint, but he could see that the engine had been completely rebuilt. "Sweet machine you have there. Nineteen fifty-five?" He bent down, inspecting the chassis. "Mind if I...?"

The man nodded and Davis ran his hands over the metal. The bike reminded him of Jane. Not perfect, but with care the beauty of her nature would shine through. An image of Jane formed in his mind. He snagged his hand on a rough section of the manifold and pulled it away, seeing the scarlet droplets of blood. "Damn!" He reached into the pocket of his dark leather jacket, found a scrap of material and used it to staunch the flow.

"You right, mate?" The man looked at him intently and he nodded.

"Yeah, I'll be fine." Then he checked his watch. "Damn. I gotta go." The men nodded and Davis retreated to his bike, realizing that more time had passed than he'd planned. The Ducati roared to life once more. He needed to hurry if he was going to grab his car and pick up Frannie on time.

# CHAPTER 10

*J*ake watched the man ride back toward town. The other men murmured and hurried to mount their bikes too. Only they weren't men. They were brownies, just like himself, there to help him achieve his desired outcome—the connection between Jane and Davis. "You know, Diocail, I can't understand why you aren't just enjoying the freedom that comes with being here."

For an instant he wanted to agree, but the truth was that he was ready to go home. To see his father, stepsisters and stepbrothers. Well, at least, the ones he knew of. And truthfully? It was time for him to take his place in the pantheon. "It's time to go home." The words slipped out and the other brownies snorted.

"Ah, well. Your father presented you with the rules of how to get there. So, I guess you'd better start thinking about who's going to accept a brownie with a past like yours."

Magic filled the air and he stilled, watching as the others became statues in front of him.

"Diocail, you have received my ultimatum?"

Jake turned to look at his father, a vision of regal power glaring through a tear in the dimensions. "I have, Father. And I'm willing to accede. However, the condition—"

"It's not negotiable. Otherwise you must stay here until such time as I will your return."

He swallowed a cry of frustration. Surely at fifteen hundred years of age, he could choose the time of his own mating? But it would seem not, so he nodded. "I don't know where—"

"When the time is right, she will be there. Learn patience, my son. Just as your Aunt Cailleach has preached." He nodded as his father continued. "I see you have quite a battle on your hands with your current couple."

Diocail nodded. "The ex-husband is after her and while I can help Davis out a little, he has to do the majority of it himself. And she has such a sweet daughter." He sighed, seeing the bored expression on his father's face. "Anyway, I have a plan. I better go. Davis and Jane need a little more of a push and I know just what to do."

His father smiled benignly. "Keep it up, then." Diocail wanted to choke on the words but restrained himself as the inter-dimensional tear resealed itself.

"So, we gotta get out of here. We have good deeds to do tonight and good times to enjoy!" The brownies snickered, not realizing that they had been frozen in time while he'd been communicating with his father.

They started the bikes and he watched them ride away.

# CHAPTER 11

$\mathcal{J}$ane fretted, walked up and down the length of the apartment and peered out the old windows onto the street below. She ached with need the whole time Davis was away. *Hours.* Hours of misery and unfulfilled hunger gnawed at her belly like some monster. There was not one darned thing she could do about it. Except... Maybe...

The thought lingered and she angrily turned away, feeling the fever crawl over her too-tight skin. She refused to take any enjoyment on her own. Whether or not it was helped along with some instrument she'd had locked in her bottom drawer for years, she refused to give in to the urges of her body. But that didn't stop the maddening ache and yearning or the emptiness deep within her.

The memory of the scorching kisses kept rewinding and playing in her mind. "Stop it, Jane. It's been years since a man's touched you and now you're old! Too old to be thinking those kinds of thoughts!" But that scolding didn't stop the feeling that coiled through her belly like a mass of writhing snakes. Neither did it stop the heat that left her clenching her legs together, hoping to somehow staunch the dampness that seemed to just...happen. But it didn't work—the gentle abrasion only made things worse.

Jane accepted defeat. Davis evoked a primal hunger within her, it was true. She retreated to the bedroom and sat down, but his scent was there. Enveloping her. Urging her body to greater levels of arousal. She groaned loudly.

A quick check of her watch told her three long and miserable hours had passed since he'd left, striding out of the door. And, heaven help her, she'd surveyed his butt, firm and tight in the jeans as he'd left the room. The memory sent her blood pressure spiking once more.

Her hunger ate at her. Called to her. She groaned again. Jane knew she'd have to do something, anything to alleviate the lustful thoughts rolling through her mind and to fill the emptiness in her core.

Jane flopped back onto the mattress and the shudder from the bed sent skittering zings through her already aroused body. *"Ohhh."* If only Davis were here. She tried to stem the thoughts, but they continued, ramping up her sexual frustration. What would it be like if he were here, naked in the bed too? With her? Her gut clenched and she squeezed her eyes shut for just a moment.

"Oh God!" Her strangled cry filled the air. She jerked up tearing her shirt over her head. "Please... Please don't come back yet."

Her bra joined the shirt at the end of the bed and she shivered as her breasts sprang free. She raised her hands to cup them, her nipples tighten into hard buds of desire, and her body shuddered.

Slowly Jane slipped one hand down her stomach, knowing what she needed. She arched her back and the bed moved again. For a moment the thought of Davis being here with her stole her breath. The snap released and she parted the zipper. "Davis..." She whispered the words and her body tensed once more.

Slowly she burrowed beneath the waistband of her knickers, knowing it would all be over quickly. The scent of her arousal grew stronger as each second passed. She found the curls that covered her heat, parted them with a shaking finger...

"Hello!"

Jane froze. *Davis.* She gulped and withdrew her fingers. "Oh God!"

She jack-knifed upwards, refastening her pants while she grabbed her bra and shirt from their spot at the end of the bed.

"Jane? Are you here?" His voice was louder. Closer.

She blushed even as she struggled back into her bra, fumbling with the clasp and finally getting her arms into the T-shirt. "Just—" She cleared her throat as she pulled the light cotton over her head. "Just a minute!"

He knocked on the door as she straightened herself. "Umm… Come in!" The scent was still there. The movements of the bed stilled as he pushed the door open and he looked in.

*That was close*, her mind screamed. *Too early*, screamed her unfulfilled body and her stomach roiled even more wildly. Another five or ten minutes and she would at least have finished. She cleared her throat once more as he narrowed his eyes.

"How can you help me?" Her words stopped her. *How on earth had that slipped out?*

T he scent of musk was heavy in the air. A blush stained her cheeks and her hair was in delightful disarray, fluffed out here and there. If he didn't know better, he'd say…hot afternoon sex, which he knew wasn't an option. She looked away from him, little more than ducking her head but now he knew: Self-pleasuring. He had to gulp hard to relieve the instant hunger that rose within him. But it didn't work.

His stomach tightened. He wanted to reach out, to touch her, but he couldn't. She could be married. Hell, she didn't even know…

The thought brought him up sharply. Married women equaled trouble. His body had a hard time remembering that. He groaned as she cleared her throat and looked back at him. "Did you pick up Frannie?"

He nodded quickly. "Yeah. She's just putting her stuff away."

"I ah… I wanted to thank you for everything you've done for us." Her voice was little more than a whisper and he wanted to get closer. But that would lead to trouble, he told himself firmly. He stepped backwards, hoping the distance would help, and stepped straight into the heavy wooden door. "Oww!"

She sprang up. "Oh, Davis. Are you okay? Here, come sit down while I check your head." She dragged him to the bed while his mind whirled at the possibilities her words evoked—visions of her touching him intimately. Touching the head not atop of his shoulders. His mind stopped working and his body took over.

Jane pushed at him and he could feel the bed rock behind him, the backs of his knees catching on the edge of the surround. His sense of balance failed and he hooked an arm around Jane's waist, meaning only to hold onto her, but instead he toppled backward, taking her to the bed with him.

"Oomph!" The sound escaped his lips, as she lay against his chest. She was warm and curvy. Then he kissed her. There was no way he couldn't. Not now. She was too close. She was in his arms.

Sparks flew.

His mind blew apart.

Davis moved his mouth over hers needing her taste. He groaned, and he slid his tongue within the warm, sweet cavern. He firmed his hands over her buttocks, learning the indentations and curves of her sweet form. His body tightened, his erection strained painfully against the placket of his pants. His heart beat wildly and he could feel her growing need.

The points of her nipples grazed him as she squirmed over him. The way she gripped his shoulders and pulled him closer as she opened her legs to cradle him against her mound.

"Mum!"

An outraged voice stopped him cold. *Shit! Frannie!* His chest still moved quickly as he sucked in the oxygen, hoping to clear the fog of desire from his mind.

Jane tensed in his arms then pulled herself away, the tendrils of arousal and frustration clear in her eyes. He saw something else and a chink in the armor around his heart grew bigger. He lifted his hands to help her up, but she skittered away and turned, raking shaky fingers through her hair. "Umm, Frannie, this isn't..." Her voice petered away and he could nearly finish her statement for her. *This isn't what you think it is.*

But of course it was. He'd nearly ravished her on the bed while her teenage daughter waited in another room. He breathed deeply, lying still and closing his eyes. He lifted his arm and covered his face. For just a moment, he relived the feel of her against him in his mind and the instantaneous spark was there again. Then Davis willed his body to settle, to calm.

He listened carefully as she ushered her daughter out. "Oh God, Frannie. I don't... Come on, it's time you got settled and started on your assignments."

*What the hell am I supposed to do?*

He rose slowly, levering himself off the bed. This constant state of want was driving him up the wall. But she had to stay. He just hoped he could survive. *Intact.*

In the back of his mind, he wasn't so sure that was possible.

# CHAPTER 12

*J*ane fretted and burned while lying in bed on Saturday night. It was tortuous. She remembered the way Davis felt beneath her and her core pulsed and ached. Emptiness clawed at her. *I have to be strong. For Frannie and for me.* Her pep talk failed.

Knowing he was sleeping on the sofa just beyond the door, she tossed and turned all night. A million times she nearly got up and went to him. Each time she told herself she was a fool.

She won the battle.

On Sunday morning she rose early, collected the dirty clothing she and Frannie had stuffed into one of the bags.

Jane had found the small laundry cupboard while he was out the day before, so she proceeded to scrub and rub, dry and iron until everything was perfect.

Next, Jane cleaned the bathrooms, tackling them with force until everything shone and glittered. It wasn't enough. The spring that coiled tightly within her kept tugging her eyes back to Davis, who watched her as if she was some kind of ticking time bomb.

"Jane, I…" She saw something in his eyes. It could be yearning, her heart murmured, but her brain ruthlessly reminded her that men wanted sex. Needed it. That was all they needed women for. So, she shook her head and asked what he wanted for lunch. He'd looked lost and more than a little confused but she ignored that too.

Frannie entered the room, her expression arch, and very much out of character her daughter stayed silent. Jane was grateful. She didn't need to tell her teenager that she was horny for this man. No, she'd spent years warning her daughter of the dangers of men and their wiles. Instead she retreated to the kitchen, pulling open the pantry doors and scanning it nervously. Flour, salt, yeast—bread!

Jane weighed and measured, mixed and pounded, just like she would have in their tiny apartment above the diner, when her anger overcame common sense. Frannie set up at the kitchen table while Jane baked furiously—muffins and pies, bread and cakes. They lined the pristine kitchen counters.

"Mum, I need to work out how to see if the family has enough water in their tank to last them the month." Frannie's voice broke through her introspective haze.

She cleaned the counter and took her place next to Frannie. "Well, what is the usual usage?" Frannie started on the usage per individual and the rationale as Jane listened. Her mind was occupied and her body ached from physical exertion but she needed more. She wanted something she couldn't have. She wanted something she wasn't supposed to have.

Dinner consisted of a hearty stew, using the ingredients brought from Jane and Frannie's well stocked kitchen. Afterwards Jane reminded Frannie to prepare her bags for school the next day. Once the apartment had settled for the evening, Jane headed for the bedroom.

Davis hovered in the doorway. "Wait! We need to talk."

She stopped. "I don't think that would be a great idea."

"We need to get this out in the open, Jane." She could hear his footsteps and wished she was strong enough to move away. He rested his hand on her shoulder, the warmth filling her. "Please."

That one word was both insignificant and yet so powerful in her mind. Tears pricked but she blinked them away. "Okay."

She turned back and saw the shadows beneath his eyes. "What do you wish to say?"

A ruddy glow crept across his cheekbones and her stomach quivered. Her fingers itched to trace the heat. Instead she clenched her fist tightly.

"I'm sorry. I've embarrassed you. That wasn't my intention. All those weeks... I came to the diner because I wanted to see you. I needed to see you again."

She waited quietly while he spoke.

"Then once I kissed you, I needed more. Wanted more. But you don't want that, do you? You don't want me."

The last statement carried a barbed tail. She could say no, but that would be a lie. And she couldn't lie to Davis. She searched his face. He waited silently as if able to read the truth in the stillness.

"No. I want you too." She choked over the words. "But I can't. What if...?" It was too much.

"What if you're married? Then we can wait. I will wait for you." And she knew he meant it. The way he leaned in and gazed at her. "Because there is something about you I can't do without."

She was sure he was going to kiss her. Heat infused her body, but he only dipped his forehead to hers and she felt a keen sense of loss. "We'll wait. Then we'll do it right. For you and for Frannie. And for me."

*Dang. If I didn't know better, I'd say that was a vow.*

The sun glittered through the open curtains. Jane roused and chanced a look at the clock: Five a.m.. She should be up, getting Frannie ready for school and getting ready for work, but the truth was she felt tired. Tired of running. Tired of being alone. She felt weary to the bone.

Today was the day she would find out if her planning had followed through to the end. Could she start looking for a new way to live her life or would she need to begin the process again? A heavy sigh emerged. *Davis.* What the hell was she going to do about him?

Her, hopefully, ex-husband aside, she could move on with her life. Perhaps it was time. Thoughts chased around in her head and she stood. Maybe she should take a chance. Her stomach fluttered but she firmed her shoulders. This man, the first since…since before Frannie was born, for heaven's sake, who thought her sexy. The morning air skated over her skin, cool and arousing. Frannie wouldn't be up yet. She had nothing to lose. After his words last night, well, she knew he wanted a relationship of some kind. So, she scuttled across the room and opened the door a crack.

He was there, on the sofa bed. His chest was bare and didn't that just steal her breath? "Davis?" she whispered, half scared that he would still be asleep and totally terrified that he'd changed his mind. He opened his eyes and looked at her. Muscles rippled as he sat up.

"Is everything okay, Jane?"

She nodded, feeling suddenly foolish and shy. Her mouth dried as he pushed aside the covers and rose. His skin looked smooth and unmarked except for a small bow and arrow tattoo on his hip—his gloriously naked hip. Then she released an exhalation as he uncovered his boxers, which were riding low. She quaked.

"Jane?" His voice was deep.

She shook under his burning gaze. "I-I wanted…"

A slight smile quirked his lips. It was enough to tell her that he knew. Her face burned as she let herself search up his chest, to his eyes. They were watching her—smoky and hungry.

"I want… I want you to kiss me."

He advanced, moving slowly, and she accepted his touch. Carefully, he drew her to him so their chests connected—her breasts were heavy. Her nipples buds of erotic sensation, while zings of pleasure flickered through her body, and she shook again.

He dipped his mouth to hers. "This time you asked. And I will do anything to please you. To protect you." As their lips touched, her knees buckled while he surrounded her with his strong arms. They were like bands of tempered steel. She opened to him, knowing there was no backing out now.

As quickly as he had touched her, he moved away. "That's a promise. And so is this." He raised his fingers to her chest, finding the ribbon closures and slowly tugging at the first. He slid his hand to the next ribbon and the one after until the gown gaped open. She didn't stop his actions. Her heart reminded her that he asked, didn't demand.

"You are mine. We'll take it as slow as you need, but one day soon, I will share your bed. I will touch your body and make you burn and cry out for me. I will fill you and feel your wet heat around me."

He slipped his fingers through the opening and slid down to gently cup one breast, his thumb grazing the sensitive nipple. She melted at the core. Dampness seeped out, coating the lips of her intimate flesh.

She reached out, placing her hand flat against his chest and slowly slid it across to find one of his nipples. "And I hope that will be soon," she whispered and saw surprise and pleasure bloom on his face. "Hopefully today the news will be good and then it can be sooner."

He nodded. "Soon."

Jane dropped a hand. "Come with me. Just for now."

He raised his eyebrows but he followed her back to the room, entered and she closed the door. "I don't want any interruption for this."

Once more she stepped forward and he opened his arms. She felt the cling of their lips, the erotic sensations fizzed through her veins as she gloried in his touch. Jane reached upward and captured him with one hand, keeping him where she needed him. The kiss was long; drugging. The effects stole her senses so that she reeled beneath the onslaught of their combined passion.

After long moments they moved apart. "I'm hard work, I know. But… I do want this. Soon."

He watched in silence, as if waiting for the rest of her promise.

"I just want to come to you free of his taint."

"You'd better, I mean come to me soon." He stopped and his gaze darted south. "Oh, man. If you are going to come out like that, be prepared to be ravished, or cover up." A hint of amusement filled his voice.

She giggled. "I'm a bit old for ravishment."

"No, you aren't." His firm words pulled her up.

She looked at him, questioning his gaze. "I'm thirty-six, Davis. I'm not some young girl with her first crush."

"That's not old. Many women are marrying for the first time and having their first child."

She pulled away, refusing to accept his words.

"Jane? What's wrong?"

"I wanted more. More babies but he never did. I got pregnant once. But…" Her stomach tied up in knots at the memory and she shied away from the pain that came with remembrance.

"Oh God! Sweetheart. The bastard!"

The savagery in his tone surprised her and, coupled with the fury on his face, she forgot who she was with. She shrank back then realized this was Davis, not her husband. "Please. It's done. It can't be undone." But the tears gathered in her eyes and leaked down her face.

He was there, enfolding her once more.

"Never again will he hurt you. I won't let him."

She shuddered in his arms, held on and hoped he could make his words come true.

# CHAPTER 13

*D*avis contained his rage, refusing to give in to baser instincts that screamed he go find that useless son of a bitch and grind him into the pavement for the things he'd done to Jane. Instead he leashed the fury, banding it with titanium will, until later.

They delivered Frannie to school, ensuring that the office staff was apprised that Davis was now on the list of contacts and would be collecting the girl at the end of the day. A short car trip in silence delivered her to the solicitor's office. The arrival was anti-climactic as they discovered the building had been demolished. Some judicious questioning informed them that the solicitor had retired after selling his practice to a larger law firm in the city.

"Oh God! What would they have done with the files, Davis?" Her words were thready and his heart bled. *How the hell can I fix this for her?*

The small tablet device sat on the back seat, where it had laid since his last visit to the diner. "Just give me a minute. I have an idea." He turned it on and quickly searched, but it was obvious that it wasn't that simple.

A policeman pulled up next to them, so Davis depressed the window button.

"You can't stay here. This is a no standing zone."

Davis grimaced at the older balding man, who somehow looked familiar. He had to be in his late fifties, with wrinkles and a pot belly, but there was something about him.

"We were just trying to work out where the solicitor from here would have gone. We'll—"

"Oh that's easy—old man Davidson sold up to his son-in-law, David Hellmond. Kauffman and Associates. Over on William Street."

Davis grinned. "You have no idea how much you have helped. Thanks so much." They waited until the official vehicle pulled out into the traffic and followed suit. "Can you use that and find where we need to be?"

Jane nodded and his heart lightened. They had a chance. When she found the address he had her use the cars map facility.

They drove following the instructions from the GPS, then hunted for a parking spot, eventually settling several blocks away. He ushered her toward the offices, keeping an eye out for her ex-husband. He knew it was unlikely that he would find her, but then he didn't trust the man as far as he could throw him.

They hurried within, even though something felt off. The back of his neck itched and he chanced a look around but there was nothing there.

Davis ushered Jane towards the large marble desk in the foyer and addressed the woman. "We are looking for Kauffman and Associates."

She smiled blandly, pushing her impeccable blonde hair behind one ear. "Do you have an appointment?" She leaned forward, and he could see her cleavage. Not that he was interested. Instead he hooked an arm around Jane, who sagged into him.

"No, but we need to see David Hellmond."

The woman pursed her lips. "I'm sorry. Access to Kauffman and Associates is limited to appointments only. Have a lovely day." She dismissed him with a false smile and he had to stop a growl emerging from between tightly clenched teeth.

He seethed and wrenched out his phone, before dialing the number as he ushered Jane to the deep loungers by the exit. "Just give me a minute. I'll get us in."

She smiled, but it was only a ghost of one. Her shoulders drooped along with her lips.

He found the number and dialed.

"Kauffman and Associates. How can I help you?" The artificially bright voice called down the phone. He hoped to infuse his voice with some kind of enthusiasm, realizing that he needed to bluff his way in. "Hi. Davis Formosa here. I'm wondering if I could talk to David Hellmond."

The woman on the line squealed. "Davis Formosa? The author?"

He grinned and winked at Jane who straightened in her seat.

"Yeah. Look, I need to get in to see David Hellmond. Is there any chance? I'm downstairs and I really need some advice…" He let his words trail away, knowing she would assume he needed help with his current book.

"Oh my. Just one moment." She flicked him onto hold.

He glanced at Jane. "They're going to see about getting us in."

The music on the line stopped. "David Hellmond here. Mr. Formosa, it's a pleasure—"

"Yes. Look, I have an issue and I need some help. You were suggested to me. Can you see me now? I'm downstairs in the foyer with a friend."

"Sure. I'll have them buzz you up." The eagerness in the voice warmed Davis as much as made him feel like a fraud. But he'd do whatever to help Jane.

He sauntered back to the receptionist just as the phone at the desk beeped. The woman answered it, her eyes becoming round. "Uh, sure. Mr. Formosa and his companion are on their way up right now." Her breathless voice filled him with triumph as she handed them both a tag. "Fifth floor. Mr. Hellmond will be waiting for you."

"Thanks." He waited while the woman on the desk gave a hundred-watt smile, all teeth and flash. But it left him cold. He ushered Jane to the elevators and stepped within, swiping the plastic tag that allowed the lift to rise. It opened to a lushly appointed foyer with maroon carpeting, dark wood and gilt trim. A man waited, late forties, rounded belly firmly encased in a light grey suit and teamed with a red tie that matched his ruddy complexion.

"Mr. Formosa!" The man shook his hand and led them to a small office. "You need my help?"

"Indirectly. See, Mrs. Church here—" He grimaced at the name. "Your father–in-law was acting for her in a family court matter."

The man looked at him then glanced back to Jane, narrowing his eyes. "Mrs. Jane Church?"

Jane nodded furiously.

He sighed. "One moment, please."

He left the office. The low buzz of voices and the sound of scraping draws emanated from outside then he returned with a large file, tied with pink ribbon. "I believe this is what you are looking for?"

He opened the file and there lay a range of envelopes marked 'Return to sender'.

"Oohh." Davis looked at the pale countenance of Jane. She reached out a hand and picked them up. "Can I…? Can I open them?"

The solicitor nodded, "As soon as I see some identification, Mrs. Church." She gritted her teeth and nodded. "Of course." She fished around in her handbag and pulled out a battered passport, handed it over and waited precious seconds as he inspected it.

"Thank you. It's standard practice," he muttered.

"Yes, I understand," whispered Jane as she reached for the packet. She opened the first, scanning the contents. Then the next. Slowly, one by one she inspected each then picked up the package and slipped them within her bag. "I'm free," she announced then she burst into tears.

# CHAPTER 14

*J*ane sighed. She wasn't usually a waterworks kind of person, but after all these years, she finally knew. She was free. And so was Frannie. The solicitor had worked efficiently, using the photos, doctors' evidence and even neighbors' statements that told the truth. Carstairs Church was an abusive husband—one who had also hit his daughter. She was a divorced woman with full custody of her child, according to the letters.

Even though he had petitioned for an appeal, the appeal had been lost given the weight of evidence.

Davis pulled into a spot and got out, they planned on collecting Frannie from school. She quirked an eyebrow at him and he smiled. "I'll come with you."

The satisfied look on her face must have caught his attention because he stopped and leaned in for a quick hard kiss. "What was that for?"

His laughter rumbled. "Because you're beautiful and look happier than I have ever seen you."

An inelegant snort erupted and she laughed again. "Come on, Mr. Silver Tongue." She gripped his hand and dragged him towards the entry. Her back prickled and she stopped dead.

"Wait!"

She turned, and there he was. *Carstairs Church.* Behind him was Frannie, being manhandled into the long stretch limo. "Looking for my daughter, are you?"

"Carstairs. Let Frannie go! She's not going with you." Her voice shook and her insides trembled.

"Francesca is coming home with her father. The one you stole her from!" He advanced and Jane's stomach wobbled with fear.

"Hand Frannie over, or I'll make you a very miserable man." Davis stepped forward and the look on his face, dark and foreboding, must have transmitted something to Carstairs, who blanched.

"She's my daughter. You can't do anything." But the words were bluster because he moved.

Jane recognized one of the men stopping Frannie from getting out of the car. "Michael, you need to let Frannie go. The courts awarded me custody because he beat us." The man looked uncomfortable and unsure so Jane decided to work on him, somehow knowing that Davis would deal with Carstairs.

"I…" His eyes were round.

"I have proof. Right here." She reached into her bag and grabbed the papers she'd taken from the office. Pulled out the what she needed. "See? This is what he did to us!" She held up the photos. They showed both of them, beaten and bloodied.

Michael didn't look over, even as he heard Frannie yelling at the man holding her. "Let me go, you ape!"

The indecision on Michael's face spurred Jane on. "Three broken ribs, fifteen stitches and a broken arm for me and a miscarriage. Five stitches for Frannie and a cracked rib. Concussion." She breathed in heavily, feeling the ache in her chest and the sting of tears. "Is that what you want her to go back to, Michael?"

Jane tried to block out the sounds as awareness of those around them impinged. Bystanders. Many muttering and a lot of shocked comments. Some just watching the scene unfold and others on their phones, hopefully contacting the police. She stepped forward. "Let her go. She's an innocent in all this."

Frannie pushed on the door and ran, heading towards Jane, but Carstairs was there, grabbing her by the arm. "She's mine now." His voice was triumphant.

Davis stepped towards her ex-husband.

Carstairs pulled Frannie against his chest. "Come any closer and she will regret it." Frannie cried out in pain.

The lump in Jane's chest became a boulder. Pain and anger warred. "She hasn't done anything to you, Carstairs. Let her go." She could hear the pleading in her voice. This was her daughter. She couldn't just watch him take her away. Couldn't let him hurt Frannie, like he had done to her for years.

"The two of you ruined my life! I didn't want some squalling brat or a wife. You got pregnant and I had to marry you. It ruined everything I planned! But now I'll get even with you!" She could tell he was on edge. Spittle gathered at the corners of his mouth and that signaled danger for her and Frannie.

His cold blue eyes held a freezing remoteness that seemed to appear just before he tipped over the edge. Her muscles clenched. *Not Frannie*, her mind screamed and she knew she'd do whatever to keep her daughter safe. "Carstairs, let her go and I'll come with you." She stepped forward and he jerked on Frannie, pulling her hard enough that her head flopped and she cried out.

Jane's stomach roiled and Davis stepped closer. "Let her go!"

"I don't—" A distant sound of sirens filled the air and he flipped his head up. Michael hovered, looking ill and lost, and Frannie stomped on Carstairs foot. Jane extended a hand at the same time as he released their daughter. Frannie darted forward and Davis caught her to him.

Carstairs growled and reached out, snagging Jane's arm with a crushing grip. "You'll do for now." He hauled her in his wake and she fought, kicking out with her legs, then twisting and turning. His loose arm flew, catching her with a brutal blow at the side of her head and, even though she ducked, it hurt enough for her to stop fighting.

A sound of anger and fury cut the air. Jane's dazed senses saw movement but her brain didn't connect immediately that Davis had moved and punched Carstairs. Cars rushed up and she heard words as she fell.

"Police! Stay still!" Her senses greyed and she fell.

Heart in his throat, Davis saw Jane slump to the ground. His quick spring wasn't fast enough as she hit the pavement, though he did stop her head cracking on the concrete. The police moved in and quickly cuffed Carstairs Church. The round little policeman with no hair was obviously in charge, but Davis didn't waste too much time worrying. Right now, his concern was for Jane, who lay still with her eyes closed.

His stomach churned as he searched for blood, but he didn't see any. So why the hell, wasn't she opening her eyes?

Carstairs Church muttered and argued as the police gathered around, hustling him quickly from the scene. Even as he was led away, he continued his diatribe. "You can't do this to me. Do you know who I am?" In response, the police, tight-lipped, pushed him towards their car.

Others spoke to the bystanders, taking their statements and one officer assured him that the ambulance had already been dispatched. The crowd started to disperse as more than one police car headed away from the scene.

"Come on, Jane. Wake up." He sat on the ground whispering at her, her head resting in his lap. She moaned and his heart lightened. Frannie cried and wrung her hands and Davis wanted to comfort her, but right now Jane was his priority. Jane's eyes opened and he knew in that instant that she knew where she was. She struggled to rise.

"Stay still, Jane. The ambulance is on the way. They need to check you out."

Frannie hurried to the ground, crouching alongside him. "Mum? Oh, Mum, are you okay?" Tears trickled down her face and she reached out with a shaking hand.

"Honey...I'll be fine." Once again, she struggled to rise, but he held her still. Her words were faint but he heard the steely determination in her voice. Saw it in her gaze, he sighed and thanked every deity he could think of that his woman, warm and more importantly alive, lay in his arms. *If not totally unharmed.*

The bones in his body wanted to turn to mush. They wanted to shake, but he locked his joints in place. He'd hold it together for her and Frannie.

The ambulance arrived, two paramedics hurried over hauling their heavy white bags with them. Davis stood and let them do their thing while he watched anxiously. They suggested taking Jane to the hospital with them but she shook her head. Davis stepped forward but Jane held up a hand. "No. I won't go to the hospital. I'll go to the doctors if necessary, so we can have a report filed against him."

He worried about her, but she stood firm. She must have seen a hint of his concern on his face.

"I promise to make a statement to the police. But I'll do it tomorrow. Right now, I just want to go home."

He waited for her to clarify the comment for him. Which home did she mean? The dingy flat where she had lived with Frannie? Her house where she had lived in the past? Or his apartment?

Frannie broke the silence. "You mean back to the flat?"

Pain lanced through his midsection. They wouldn't stay.

"No. I mean…"

Davis glanced down at Jane. "What? Where do you want to be?"

"I want to go home. To your place. But only if you want us there."

He grinned, knowing there was no question what suited him best. Davis couldn't contain the joyous feeling growing in his chest, heating him from the inside out.

"You bet." He hoisted Jane. "Frannie, could you grab your mother's things?"

The girl bent and retrieved the battered handbag and held it out. "Why are we going back there?"

Jane laughed, then groaned. "Ah…I'll explain later, honey."

# CHAPTER 15

*J*ane ached. Her face had the stiff feeling that only came with the swelling and bruising from a meaty fist punching on flesh. Her back twanged from the fall, but for some reason the bruising around her cheek and the puffiness of her eyes didn't seem to put him off.

Davis watched intently, the way he'd followed her around the apartment while waiting for Frannie to head to bed made her shiver. He'd certainly been solicitous. Ice packs and drinks had been ferried and the second she had so much as moved he was there, patting pillows. He'd even organized dinner for her while he'd entreated her to rest. A situation she was wholly unfamiliar with.

Francesca meanwhile had obviously worked out the shared interest between herself and Davis. The horrified look on her face and her outburst of "Muuuum!" cleared up any misconceptions Frannie had. The wail when Jane had sent Frannie to bed had been uttered with all the shocked disbelief that only a teenager, realizing her parent might actually want to be sexually active, could muster.

Then Davis had taken her hand, helped her to rise from the comfortable armchair and led her towards the bedroom. "You should be in bed." The lump in her throat had grown larger.

"I need…" Jane swallowed her nerves. "I'd like to take a bath first."

The look he shared was just this side of smoldering. In fact, if he didn't leave soon, she'd be a pile of ashes on the carpet, so when he turned on his heel and left the room, she inhaled a deep shuddering breath.

Her body was tight with arousal. Staggering towards the bathroom door, she pushed it open and dragged off her clothes as she moved into the luxurious blue and white tiled area. She plugged the drain then hauled on the handles. Warm water gushed from the spout. She rattled about in her toiletries bag, finding a small bottle of bubble bath Frannie had given her for Christmas.

The musky scent filled the air as the water rose and eventually she was able to turn off the taps and climb into the large, square and obviously custom-made bath. Jane hissed slightly, lowering herself, and the warm water lapped at her body.

Muscles slowly relaxed. She leaned back letting the worries and concerns float away. It had been so long since she'd been able to immerse herself and the feeling of well-being had her drifting in a haze of comfort. A sound intruded.

Jane shot up and water splashed onto the tiles. "Who is it?" But inside her mind she already knew.

She looked at the door, which inched open farther. "Can I…? Can I come in?"

*Davis.*

Now was the time to tell him yes or no. She breathed deeply, filling her lungs. She admitted to herself that she wanted this. Wanted him. "Yeah." Jane heard the frightened croakiness of her voice and winced as the door opened. Her tummy jumbled but she waited, knowing she'd passed the point of no return.

Then there he was—framed in the doorway, carrying two glasses of wine. He looked concerned, hesitant even. She felt that warmth creeping through her limbs spread a little further.

"Is that for me?" She nodded to the glass of wine in his hands and he nodded with a jerk.

"Yeah. That is… Did you want a wine?"

Jane cocked her head to one side. "Yeah. But I'm nearly done here. Just let me rinse my hair." As far as romantic lines went, it probably wasn't a winner, but she needed to be herself.

"Let me."

She cast him a quick fiery look. She wanted him to stay still and silent to keep the hunger at bay, but it wasn't working, judging by the look in his eyes. Jane shivered with anticipation that curled through her belly. This time, she could be in control of her own destiny and she waited as he tussled with the hand-held shower attachment, rinsing the suds from her tresses. The action telling her wordlessly how much he desired her.

Finally ready, she rose, noting the way his eyes darkened. His gaze travelled over her body.

She knew what he could see. Breasts that had once been firm globes now showed signs of age as they sagged with the help of gravity. A belly that was reasonably trim if showing some padding, no matter how carefully she ate or how many miles she walked.

He turned around, grabbing up the glasses of wine from the ceramic vanity unit with a quiet *clack*.

As she stepped from the bath, he extended one to her, waiting until her fingers curled around the stem, then with one swift motion he pulled her into his embrace.

The most beautiful woman he'd ever met had accepted his help. His mouth had dried as she'd risen from the water and the suds slicked down her body, leaving him one massive ache. The bubbles that clung to her wet curves called to him like a siren.

Her pretty pink nipples budded tightly under his gaze and he caught sight of the trimmed hairs covering her mound.

His body burned.

A tingle ran through him—his erection pushed on the cotton briefs he wore and his heart raced. She was beautiful. Stunning.

And she was now his.

With a careful slow action he enfolded her wet body, savoring the feel of her silken skin beneath his touch.

The wine slipped and he sighed. "We should put these down I guess."

"Yes, we should." Then she lifted the glass to her lips, gaze firmly set on him and sipped.

He shivered and reached out to place his glass on the vanity as she did the same, then he moved forward, slid his hands down her front, finding the dips and hollows. His fingers trailed over her skin, leaning the flare of her hips and slid them around to the firm muscular buttocks while he kissed her. Deeply. Hungrily.

When he finally pulled away, she panted, telling him wordlessly that she too felt the desire that clawed at him.

Rational thought fled in that instant. He wrapped his arm around her and tugged her gently to the bedroom, where only the bedside lamps glowed. Slowly, he unbuttoned his shirt, watching for any sign that she had changed her mind, but instead her smile broadened.

The material parted, and he slid it off his shoulders and let it slither to the floor. His chest rose and fell with the force of his need. He reached for his belt, fumbled with the metal clasp until it gave way, then he unfastened his jeans, pushing them and his briefs down over his hips.

His erection sprang free and finally he was as naked as she was.

In her eyes he read the same burning hunger and he smiled, before advancing slowly. Her gaze dipped, and he knew the instant she focused on his cock. The length jerked and he had to swallow the instinctive groan that rose at the sensation.

Jane reached out, her fingers glanced over his head of his erection and he couldn't contain the hiss that escaped.

She pulled away and swallowed.

"I'm not hurting you?"

In that instant, he understood. She may have been married and given birth, but she knew nothing about loving. He damned the bastard for his unfeeling use of her body and Davis promised himself that she would feel only pleasure at his touch. "You can't hurt me like that, Jane. Let me show you pleasure."

"I-I don't really know."

Anger warred with his need to soothe her. To touch her. To school her. "I'll show you pleasure… Make you want like you've never before experienced."

He didn't wait for her to answer—instead he touched her breast. Cupped the weight and slowly rubbed his thumb over the distended nub. She moaned quietly.

"By the time tonight is over, you'll want this and so much more. Your body will crave the pleasure I want you to experience," he muttered as he caressed her belly. She sucked in a deep breath while he rested against her for an instant, felt the tensing of muscles then slowly started to trace circles.

"Oh, Davis…" She groaned while he fondled her breast. He kneaded her skin, learnt her responses and exulted each time her breath caught.

This time, when he shifted his touch, slipping his arm around her waist, she melted into his embrace. The skin to skin feeling nearly overwhelmed him and he had to stop. To suck deep breaths in.

God help him. He was caught in the sensual web. The one he'd planned to wrap around her. It flung him into a world of feeling he had never before experienced.

He ached to fill her, but he had to go slowly. The thought lapped at his beleaguered mind.

She slid her hands over his flesh, gripping his hips as she undulated, lost in her passion. His heart beat wildly in his chest. He shuddered as he pushed her towards the bed. She lost her balance as the edge caught the backs of her knees, crying out and pulling him down with her.

He angled his mouth over hers, sought entrance, and he surged within the moist cavern. He tasted her desire as she pulled at his shoulders. He tore away, gasping.

"Please, Davis," she entreated and, heaven help him, he lurched up, fitting himself at her center, felt the scalding heat as she parted her legs for him. He thrust once and seated himself to the hilt.

She cried out and he stilled. *Dear God! What have I done?*

Then he felt her movement as she circled his waist and gripped behind him with her legs. She moved and he was lost to everything except the need to fill her. Pleasure her and make her scream.

His thrusts sped up and she undulated against him. Her nails bit into his skin, but he didn't care. They remained fused together while her tongue danced wickedly with his in the heat of their intimate embrace.

Finally, unable to stop, the pressure grew in his lower back and he stiffened, while she orgasmed, rhythmically milking him. Her abdomen clenched strongly, and she yanked her mouth away with a cry. She stiffened in his arms as he emptied himself within her body.

# CHAPTER 16

*A*wareness came slowly. She stretched and the unfamiliar weight of a man bore down on her.

Her body ached, differently from the way it had earlier. *In a better and more fulfilling way*, she thought with a smile. This time, it was the after effects of sex. *Sex with Davis.* Wild hot sex that was both sweaty and satisfying. Something she'd never before experienced. Her mind struggled with the ramifications of their actions. *Unprotected sex.*

She sat up, or at least tried to as she became aware of that truth. She pushed at him and he grunted groggily. "Wha—?"

"Davis, wake up," she whispered, hearing the agitation in her voice and hating it. "We've— Oh my God!"

He jerked up, his hair a wild bird's nest. "What's up?"

"We didn't use any protection!"

He stilled. "Damn. I'm sorry, Jane. I meant to." He touched her shoulder as he levered away. "I just... I got carried away." His voice was hoarse as he leaned over, reaching into the bedside drawer. "I actually bought some for us."

Shame and horror filled her. She'd been there once before. *Haven't you learnt your lesson?* "I'm..." Jane shook her head as shame burned her. "I'm so sorry."

He looked back at her. "Why? We both wanted it." He must have seen something in her eyes. The guilt she refused to hide from. "We are both adults. Horny adults who both consented to the sexual act. Neither of us is guiltier than the other. That's what relationships are about. Accepting each other and our actions for what they are."

She stilled. *Was that what they had? A relationship?*

Fear snaked through her. She'd been in this position before with Carstairs and she'd paid heavily for her mistakes, not that she had ever regretted having Frannie. And if she was pregnant, not that she should be at her age surely because didn't fertility decrease? But still... Would he think it was her fault? That she'd trapped him? After all, that's what her ex-husband had accused her of. *What if Davis was the same?*

"Jane. If there are consequences, we'll face them together. And, to be honest, I'd welcome it."

A knot formed in her belly. *He says that now. But what if...?*

Davis hooked one of his fingers under her chin so that her eyes were level with his. "I mean it. I don't care what that coward ex-husband of yours did or said. I'm..."

She heard a sliver of fear in his voice and inside her a small piece of the armor around her heart broke away.

"I'm in love with you."

She absorbed the blow of his words. "You... You *love* me? How can you? You don't even know me." The words trailed away with a squeak. She closed her eyes.

Oh God. How she wanted to accept his words at face value. She really wanted to believe what he said and the emotions that were contained in them. But after the mess she'd made of her marriage, she needed more than just the words and hot sex.

She needed time and commitment.

"I don't know that I'm—"

Davis pulled her to him and she stiffened for a moment before melting into his embrace.

"I understand. You need time. I'm willing to give you as much as you need. Even if it means sleeping on the couch—"

"No." She cut off his words. There was no way he was sleeping anywhere but with her. She didn't understand why, but it felt wrong on so many levels to not have him beside her. "I..." Jane cleared her throat even as he looked at her quizzically. "I need you here."

He nodded silently and relaxed, just a little, against her. "If that's how you need it..."

"Yeah. It is."

Morning dawned, fine and bright. Jane felt an unfamiliar sense of well-being.

She stretched in the bed, her arm connecting with a solid item. A hard and warm something, her brain unhelpfully offered. "What the...?"

Slowly she opened her eyes and turned her head. Then she saw him, watching her. Davis. The sexy, gorgeous writer with a morning shadow covering his jaw and glinting eyes turned to face her.

The man she'd been dreaming about for weeks. The one who'd left her hot and bothered and so ready.

Had she...?

Did they...?

Surely they hadn't had sex together last night? It was just another erotic dream, wasn't it?

Jane couldn't help herself, looking down the bed to see only from the waist down covered by the pristine white sheets and her mouth dried in reaction as her gaze trailed over miles of sexy, well-toned and muscled man flesh. They had.

Awareness of her own nakedness impinged and she tugged on the sheet, thanking whatever instinct within her had kept her breasts and body covered by the same material. Memories of the night before flooded her mind and she couldn't stop the blush that heated her face.

"Good morning."

A quiver started deep in her belly at the sound of his strained voice. Warmth flowed through her, in every part of her being. He reached forward and brushed a loose strand of hair from her face. She shivered as desire coursed through her system. She nuzzled against his hand, unable to stop her body's instinctive reaction to his gentle touch.

How on earth could she possibly feel this desire after last night's wild and fast lovemaking session? But the truth was, it was there. It hadn't gone away—if anything the spark between them burned brighter. The way he moved his fingers over her face pulled her nerves tight and she leaned in, needing the embrace that he offered.

The kiss was fiery and she was once more ready for whatever he offered.

He moved his lips over hers, tasting lightly before deepening the embrace.

He feasted and she reciprocated, holding him close, while her body ached for fulfilment. Her nipples budded against the firm wall of his broad chest, and the hairs on his legs abraded hers as they twined together.

Somehow the sheet between them disappeared. Had it evaporated, or been pushed aside? She didn't care. She wanted to run her hands over his chest, to haul him up and to feel him within her body.

"Davis!" She couldn't contain the whispers and groans that burst forth while they touched and tangled—each glancing caress a promise of pleasure to come.

Musky scent filled the air as did their cries of hunger and need. She dug her fingers into the muscles of his shoulders while his whiskers rasped over the smooth column of her neck. She tipped her head back, wordlessly asking for more, and he obliged—he kissed his way to her collarbone before continuing his exploration. When he settled his warm mouth over her breasts she bucked and he laughed. It was little more than a husky whisper but the heat in her chest rocketed to white hot.

Her core melted and reality fled.

"There's more to come yet, my love." He flicked his tongue over her distended flesh and she bucked again, as pleasure, lightning-bright, streaked through her nervous system.

Letting go had never felt so good. She pulled one of her hands away from his shaking shoulders, to trail down the middle of his body, tracing a path over muscles that clenched, dipping into his navel. He hissed as she found what she was searching for, circling his fully aroused cock and gently squeezing.

Now it was his turn to buck and she shuddered, knowing what both of them needed, but hoping valiantly to prolong their love play.

He found her center, trailed through the damp curls covering her core and she felt him slip one then another finger deep within.

"Not yet..." she panted, but he continued dipping slightly, the light friction tightening the sensual wire. His strokes were gentle but sure. She quivered as her body convulsed with a fast orgasm.

"Not enough," he muttered, while he made his way down her torso, nipping lightly at her belly, laving the small indentation he found. She arched into his caress, her hands now fisted in the sheets, unable to contain her cries of pleasure.

Down he moved, his body rubbing against hers, skin against skin until slowly he reached the top of her mound and he stopped.

She was a mass of sensations as she lay there, chest heaving. She looked down to see why he had halted, and the fog of desire lifted lightly until she glanced at his face. It was graven with passion and he surveyed everything he had discovered with a hot, hungry gaze. His fingers were still buried within her, then he winked, grinned broadly before he dipped his head between her legs.

She squeaked at the unfamiliar sensations, but her breath fled as he exhaled over her, his fingers busy, urging her on while he licked, using his tongue to work magic on her. He sucked and licked, lapped and feasted. She rose up, back arching off the bed while he devoured her. She splayed her legs wider for him.

"Oh God! I can't..." Once again she shattered, the rolling waves of pleasure overcoming her while he worked at her, mercilessly. Just as she was sure she couldn't possibly take any more her body slumped back to the bed and she lay there, boneless.

Davis froze, the harsh sound of his breathing telling her just how aroused he was and she lay still, eyes closed. *Surely there couldn't be more?*

The touch of his kisses on her belly stopped her before the pressure ramped up again. How could she possibly survive more torture? The pleasure hadn't yet fully subsided. He sucked at her breast and she mewled weakly. The rattle of the drawer barely impinged, but she heard him and knew. This time he was going to use protection. In a single corner of her mind she wanted to cry out no, but then he touched her again and her thoughts fled.

The graze of teeth stole her breath but he gripped her hips, merciless and hard and she didn't care. She wanted him. Every small part needed him to fill her.

"Please..." she moaned and heard his growl as he rocked.

He slid deep within her body, which opened and welcomed him. Jane wound her shaking legs around his midsection, pulling him closer and cradling him intimately.

When he touched his lips to hers she could taste herself. She gripped him with curling fingers while he continued to thrust deeply within her, and she met each movement. Wanting more. Wanting everything.

The tone changed, becoming urgent. Heaving sounds filled the air along with their broken cries.

She felt the arousal winding tighter and finally there it was. Her body splintered around him, she stilled herself, holding him close as he surged home one last time.

"Mine!" His hoarse cry and fierce hold filled her with a warmth she couldn't ever remember feeling before.

Then the world slipped away.

# CHAPTER 17

*A*t breakfast Frannie kept shooting odd looks at Jane and Davis, and he knew she'd worked out what they'd been up to. On one hand it was embarrassing that this teen had even a clue of their intimacy, but on the other he didn't much care who knew his feelings for Jane. He loved her.

By the time Jane had chased Frannie up, collected lunches, her school bag and ushered her into the uniform, Davis was exhausted, and he'd only been watching, waiting to take her to school.

But then, he conceded, some of that exhaustion could be from the athletic sessions they had shared. Each time he thought that, he had to struggle to contain the grin that grew on his face. Then Frannie would take one look at him and make a gagging noise and he was back to square one again.

He chanced a glance at Jane's face, and saw the shine in her eyes, the rosy flush on her cheeks, and it made him feel whole. Complete.

"Come on then, we should drop you off. Then we have some things to attend to."

He snatched up his keys, wallet and phone and waited for the two females in his life to precede him to the door, down the steps and into the car park. With a beep the car unlocked and they climbed into the large vehicle. "Everyone ready?"

He clicked the lock button and they left the parking bay, entered the street and started in the direction of the school. He felt good. He and Jane were going to see a solicitor about hopefully getting control of her pre-marriage assets, then they were going out for a long leisurely lunch, before heading back in time to collect Frannie.

They were only three blocks away when the phone trilled. He pressed the button on the steering wheel. "Davis Formosa."

"Mr. Formosa? This is the police. We're ringing to inform you that Mr. Church has been released on bail, against our request." A shiver of unease rippled through him and Jane gasped.

"How the hell did that happen?" Deep in his heart he knew neither woman was safe with Carstairs Church at large.

"He has very good solicitors, Mr. Formosa." The dry voice on the end of the line waited for a beat. "Look, there isn't much we can do right now. Just make sure Mrs. Church and her daughter have some kind of protection."

Anger coursed through him and he gripped the steering wheel as the call ended.

"Davis? What are we...?" There was fear in Jane's voice.

"We'll go to the solicitors. But maybe Frannie should come with us."

He felt rather than saw the convulsive nod she gave, and anger burned in his chest. How could the law fail them so completely? But he knew right now wasn't the time for recriminations. What he needed was a darned good solicitor. Thankfully Dee had come through for him. And for Jane and Frannie too.

They passed the school and kept going, the trip taking around forty quiet minutes as no one talked or laughed. Jane sat gripping her hands together, but he could see how they shook.

He pulled into a vacant parking spot and waited while the women climbed out. Davis ushered them towards the dark brick building. It looked old though well maintained with a high black wrought iron fence. An intercom was mounted beside the gate, above a brass name-plate that simply read 'Nathan Anderson, Solicitor'. He buzzed and waited.

"Nathan Anderson's office. This is Simone."

"Hi, Simone. It's Davis Formosa with Jane Church and her daughter Francesca. We have a nine o'clock meeting with Mr. Anderson."

The line went dead and he was sure Simone was checking his paperwork. A buzz told him that the gate had unlocked. "Please come straight to the door."

They pushed through and it latched behind them as they made their way up the cobbled path to the door, which swung open.

A blonde woman, small but with an air of assurance, smiled at them. "Come on in. I'm Simone, Nathan's assistant. He'll be with you shortly." She led them into a small comfortable waiting area then retreated to another room, leaving them in silence.

"Jane, we'll sort this out together." He murmured, and her chest ached. One short night of passion with Davis and she had to move on again. She damned Carstairs for his inability to accept that they were over as much as she damned herself for staying as long as she had.

Jane shivered and shook in the seat of the car. The meeting with the solicitor had gone as well as could be expected, given the circumstances. He was sure he could arrange for her to regain a portion of her assets and maybe also make a reasonable claim on some of Carstairs'.

Not that she wanted it for herself, but Frannie needed stability—the kind that came with a real home. A future.

The thing that really concerned her was whether or not the restraining order would work. Would it be enough to keep him away, now that Carstairs had been released, even with the so-called strict bail conditions?

"You know, we're going to have to find somewhere new. Somewhere that Carstairs can't find us again." Jane glanced out of the window, watching as the cars zoomed by them on the highway.

She seriously doubted that he'd back off. No, he'd never been good at being told to do something he didn't want to. She knew first-hand what happened in those instances. And to be honest, things like restraining orders and distance had never worked in the past.

"Mum, I don't want to move again. I have friends." The alarm in Frannie's voice left her wincing. Jane really didn't want to have to do this to her daughter. *Damn it, it's just not fair.* But what other option did she really have?

"Let's just..." She breathed deeply, trying to dispel the pain that had lodged in her chest. "Let's just wait until we get home. Then we can talk about it."

Davis glanced at her quickly and she knew he had an inkling of what she was thinking and planning. The way he flattened his lips, forming deep white creases, was more than just a hint and the ache in her chest grew, crushing her breath. But she refused to give in. Refused to cry even though her eyes burned.

The warehouse district lay ahead. And with it the end of what she had been so hopeful of: A future with a man who treated her like a queen and who professed to love her. In her mind she was already tossing over possibilities. Where could she and Frannie go that would be safe from Carstairs reach?

And how could she survive without Davis? Jane curled her hands into fists, feeling the bite of nails in the soft flesh of her palms.

That was when she spotted it. "Davis, wait!" She flung her hand out, touching his arm.

*God damn Carstairs to hell!* She saw his car and his people at the entrance to the converted warehouse. "How could he have found us?"

"Mum?" Frannie wailed from the back seat.

Jane turned, noting the fright on her daughter's face.

"We need to get out of here." She looked back and Davis wrenched on the wheel, tugging it over to the next lane amid the blare of horns.

They passed the building accelerating but she saw Carstairs. He focused on the vehicle and dived into his BMW convertible. But they were past him now.

She turned to look through the rear window, watching as he shot into the traffic. "He's following us, Davis. What the hell are we going to do?" Jane heard the fear in her voice, the way the panic ticked her words up at the end.

"Lose him," Davis grunted, turning off the main road into a side street and travelling quickly up to the end, but she could see that Carstairs was following them still.

*Oh God, I'm never going to be free of him. And now I've drawn Davis into danger as well.* She held her trembling fingers to her mouth, smothering the moan that nearly escaped.

Frannie's white face caught her attention. She needed to be strong for her daughter.

"Pull over, Davis. Let me out and get Frannie away from here." Perhaps she could draw him away.

"No way. Now sit down while I ring my agent. She's manic for recording conversations, which will be ammunition if he tries to wiggle out of any charges. Deanna can use her phone system to contact the police at the same time. She can also ring the solicitor who arranged the restraining order." His gruff tone had her retreating back into her seat. "And don't ever think you are going to sacrifice yourself. You're mine now. And I'm not going to let you take chances with yourself and our future."

Davis yanked the steering wheel again, and they were on the highway leading south. He pressed a phone and the sound of ringing filled the small area.

"Davis? What's up?" The woman's voice was perfect, silky and smooth.

"Dee, I need you to ring the police. I've got Carstairs Church following me in a black BMW convertible. I've got Jane and her daughter with me. He spotted us going home and I'm worried for their safety. We're heading south. Also ring the solicitor Nathan Anderson. Clue him in. Get me some help and do it quickly."

"Okay, Davis. Are you safe at the moment?"

"So long as I don't stop and he doesn't catch up." He gave a mirthless laugh and Jane shivered at the feral tone in his voice.

"I'm going to put you on hold and get onto the police. I'm also going to tape the conversation. Okay? Just in case there are any questions down the track."

"Sure. And Dee? No photographers."

Jane was surprised to hear a tinkle of laughter. "Yeah. But just this one time, Davis."

Davis was angry. Actually he was beyond that. He was furiously and incandescently enraged. How the hell had Carstairs Church managed to get bail? He damned solicitors, the justice system and everyone he could think of under his breath, tightening his grip on the steering wheel.

He glanced in the rear-view mirror again. Jane's idiot ex was gaining on them. The thought that he might try something even more dangerous skated through him, leaving a chill down his spine.

"Jane, make sure you're in really tight, okay? Frannie? Are you okay back there?" He couldn't spare the glance back again, as he focused on the tight winds ahead of them. He heard her anxious sobs, though, and the knife twisted more deeply in his chest.

"Yeah, we're good. But where are we going?" Jane's voice trembled and he cursed again. His mind skittered in multiple directions as he tried to plan where they should head.

"Davis? Where are you now? The police are sending units but they need your exact location." Dee's voice punched through the hold music.

"Taking the road south. By the water. We're about thirty kilometers from the city center now. About to start on the windy sections of the waterfront link." He slowed cautiously, navigating the tight corner as quickly as he could and chanced a look behind them. The idiot had barely slowed. "Shit!" He'd gained on them.

"Davis? What the hell is going on?" Dee shouted through the phone system and he braked again at the next approach.

"He's still gaining on us. If he gets in front of us, he could block the road. Then we've nowhere to go." There was no way he was going to let that happen to them. Not now.

"Okay, give me a few minutes. I need to let them know where you are."

Davis breathed a sigh of relief as the annoying music filled the air once more. He needed to think and Dee didn't help. She just splintered his concentration further.

The madman was now right behind them and another hairy curve lay ahead. His stomach cramped and the knowledge that they were committed to following this path rode him like a demon. There was nowhere safe to turn around. They had to go forward.

Why hadn't he thought of that before? Why hadn't he planned this better?

*Because you didn't expect the man to follow you*, whispered his subconscious.

He braked slightly, this being the worst corner yet. He judged it to be something like one hundred and fifty degrees—it needed skill to negotiate safely. He was nearly out of the turn when he caught the flash of black at the side through the car window. He had to curb his instinct to haul the car away, knowing what would come next.

"What are you doing?" he bellowed but it was rhetorical. The idiot driver pulled back, but not before jagging the side of the car and forcing the larger one to swerve slightly towards the left-hand side of the road. Both women squealed as a vicious tearing sound rent the air.

The wagon jerked and shuddered and he fought for control. He breathed lightly and puffed, once back into his lane. He glanced again. The side mirrors showed the car pulling back a little and he thanked the Lord as he saw a removalist truck heading in their direction. It passed with a whoosh. Davis checked the rear-view again, but the car was gone.

Frannie screamed. "He's going to try it again!"

Davis set his mouth and held the car true to the traffic lines, fighting the two cars. A jerk and a bang. But this time, they were approaching another corner and he sweated.

"Oh God! Hang on!" he yelled as the music stopped.

"Davis? Are you okay?"

He ignored Dee, who hollered down the line while he pushed back into his lane. He knew they were close to the road edge. In this section it hung over the jagged coastline with boulders and rocks dotting the white sands below.

Davis stomped his foot on the brake.

The black car shot ahead of them. But it was going too fast and continued straight.

Their vehicle shuddered to a halt and he turned off the engine automatically.

Their last sight of the black car was as it rammed through the white fencing. He watched as small bits of white wood splintered and sailed through the air in slow motion.

The car, however, didn't stop.

Instead it shot over the edge before nosing down.

Then it disappeared from view.

A plume of something sputtered into sight.

Davis sat in the seat shivering and shaking. It could have been them. Him and Frannie. And Jane.

He closed his eyes.

J ane couldn't believe what she saw. She moaned and clapped a shaking hand over her mouth.

Carstairs, the man she'd married, slept with and run away from, had flown through the fencing and the car had plummeted to the rocks below. The roaring sound came later. She wasn't sure how much later. Just that it came. Her stomach roiled madly and bile rose. But she still watched as if hypnotized by the horrific scene ahead of her.

Then came the smoke.

Black and oily. Rising in puffs.

Sirens wailed in the distance but she ignored them, focused intently on the scene unfolding before her eyes.

A hand slipped into hers. Soft. Small.

Frannie. Her daughter. She turned and saw the beloved white face staring into hers.

"Is everyone okay?"

She turned back to Davis and nodded, opening the car door. She moved to the back door and Frannie was there, sliding into her arms.

They clung to each other, soaking up the relief of knowing neither was harmed. Davis joined them, winding his own arms around both of them.

The police pulled up, hurrying forward, but she ignored them. Needing the security of these two vital humans who meant so much to her.

"Frannie? Honey, I love you," she whispered to her daughter who nodded and started to sob noisily. She caught Davis' gaze and looked at him, hoping he would read the similar message in her eyes.

A nod from Davis relaxed her, then she pulled away. "I need…"

He tensed, arms around the shuddering Frannie. "No…you don't…"

Jane shook her head. "Yeah, I do. I need to know it's really over." She stepped away, noting the crunch of gravel below her feet. The surreal quality of the moment left her feeling as if she were floating. That nothing was real. She made it to the edge before anyone stopped her and looked over. The twisted wreckage was engulfed in flames, bits strewn here and there on the sandy beach. Police cordoned off the area and started the redirection of traffic.

One of the men in a blue uniform looked familiar. He pulled off a police hat and rubbed his bald head and she thought immediately of the regular at her diner, Jake. But he obviously wasn't that man, though they had similar dark eyes and a rounded face. Maybe they were related? Jane shrugged the thought away as she returned to Davis and Frannie.

Police gathered around them, needing information. Davis stood by, having retrieved his phone from within the car. He gave them directions for how to contact Dee.

# CHAPTER 18

Finally they were free, climbing into the large vehicle, he turned it around, heading back towards the town. Frannie was silent as was Davis, and Jane felt no compunction to fill it. Instead she watched the other cars on the road, watched as Davis drove carefully and sedately.

Once they had parked in the parking bay they made their way upstairs. "Frannie, sweetheart, why don't you go have a shower? I'll make us all a cup of tea." The girl left the room with only a silent nod and Jane sighed. "Davis... I don't know..."

With several silent steps he came up to her, slipped strong arms around her and pulled Jane close. She savored the touch, soaking up his warmth.

"I was so afraid. You and Frannie have become the most important people in my life and I couldn't face losing either of you."

She gulped down the greasy waves of fear she'd managed to strangle. "And I need to tell you how much I love you too. I refused to do it before because I was scared. In the car it would have been wrong. To only tell you when we were in danger. To distract you. But God knows I am so pleased I can do that with a clear conscience, Davis."

She stepped away and brushed at the burning droplets that hung from her lashes. "I love you because you love me. The real me—the one no one else wanted before. I love that you put my needs first. I love that you protected Frannie, even though she's not your daughter. And I love you because you are a sexy and awesome lover, an amazing man who is giving, clever—" She stopped. There were so many reasons why she loved him. Too many to tell right now.

He smiled and his eyes glinted with a damp light. She went into his arms willingly.

The light dimmed and Jane lay on her back, the soft cushioning of the mattress beneath her. Frannie was in her bed, finally having sobbed herself to sleep. It broke Jane's heart that Francesca would now never have a normal relationship with her father. But much as she wanted to avoid the truth, she knew he'd made the decision that had ultimately ended his life.

A sudden dip of the mattress pulled her from the introspection. "Everything okay, Jane?" That he was so worried about her made Jane smile. What had she done to deserve this wonderful man?

"Yeah. I'm okay. I feel sorry for him, though."

Davis gathered her up, pulling her snugly into his embrace.

"He'll never know that Frannie has a wicked sense of humor. That she speaks almost fluent Italian or hates math. He'll never taste her lasagna or watch her get married."

"It was his choice." Davis' voice rumbled against her ear, while he rubbed circles on her belly. "He missed all the things that I'm going to be there for. And I'm going to be there for her and you..."

Jane smiled at the fierce tone. He loved her, this fine man.

She turned in his arms. "Do we have to discuss this right now?" Her gaze zeroed in on his lips and suddenly a ravenous hunger swept through her.

"Yeah. Actually, before we go any further I have a question. I really should ask both of you, but..." His voice trailed away and he cleared his throat. "So, I want you and Frannie to stay here. With me. I know the apartment isn't the right size for a family, but I own the one next door too." He looked away, blushing slightly.

Her stomach quivered with nerves.

"I think if I renovate this place, we could give Frannie a room on the other side of the apartment, you know, expand it a little. Maybe…" He turned and started hunting in the bedside drawer. "Maybe you would marry me?"

Davis held a small sapphire blue jewelry box in his hand. He held it out and Jane extended trembling fingers, brushing them over the velvet covering. She gazed into his eyes and saw uncertainty as he nudged the box towards her.

"Please?"

The lid opened with a tiny creak and there, on a bed of white velvet, was the most exquisite ring she had ever seen. The deep gold glinted in the partial light while the rubies and diamonds winked. "I… Oh, Davis!" She lifted the tiny ring and felt the trail of happy tears slid down her cheeks. "Will you… Will you put it on for me?"

With a fumble and some pushing, the ring finally settled on her finger, a weight that bore testament to their love. She gripped his face with her shaking hands and tugged him to her. The kiss was soft, achingly tender as she told him wordlessly just how much she loved him.

The box fell to the sheets, unheeded as he brushed the strands of hair away from her face, running his fingers through her tresses, before they settled on her shoulders. His touch soothed her.

He trailed his thumbs over her jaw line. Caressing lightly as she sighed her pleasure.

He leaned in, so very slowly, and the touch of his breath whispered over her lips, warm and exotic. She shivered; her nipples puckered.

But he didn't kiss her. Not yet. Instead, he gazed into her eyes, mesmerizing her as he whispered. "I'm going to kiss you all over tonight. Make you scream. Then when you think you can't feel any more pleasure… Only then will I slip inside your body."

His darkly erotic words ratcheted her need to a higher level. He ran his soft hands down the cotton of her nightgown, caressing the globes of her breasts, tugging the fabric taut so he could see her clearly through the worn material. "Beautiful nipples. Pink and begging for my touch." He blew slightly and amazingly they tightened further, the buds aching for the touch of his skin on hers.

She shifted in the bed and he grinned, but didn't stop his stimulating exploration of her body. Jane lifted a languid hand and rested it on his shoulder. "Can two play this game?"

When Davis raised his head and stared intently, a raw bolt of electricity ran through her from head to core. She tingled with the fire she saw burning in his eyes. "Not yet. Soon." Then he flicked the tips of her nipples with his hard fingers and she gasped and gripped the robe he wore.

She tugged and pulled, finally finding the way under the velvet to find his warm skin, where it had been hidden. She inched her hand up under the material to his shoulders and pushed it back, baring most of his chest.

The breath he sucked in ended with a soft hiss. "Stop. I want this to be special for you."

Jane stilled her movements. "Every time with you is special, Davis. Because you love me."

Starved for the taste of him, she kissed him hard, pushing at the seam of his lips with her tongue until he admitted hers. They moved together, feeding the cravings of their bodies as she skated her fingers over him. Seeking flesh. He pushed the gown from her shoulders, baring inches of skin to the cool night air. She shivered with delight until he warmed her, enfolding her in his arms, brushing skin against skin.

The cotton stopped at the top swells of her breasts. He shoved at the cloth, pushing with jerky motions. The sound of ripping threads had them both pulling back. "Oh God," Davis panted, leaning his heated forehead against hers. "I'll replace it."

Jane smiled. "It was old. Don't worry." She gripped either side of the fabric and tore it down the middle. Then he smiled.

"Good. Now I can get to all of you."

She laughed, letting the sound fill the air, and he grinned. "Well,

Jane. You are a gorgeous specimen, but I don't want you to get cold." With a wink he undid the cord at the middle then shoved the velvet fully off him. He flung it over his shoulder, uncaring of where it landed, then with firm hands he pushed her back down. He settled his mouth on her breast, grazing her with teeth and worrying the nub with his tongue.

He settled his hand between her legs, sought the entrance to her heated core, and she moaned at the touch of his fingers, brushing the curls to one side.

She opened her mouth, but he stilled her, placing his finger against her lips. It was the one he'd just used to drive her wild.

She licked.

Jane watched the reaction in his eyes as they burned brighter. She noted the subtle flaring of his nostrils, which told her that she was doing okay in the seduction department. She refused to be a passive participant anymore. No, she wanted to experiment and experience with Davis.

She sucked his fingers into her mouth, teasing the skin with her tongue, slipping it around them, tasting the musky essence.

He slid his hand from her mouth and kissed her. The kiss was searing. Devouring. All consuming. It stole her very breath from her body, and when he raised his head to settle back, he was panting as much as she was.

With one raised hand, Jane pushed him back. He fell with an "Oomph" to the bed. She moved, scaling his body, running her fingers up and down the luscious skin laid out before her. A tiny teasing line of hair ran from his navel down to the much larger thatch at his groin. His erection stood to attention and silky liquid seeped from the slit.

He lay still while she checked his body, licked her lips. He groaned and her tummy jittered. She gazed at him in amazement.

She wondered if Davis understood that she'd never done anything like this before as she lowered herself down to his waiting cock. Then, slowly, she licked the tip, tasting the saltiness of him and smiled, emboldened as he jerked.

"Do you want me to stop?"

His growled answer filled her with heat.

She kissed the head, opening her mouth before sucking him further within. He bucked against her ministrations, winding his hands through her hair and holding her close.

The velvety hardness and slow movements made her wonder how she could have missed this pleasure. But the thought fled as Davis abruptly pulled her up the bed, over his body and kissed her again, so deeply, while he shoved her legs apart.

She groaned as he positioned himself and he stilled, raised his head. "Oh God. Condom…"

Jane panted "No. Do we need one?"

He cupped her face. "But what about pregnancy? I don't want to rush you, but…" The hunger in his voice stopped her in her tracks. Yes, that was what she wanted too.

She shook her head, feeling the swish of hair around her shoulders. "No. I want that too. Your baby—what could be better?" Then she moved her hips, needing him to fill her.

Davis released her face, dropping his hands to hold her hips. Slowly he lowered her down, so that she encased him—all the way to the hilt.

Her body shook and shivered and she wanted to move on him, to feel the release she knew hovered just beyond, but he stilled her.

"Not yet." A subtle nudge of his hips made her moan and he laughed throatily. "You like that, don't you? Watching you explore what we have makes me hot."

Jane had to close her eyes, unable to cope with the intense sensations brought on by so much stimuli. She could smell him, and feel the way he moved slowly between her legs. His erotic words and the sight of him, his face drawn, was almost too much for her beleaguered senses.

Her breasts tingled from his touches and caresses. Her core burned with molten yearning and she needed the release only he could offer.

"Davis… Please!" she pleaded then he moved. Hard and fast, thrusting deeply.

"I love you," he chanted at each movement.

She threw her head back, glorying in the sensations, in his words and finally… "Oh God!" She orgasmed. The strong muscular pulls urging Davis to move faster, wilder and deeper in search of his own release.

He dug his fingers into the skin of her hips, gripping her as he plunged one last time, before holding himself still and emptying within her with a groan.

They waited, wrapped around each other, in the nearly silent room. The only sounds were their heaving breaths as settled.

"Wow." It was all she could manage as she slid into a boneless heap beside him.

"Yeah. So, I guess that was a yes then?" His dry words caught her as hilarious and she laughed.

"I guess it was."

She cuddled up against him and her eyelids drooped heavily before she drifted off to sleep.

# CHAPTER 19

*J*ake lifted the coffee cup to his lips. He felt good. Damn good. But now the job here was done. It was time to look for his future bride—the woman who was his perfect mate. The only woman his father would allow him back with.

The new waitress in the diner, the woman who had served him, scurried around, wiping tables quickly. Now that Jane was settled, she'd resigned. While he would miss her smiling face and efficient manner, it pleased him to know that he'd done a good job. Davis and Jane would marry and at least one baby Formosa would arrive in due course. Francesca had come to terms with the situation and was blossoming with a male role model.

A banging of the door heralded the entry of a woman bursting into the small diner, her face streaked with tears. She sniffled and snorted into the tissue wadded tightly in her hands.

The woman was familiar. Then he felt a tingling sensation—one of recognition. It was Cara's friend. Simone. She was a perfect siren with long blonde hair worn in a simple braid. As always she was impeccably turned out, in her expensive red wool suit and high heels that screamed *'I'm a sex goddess.'* He'd noticed her before when he'd overhead Cara's plot to get closer to her now husband, James.

Cara and James Veha scurried in after her, taking a seat at the cubicle behind him.

At the other end of the faded diner, he could see the small celebration Les, the owner, was holding for Davis, Jane and Francesca, now that their union was about to become formal. But his eyes kept straying back to the noisy and very distressed woman.

"Simone, what happened? How could he end it all?" Cara patted her friend on the back and Jake strained to hear more, stabbing himself on a fork tine.

He raised his finger, inspected the small droplet of blood and lifted the offending digit and sucked absent-mindedly.

"He said…" Simone was talking and he knew he needed to hear the words.

Even as Simone started to recount whatever the tale of woe involved, he felt the touch of a nail upon his arm and turned. *Cailleach. Fabulous.* "What the hell do you want now?" He couldn't contain the anger in his tone. He didn't need her interrupting, not now.

"Well, I see you've found yours." She indicated to the fork with a grin and for a second he felt a vertigo-like sensation.

Found his what? Then understanding intruded. "Shit! You've got to be joking!"

But Cailleach, the goddess who didn't look a day over twenty-five, grinned broadly as she clutched her perfect South Sea pearls. "Never less so, Diocail. Now, how are you going to cope with this?"

Bewilderment filled him. Cope? She was blonde, she was gorgeous and somehow he had to make her want him. Fear filled him for the first time in a long while.

The blonde with the perfect figure was his soulmate. Cara's best friend? At least he'd kept his true human-like visage to himself. He was sure he would need it.

"By the way, your father is incredibly proud. You only intervened enough to ensure they found their own path. Only a truly enlightened being can manage that." A bottle of water appeared in front of her. "Of course, I'm pleased she took my advice about the hair and clothing. She looks so much better. So much younger." Cailleach peered intently at Jane and frowned. "Either that, or she did a very good job at hiding her age. Anyway, time won't wait for me. No matter how much sex I promise."

She waved a languid hand and disappeared with a shimmer of power. Jake turned around to see Cara and James ushering the crying woman from the diner. He'd missed his opportunity.

Then he laughed. She was his future. Another opportunity would come along. He just needed to help it a little. Then he stood and headed for the street.

# REVENGE ON CUPID

## CELTIC CUPID BOOK 3

*Sometimes magic isn't enough when love is in the balance.*

After years of hiding, it's finally Jake's turn to find love... Or is it? Will Cupid's arrow bite him or bounce off the woman who could complete his life?

Diocail, in the guise of Jake, has to deal with the ultimatum his father, the God Lugh, handed down. Before he can return home, he must find his predestined mate and make her fall for him.

Simone is hurt when she realises that her long-term lover Nathan has cheated on her. An encounter with Jake fuels her desire, but she's not sure that she is willing to risk her emotions again. But when Senuna, a goddess from Jake's past, starts to mix things up, the situation goes from bad to worse

.

Now Jake has to make Simone see that they have a future, and he has to deal with a deranged goddess—and all without the magic of Cupid.

# CHAPTER 1

# *M*onday 9th

*Dear Diary,*
*Some days are just not meant to work out right, are they? Of all the days for*
*my alarm clock to fail...*
*We had a new client turn up today. A seriously horsey-looking female, with a*
*long face and solid teeth. Nathan is cross with me for being late and I broke*
*the heel of my fave shoes! Talk about a sucktastic kind of day!*
*Topping it off is tonight's cancellation. I hope tomorrow's better!*
*S*

Monday morning, Simone rose having somehow managed
to break the alarm clock the day before. It didn't beep as
it usually did. So there was nothing tugging her from the
arms of Morpheus, except the buzz of her phone. It woke her from
the pleasant dream she'd been lost in. The one where she'd been lying

on the beach next to the man of her dreams. *Only he didn't look anything like Nathan. He had red hair!*

She groped for her phone hoping to quell the mechanical buzzing of the alarm, which she'd wisely set to tell her she had ten minutes to be out of the door and on the way to work.

"Shit!" She scurried out of the bed, tearing off her pug print pajamas, hurried through her ablutions, thankful that her personality required having everything laid out the night before. Within twenty minutes she ran out of the door, hair scraped back in a bun and with immaculate makeup.

In the car, she quickly dialed Nathan—her boss and lover. "Hey, Nathan! You won't believe this. The alarm didn't go off this morning, so I'm running late." An expletive met her comments and she winced.

"What? Simone, I can't condone you being late. I explained that when we started." It was an ongoing source of irritation that things others did purely by accident always seemed to end up being associated with their relationship and her taking advantage, somehow.

A deep blush burned her cheeks and her stomach tightened into a hard knot. "Yes, I know that. It wasn't my fault. Honestly. The good news is, the case files are packed and on my desk." Simone braked at the red light, waited while Nathan muttered loudly and as soon as it turned green, she moved the car forward. "If you grab the briefcase, I'll meet you at the courthouse. That way neither of us will be late." She knew she was pleading with him—surely he'd respect that she'd had everything ready?

"Fine." He sighed heavily and she had to fight her reaction to his comment.

"I'll park and be on my way. I'm only about ten minutes away from the courthouse."

"Right." His curt answer angered her slightly, but she shoved aside the emotion. Instead she breathed deeply, letting her nostrils flare a little.

The multi-story car park was just ahead and she nipped in, finding the first available spot. At least it was easier, now that they had little green lights alerting her to the next vacant space. She noted the level, area and number, quickly tapping the details into the memo section on her phone, and with bag in hand, she moved quickly towards the exit sign.

Her feet tapped on the concrete as she hurried down the steps, long experience telling her she'd gain no extra time with the lift.

"Oh, man!" At a red walk sign she checked the time on the phone and relaxed slightly. She still had time to make it before they had to be in place for their first meeting of the day.

When the lights clicked to walk, she scurried over the road in the direction of her destination. Within minutes the imposing courthouse rose in her vision. She hurried up the steps and there he was, waiting for her—scowling.

"Made it." She beamed, hoping to make Nathan smile. Instead he frowned and turned away. It wasn't the greeting she had hoped for and her stomach plunged.

Simone trailed behind him as they headed inside and over to the lift. People crowded and voices echoed. Refusing to catch Nathan's eye, she fished in her bag and dragged out her diary. "So the nine o'clock is the Wilkerson case. Room three-two-two."

The doors opened and once inside, Nathan punched the button without a word. No one else joined them and Simone leaned in his direction.

"Would you like to say good morning?"

Normally she would have expected him to bend down and accept her kiss. Not today. Instead, he turned away and she sighed. "Right then." Her stomach roiled just a little at his reaction and a dull pulse began in her head.

As the doors opened they stepped out.

The negotiations were long and messy. Simone hated dealing with these civil cases. In this instance it was questionable whether Nathan's client was guilty or not. *At least it isn't a rape or murder case.* Instead she focused on the files piled in front of her. This one revolved around an alleged fraud of several hundred thousand dollars.

"Where do you want to go for lunch?" She turned to him, having gathered all the papers and filed them in the bag.

"I have a lunch meeting today. A new client. She came via a recommendation. It's a family court matter. I've set the file up and I'll take it with me."

"Oh." *This is unusual.* Normally she would attend and take notes for him. Get all the background detail before they started. "So where are we going?" Her stomach wobbled just a bit, sure that she hadn't understood what he was saying.

"We aren't. I am. I'm meeting her at La Guin."

*Our special restaurant.* She frowned. "Right. Then I guess I should head back to the office?"

He shook his head. "No. I'll be back here after lunch. I've pushed in an extra meeting. I sent you a memo this morning. One I suppose you didn't get because you couldn't get into the office." His tone was tight, as was his frown.

This time she only just managed to suck in the anger that rose. "Nathan, what's going on?"

Nathan marched forward and as they reached the bottom of the steps, she felt the bump and her feet moved without any direction from her.

*Snap!*

The heel caught in the old rusty grating, breaking beneath her, and she threw herself into Nathan's arms. "Oh God! My shoe!" she wailed and he held her while she pulled the shoe from her foot. "My favorite stilettos!"

Nathan helped her to hobble over to the seats and squatted down. "Well, they've had their day. What will you do?"

"I have a spare pair in the car. Can you nip over and grab them?"

He looked pained before shaking his head. "I have a meeting…"

"Nathan, this will only take a few minutes. Please?"

He huffed and she held out her keys, she told him the level and bay details, and he set off. She waited and watched as the crowds of people hurried around her. It was only a matter of maybe ten minutes and Nathan returned, holding out the plain black court shoes.

"Here."

"Thanks, Nathan. Look, about today… It's been a mess, I know. Let me make dinner for us tonight. Can I?"

He shook his head. "I have an appointment." His lips firmed into long white lines and her stomach twitched and quivered. This was a different side of Nathan than she rarely saw. *What on earth could have caused it?* Instead, Simone bit her lip, the tang of copper rising.

"Fine. I'll meet you back here in an hour and a half? I'll go upstairs and set up the meeting room for the two o'clock appointment."

He nodded and she wondered what he was thinking. "Right. I'll see you at two." He turned and left her staring after him. She rose and headed to the nearby rubbish bin, dumping her shoes with a mournful sigh.

She squared her shoulders and headed for the food court, grabbing an unhealthy lunch of fish and chips—something she rarely allowed herself anymore. For years, she'd battled her weight, though since knowing Nathan she'd managed to control her tendencies for fat and fast options and had dropped three whole dress sizes as a result. When Nathan was around, she'd usually stick to grilled fish with salad. Today she needed comfort food.

Alone, she crowd-gazed, and thought longingly of Cara, her best friend, who was getting married in three weeks to the brilliant but seriously geeky James. If only she were here at the café. Or better yet, if they were at their favorite meeting place. The long lunches they'd shared in the Wait-A-While Diner seemed like a distant memory as she ate the battered fish, a slight coating of oil making her fingers greasy. They'd always eaten there when Simone had worked for Veha Industries.

Frustration wound through her like a tight ribbon. "I need some new shoes." Shopping usually made her feel better so she hurried the last few bites of fish before discarding the empty paper wrapping in the nearest bin.

There was a shoe store nearby and Simone headed in that direction, ready to cast away her cares with a quick case of retail therapy.

~

Diocail watched from a table at the other end of the food court, as Simone thrust the wrapper into the bin. As always, she captured his attention. His body tightened. It usually did when she was around, but he didn't dally with humans. He really couldn't afford to in case they discovered his secret, so he never acted on the impulse.

"You know, if she eats like that, she'll be the size of a barn soon."

He jumped, startled at the intrusion, before glancing back at his aunt.

Cailleach sat on the bench beside him. Her perfect hair was coiled around her head and today she wore a pinstripe business suit of black and pale pink. The matching camisole edged with lace softened the harsh cut of the material. On many women, it would look terrible, but Cailleach, *The Mother of All*, wore it with style. At her ears and throat she wore an impressive matched pearl set. She might look twenty-five but in truth she was older than Methuselah.

"How long have you been here?" He hated when she sneaked up on him, and even more that he'd been caught watching the woman.

"Not too long, Jake, dear." In her eyes he thought he detected softness, something he rarely associated with her.

"Why? Why did you follow me here?"

"Because I wanted to see if you'd yet found the woman destined to be your match. Any woman that halts your fondness for floozies like Niamh is a sight to behold."

He winced at her blunt answer. "Well, now you can see I haven't found her, you're free to go." It was a vain hope, and she responded with a smile and a pat at his cheek.

"I don't think so. Not yet. You see, your father is concerned that you don't really have your whole heart applied to this task."

"What? Well, you can just go right back and—"

She laughed at his heated response. "Well, my dear, I can go back now and tell him that you are." Her face softened as she gripped his hand. "Just be careful, Diocail. Humans aren't like us. They take offence very easily and don't believe without proof, for the most part."

"I've asked you—"

With a broad smile she shook her head. "Yes, I know. Call you Jake." She leaned in and pecked him on the cheek. A waft of expensive perfume filled his senses. One second she was there, then she was gone—the only reminder of her presence was the empty bottle of water at his table.

He stood, looking around, only to realize Simone had disappeared from sight. He'd enjoyed watching her sashay along the cobbled eating area heading for the shops. "Damn it!"

For a moment temptation curled in his gut. He could use his abilities to find her, but a feeling—he discounted it being a premonition—stopped him in his tracks. Right now, he didn't have time to examine why, as he would have to hurry to be in the right place at the right time to watch his current couple, Davis and Jane, visit to the lawyer.

He turned and walked away, but couldn't help a final backwards glance.

# CHAPTER 2

uesday 10th

*Dear Diary,*
*Today didn't go so well and Nathan's being evasive. The appointment book at*
*work got messed up with an unexpected client visit and honestly, this week is*
*not going well at all. I hope it improves tomorrow.*
*S*

Unlike the day before, Simone woke early, hurried dressing and eating, before driving to the office. The doors were still locked and she dragged out the keys to the office. "Hello? Nathan?" She walked through the empty rooms, looking for him. "I wonder where he is? It's not like him to be here after me."

She bustled into the tea room, boiled the kettle then made a coffee. Wandering back into the office, she then turned on her computer and collected a bunch of paperwork, planning to start a new file. She could see that Nathan had started the file in the system and was intrigued. It wasn't something he usually did. When she clicked on the open file tab, a password protected screen came up.

"What? What the hell is this?" She racked her brain trying to think what the password could be, yet nothing came to mind easily. In disgust she gave up.

The files from Friday sat on the desk, waiting for her attention, so when Nathan finally arrived, she was already hard at work. "Morning, Nathan. I missed you last night."

His gaze slid away from her face and a pit of uncertainty welled in her belly. Something was seriously wrong. "I had things to do." Nathan hovered for a moment or two before shifting his weight to his other leg. "Look, ahhh… We maybe need to—"

A sound pealed and she depressed the button on her desk. "Nathan Anderson's office. How can I help you?"

"Mar—"

Nathan depressed the call indicator. "I'll buzz you in."

Simone watched in disbelief as he pressed the gate release. Then he turned back. "I promised to go over some documents with her."

Nathan opened the door to the new client and Simone watched as he spirited her through to his office. With a click, the door shut.

She returned to work as silly ideas slipped through her mind. *Is he doing something behind my back?*

The thought hurt. Nathan was an honest man.

He wouldn't creep around behind her back. Or bring some floozy into the office.

"Would he?" There was no answer.

During the morning, the phone rang and clients turned up—each time she buzzed Nathan his phone was switched to busy. She knocked on the heavy wooden door and he opened it swiftly. "Nathan, we have clients…"

He looked around the door and said, "Reschedule them."

Then he closed it in her face and she stood there feeling silly. Her face burned with humiliation.

The growing fear congealed in her belly while she rearranged his schedule. The clients were unimpressed and she soothed and pandered as best she could. One raised his voice and she had to studiously work at not blaming Nathan's lack of planning or empathy.

By the time lunch came, Simone felt ill. Once again, she knocked on the wood and this time when he opened it, the woman stood behind him. "Thanks for fitting me in on such short notice." Then the woman sashayed out.

"Nathan! You've upset your clients and I've had a long and difficult morning…"

He smiled enigmatically. "Go to lunch, Simone. Then we can get to work this afternoon."

When she opened her mouth he shook his head and refused to answer. Deep inside anger bubbled away. *He's not going to tell me anything.*

In the end, she took his advice and headed out of the door to her car, where she sat, stupefied. *What the hell is going on?*

There was no answer, and on return from lunch a note sat on her computer—*Can't make dinner. Ellie's sick and I'm babysitting.*

He avoided her for the rest of the afternoon and she worked, quietly stewing over the events of the morning. The whole time, his attitude ate at her.

# CHAPTER 3

 ednesday 11th

*Dear Diary,*
*Something's going on with Nathan. Should I ignore it? Hope it will just go*
*away? Do I try to bring this to a head?*
*I need to talk to Cara.*
*I feel so lost.*
*S*

The day passed slowly, once Simone had contacted the clients to reschedule their appointments—some for the second time in a week. A few requested their files so that they could seek another solicitor, and she couldn't blame them. More than one was angered. "I'm so sorry. This is quite an unusual event. Let me reschedule you for…" Some of them vented their frustrations to her. There wasn't much she could do.

On her own in the empty office, she had time to think over the situation with Nathan and it didn't reflect well on him.

In the afternoon she shut down the systems and slamming her coffee cup into the sink while savagely turning on the tap, hoping to vent her frustrations. "He can't do this. It's not just unprofessional. It's unfair!" In the empty office, there was no answer. Nothing to make her feel better. She hefted her red leather bag over her shoulder and stalked out.

# CHAPTER 4

*T*hursday 12th

*Dear Diary,*
*Nathan avoided me again all morning. This afternoon, he sent me an email!*
*A Freaking Email! In one week my life has spiraled out of control.*
*I feel sick.*
*S*

Simone scurried to her desk in the morning. She'd dressed in her favorite blue outfit. The one Nathan always told her highlighted the color of her eyes. She flicked a single wayward strand of blonde hair off her face and over her shoulder. "Maybe I should go back to red?" she muttered then snorted. At the moment, her hair color was the least of her problems.

Once seated in front of the computer she logged in, checked for emails and found one from Nathan.

*Simone. We need to talk. Ten a.m. in my office tomorrow. N*

"A meeting. Tomorrow." Simone ground out the words before

stilling herself. Her brain and heart stopped as she thought over the terse message. What could he want to say that warranted scheduling a meeting? And why in hell hadn't he just called her into his office to get this over and done with?

Even as she made to rise, the telephone buzzed and she answered it. After taking the details, she transferred the call to Nathan. His answers of "Yes" and "Put her through" shed no light on what was going on, except anything she wanted for the mystery client whose divorce he was handling.

Clients came and went, many of them the rescheduled ones from Tuesday and Wednesday. They kept her frantic all day long as they lined up in the waiting room, every chair filled, and sometimes their angst and anxiety boiled over, with cutting comments and angry exchanges the order of the day.

At lunch, Simone tried to catch Nathan's eye. Instead he marched through the office, ignoring her, and left the building. Fury seethed deep in her chest. When he returned, there were clients ready to see him. No chance arose where she could button him down and ask what the hell was going on.

By five o'clock, after transferring calls from the woman she thought of as 'Horsey Divorce' on another five occasions, she didn't want to see Nathan. Instead she tromped to the car and sat there. Tears burned her eyes. "I don't know if I'm ready for this to end. Not like this," she wailed in the silence, but no one was there to see. In the garden, she spied the swarthy, squat gardener who nipped in from time to time.

"You okay, Mis Simone?" His eyes shone in the dimness and for a moment she fancied there was a deeper understanding in his words, then she shrugged away the thought.

"Thanks, Duke. I'll be fine."

With a deep breath Simone drove to Cara's parents' in time for the fitting she had promised to participate in.

As she pulled up in the driveway, her mobile trilled. "I didn't realize you were leaving early. I have several urgent contracts that need drawing up." *Nathan. That would be right, wouldn't it?* Simone wanted to scream in frustration—he wanted her to do his contracts, but couldn't speak to her about what was going on between them? She stopped herself and breathed deeply.

"I have a fitting. I told you about it last week, and that I'd be leaving at five. I'll get to them tomorrow."

He harrumphed and hung up on her. The urge to crush the phone or throw it grew. It wasn't the phone's fault he was an arrogant pig. Deep, calming breaths settled her enough to cool the sting in her cheeks.

Simone placed the phone back in her bag and climbed out of the car. A swift knock on the door had her ushered in by Cara's parents amid admonishments to hurry to the bedroom. As she entered, she caught sight of Cara, who waited in her underwear. "Shall we get started?"

Simone nodded at Cara, pushing away her personal anguish and pasting on a bright smile. "You bet!"

Jake watched as Simone drove away. Something was going on, and it was hurting her. Deeply. He could see it in her eyes, the way her usual sunny smile didn't shine. An ache began in the pit of his stomach, but he shrugged it off. "Whatever is going on, I wonder if there is some way I can help her?" He couldn't help observing as her tail lights trailed off into the distance. Nor could he escape the deepening emotions he felt every time she was near.

The back of his neck itched in a way he hadn't experienced in many years and he was sure it was related to Simone. He ignored it with a shake of his head. "I have to concentrate on my own situation first. Then maybe I can get to the bottom of what's happening for her." Previously, Simone's love life hadn't really been of high priority, given her long-term relationship with Nathan Anderson. Yet he'd never been able to resist the temptation of allowing himself a spared glance here and there, over her frame, to gaze on the beauty of her face or the kind way she spoke to him.

He tossed over his own problem. He might have an idea as to who he was supposed to be mated with but the rules for his mating were very clear. Once a brownie met their soulmate, any connection between himself and the woman he was predestined to end up with had to happen naturally, without any nudging on his part. "Damn." It would be so much easier if he weren't bound by these rules when it came to wooing her.

Movement caught his attention as a black sedan rounded the corner and he stopped work again, surreptitiously keeping an eye on the proceedings. Once it halted and disgorged its single passenger, with a slam of the door, he understood. Nathan Anderson met the woman at the door and ushered her within the darkened building. There was something about the woman.

She glanced in his direction, her eyes widening before she turned away. Deep in the recesses of his mind, he was sure he'd seen her before. Somewhere... He stretched his consciousness but couldn't find anything.

"I wonder who—?" He stopped himself. He was merely here as an onlooker, keeping an eye on Cara and Jane and their men until such time as their unions were finalized.

Tomorrow would be Jane, Davis and Frannie's going away morning tea at the diner, and he smiled thinking over the way he'd helped them come together. In a few weeks Cara and James would be married and he could go and seek his own bride.

He eagerly awaited the wedding. Not that he would attend as himself. He could watch over from some vantage point, maybe as a waiter at the reception? He sighed and glanced at the garden bed in front of him.

It was overgrown. The man he was replacing for a short while kept it better than he could. He probably even enjoyed his role.

Jake didn't.

It irked him endlessly.

He could weed and clear until doomsday. The grasses kept coming back up, thick and lush. Surely he could appeal to another of his uncles to help him? But even as the thought came he banished it.

"Bloody green stuff." He crouched down, needing to keep up the impression that he was nothing more than a gardener.

"I hate plants." He cursed quietly, thankful that no one would hear him. Sometimes they juiced all over his fingers, leaving green stains that were hard to shift, even when he changed forms. And dirt gathered under his nails.

He might have been a brownie, but that didn't make him immune from the need to wash. That and the need to hide his true form were the biggest drawbacks to his time here. After all, as a roaming cupid, how could he possibly be successful in his role if everyone knew what he looked like?

The door to the offices opened and Nathan popped his head around the corner. "Duke, we won't be needing you for the rest of the month. Leave what you're doing. It'll be fine."

He looked at the man—his hair was a little disheveled—and shrugged. It wasn't any skin off Jake's nose.

"Sure, Mr. Anderson. I'll head off then."

He slapped his hands on his rump, pleased that he would be able to return to his own form soon. This persona irritated as much as any of the others he'd taken on since being dismissed to Earth to make up for his previous inattention.

# CHAPTER 5

riday 13th

*Dear Diary,*
*I'm gutted.*
*What else can I say? I never saw this coming. Well, I guess I did in the last*
*week, but still... I might take a break for a while from writing. I don't have*
*anything positive to add.*
*S*

On Friday morning, Simone walked slowly through her house. "I really don't want to go in there today." The whisper filled the air and she grimaced. *It's a miserable place to work right now.* The night before, she'd tried to keep a buoyant attitude.

"*Spill it.*"

*Simone refused with a jerky shake of her head. "No. Tonight is your fitting. Maybe tomorrow I might need a friend."*

*Cara had frowned but she'd shrugged it off as best she could. "Come on, I want to see the dress on you."*

Simone hadn't drifted off to sleep easily. Instead she had tossed and turned. When sleep finally came, dreams invaded. Dark and grainy visions of Nathan and another man. This one muscular and red headed. Visions of her twined around that unknown person. It felt wrong on every level. As if she was cheating in her mind.

She was almost relieved when the alarm went off.

Before retiring last night, she'd spent an hour searching for the right ensemble. Something had told her that she'd need to be ready for anything and in all probability, the worst. Her eyes kept straying to the scarlet power suit. The way it molded to her trim figure worked well with her currently blonde hair. She'd never worn it to the office before, deeming it too bright and eye-catching for a solicitor's PA to wear. Today there was a hint of rebellion tugging her in its direction. It wasn't the carefully tailored black and white suit-dress she'd hung off the hook over the back of her door.

"What the hell." A quick grasp pulled it from the hanger, which squeaked on the metal rod as it swung back and forth.

Next up, matching heels. Shoes were a weakness that she always gave in to. She stood by her mantra that shoes made the woman— something that was especially important in her profession. Not being a standout, but impeccably groomed always helped to promote the solicitor as professional. All part of the image, she always told herself.

With extra care Simone applied her makeup, accentuating her features and deep blue eyes, then chose siren red lipstick. If what they'd had was over, she'd go down looking her best. Finally ready she gazed at herself critically in the mirror. "If he ends our relationship, he's an idiot!" The words carried little power, finishing on a sad wobble.

With a gulp, she scooped up her keys and her bag and headed for the door.

She avoided breakfast. The roiling of her stomach had told her that it would be unwise, so she arrived at work early, headed for her computer and was surprised to see a sticky note on her screen—*Will be in at ten.*

On opening the appointment diary, she noted that all appointments for the morning had been cancelled. Unease slithered through her belly and she reached for her phone and texted Cara.

*Something is definitely up. He's not in till ten and cleared the calendar.*

Simone's anxiety levels ratcheted up while she worked in the empty office. She hurried through the few contracts she'd promised to finalize and was just printing the last one and placing it in the folder when she heard the front entrance opening.

She checked the clock, which showed five minutes to ten.

Nathan entered, averted his gaze and headed for his office, shutting the wooden barrier behind him. Simone rose, smoothed down her suit and collected the files then knocked on the closed door.

"Come in."

She gulped down a quick breath, placed her hand on the rounded knob of the door handle and twisted it. Three short steps took her to the desk.

"Here's the contracts you requested."

He nodded absently and indicated a seat. She placed the files on the heavy dark wood desk and waited.

"I don't think this is working." For the first time he looked up.

Simone waited, watching his blinking eyes. A sure sign he was nervous. She needed to hear it all, before she said her piece. She twisted her fingers together as a crimson tide crept over her face, heating it.

"I, um… I think our relationship has run full course. As such, I think it would be unwise to continue our professional association." He glanced away as if embarrassed.

Deep anger burned through her.

The need to say something scathing rose, but she beat it down, realizing that the time to argue the case had come and gone. He coughed, blinked again and squirmed in his chair. *You bastard! Creeping two-timing scum!* It wasn't nearly a strong enough term, but her mind had congealed at the knowledge that it was ending like this.

No matter how much she wanted to call him on his cowardice—she remained quiet.

"Um… Is there anything else you'd like to know?" His gaze met hers. A red crest tinged his cheeks.

"Yes. When did you come to this conclusion and on what basis?" Her voice didn't wobble. She could hear the anger—that was to be expected, wasn't it? At least she was acting professionally.

"Uh, I, umm… I don't think that is appropriate to discuss."

In that instant she knew and white-hot fury seared her from the inside. He'd been unfaithful and was trying to hide it from her!

*The phone calls.*

*The meetings.*

She curled her fingers into claws, welcoming the bite of nails on the fleshy part of her palms. "You've been cheating on me! How could you?" She stood, planting both her hands on his desk. "You know what? I don't want you if you can't be honest with me. If you can't be honorable."

He reared away as if stung.

Honor was one of his buttons and she used it, as the caustic sting of anger flowed.

Now the blush was mottled, she thought, in a most unbecoming manner. More words came to mind. She restrained herself, bottling the outburst that wanted to rise. This kind of behavior wouldn't get her anywhere.

*Not now.*

Simone straightened, needing space between them. She stepped back from the desk. "You know what? I don't even want to be here." He flinched as she threw the last word over her shoulder, and stormed from the office.

Once in the waiting area reality intruded.

*My stuff.* What should she do about the things she had furnished the office with? A box sat in a corner and she scooped it up, hurrying around the room collecting her personal items. In the tea room, she emptied the kettle into the sink and shoved it into the box together with the matching coffee cups she'd bought. The coffee and tea she'd provided. *He can buy his own damned things!*

Simone pulled the plug on the tiny microwave she'd purchased and carried it to her car, rage spurring her on.

When she returned to the office, the small silver-edged photo frames, her Rolodex and the unused appointment books she'd invested in, the book of business cards and the stationery organizers found their way into the box.

She stalked out and dumped it into the boot of her car, joining her other items. "Bastard. Cheater." The words helped her keep the tears at bay and she knew she didn't have long before they escaped her iron control. "I'll be damned if he sees me cry."

She dropped her hand to her stomach as the adrenaline began to wear off, nausea replacing it. Simone took a shallow breath before she marched in one last time. He stood by the door, and he held out an envelope. "Uh, I have a reference, your severance pay and a bonus."

"Fine." She snatched the white item from his hand and he blanched, likely at the bitterness in her voice, she thought.

"Will you...? Will you be okay to get home?"

"Go to hell!" She snatched up her bag and keys, rifled through them and ripped the office keys from the ring. She wanted to fling them at him, but instead held onto her dignity and placed them on the desk with a resounding thud.

With her head held high, she turned and left him alone in the empty office.

The diner loomed while the tears trickled down her face, tracing a burning path. She pulled the car to the side of the road and checked with extreme care that she was within the parking lines. Simone sniffled into the handkerchief she'd stashed in her handbag. The phone rang through the car stereo system as the Bluetooth kicked in.

"Cara here."

"Oh God. He dumped me! Then he sacked me!" The wail was interspersed by hiccupping sobs. No matter how dignified she'd been before, now she just felt like a puddle of misery.

"Oh, Simone! Sweetie... Where are you?"

"Outside the diner." She hiccupped again, wiped her eyes and looked at the shabby exterior of the building ahead.

"I'm on my way." Simone heard a rustle and her friend talking to her fiancé James. "Come on. It's a best friend emergency." Simone knew Cara and James would be here in a matter of minutes—after all, they only worked across the road.

She disconnected the call before clambering out of the car slowly, gripping her purse and phone. She glanced around then locked the car. It would be just her luck today to lose it along with her job and boyfriend.

With intent Simone propelled herself forward, her shoulders hunched. She reached for the polished metal bar on the door and was grateful to find that the first cubicle was empty. Simone slumped onto the deep red cushioning.

Her handkerchief was now thoroughly soaked, so she fished around in her bag and found a tissue... She wadded it in her hand as Cara and James hurried in behind her and slid into the seats around her. The place was practically empty, something Simone was grateful for.

"Simone, what happened? How could he end it all?" Cara hugged her.

"He said it had come to an end. But I know he was playing around with *her* all this time." The words were thick and wet and she blew her nose again. The pain radiated through her chest, as she dragged a fresh tissue beneath her eyes.

"Aw, honey. I wondered when you got involved with him... Yet you seemed so happy." Simone looked at her friend, her concern shining like a beacon. "You know he played around on his wife when she was pregnant with Ellie, don't you?"

Simone stilled. *Could that really be the truth? Is he a player and I've been played?* Much as she didn't want to consider it, she had to weigh up the information that lay before her. He'd go for long periods of time lunching with her, then for a month or two he'd be busy at night and lunchtime.

*He's done this before.*

"No. He wasn't like that." She desperately avoided the truth that had bloomed in her mind—even she could hear the uncertainty in her voice.

Simone glanced around for the server, but no one came to their booth. Instead she hovered near the celebration at the back of the diner. She could see the woman who'd worked there before. She racked her brains trying to remember, as her fogged brain cleared away the grief that enveloped her. It was Jane. She seemed somehow different and was sitting very close to a muscular man with a teen holding her hand. She appeared so happy and Simone felt a momentary stab of envy, which she brushed aside with difficulty.

Simone was glad she had something, anything to do right now that would drag her mind away from the mess her life was in.

"Come on. The service here has gone downhill since Jane left. I'll take you home and we can drink wine and eat chocolate." Cara's words impinged on Simone's and she smiled.

"I don't know. Should you be doing that, only weeks out from the wedding? You won't fit in your gown."

Cara giggled at her comment. "Well, I'm sure we can come up with a low-fat alternative then."

Simone nodded and they rose, Simone grateful that her best friend could be there for her. She looked back one last time before leaving the diner. The action reminded her that one part of her life was over. She sighed and walked out of the door James held open for them.

# CHAPTER 6

*H*e'd heard the door open with a bang and swung around in time to watch Simone enter the diner followed quickly by Cara and James. Under normal circumstances she was truly a beautiful woman. Usually her hair was immaculate, but today she seemed as limp as the droop of her mouth.

She was blotchy, with mascara runs on her face and she clutched a wadded handkerchief in her fisted hand.

As usual she was dressed well. On any other day it was understated and elegant, yet today the red suit caught his eye. It was totally at odds with the emotions on her face and he fought off the need to see her smile.

Inside him, a tiny bud of heat bloomed.

He'd been watching over her for some time, because she was a friend of Cara and James, and one of his many covers saw him tending to the gardens of the office space where she worked. He'd started doing that as a way of staying closer to James and Cara, after his little stint in the mailroom at Veha Industries came to an end. He still had to have an excuse to stay around.

He'd watched the way Cara and James crowded into the faded cubicle flanking Simone.

"Simone, what happened? How could he end it all?" Cara enveloped her friend in a hug and Jake strained to hear more, stabbing himself on a fork tine.

"Owwww!" He lifted his finger to inspect the small droplet of blood then sucked absently, tasting the coppery tang.

*"He said..."* Simone was talking and he knew he needed to hear the words.

He felt the touch of a nail upon his arm and turned. *Cailleach. Fabulous.* "What the hell do you want?" He couldn't contain the anger in his tone. He didn't need her interrupting—not now.

"Well, I see you've found yours." She indicated to the fork with a grin and for a second he felt a vertigo-like sensation.

*Found my what...?* Understanding quickly intruded and his stomach rocked. "Damn! You've got to be joking!"

Cailleach smiled broadly. "Never less so, Diocail. Now, how are you going to cope with this?"

Bewilderment filled him. *Cope? She's blonde. She's gorgeous and somehow I need her to want me.* He groaned. *Just my luck.* No red-haired man he knew had ever managed to find a sexy blonde for a mate.

This was a whole new ball game. Now he needed her to commit to him. Just him. Without any trickery or help. In his current persona, he was small and round. Bald. *I'll have to reveal myself fully.*

"By the way, your father is incredibly proud of you. You only intervened enough to ensure Jane and Davis found their own path. Only a truly enlightened being can manage that." Her words knocked him flat. *Enlightened?* That had nothing to do with it. After all, he'd been angry, worried and more than just a little pissed off with the foolish man who'd died. He'd been too slow. The self-castigating thoughts burned him to his soul.

Even as he considered those thoughts, Cailleach disappeared, leaving a wave of shimmering power in her wake. Jake turned around to see Cara and James ushering the crying woman from the diner. He'd missed his opportunity.

He laughed quietly, realizing this was only the first chance.

Simone was his future.

Soon he'd come up with another way to engage with her. Now wasn't the time—after all, she'd just realized that Nathan had been cheating.

She was raw.

Hurting.

He wouldn't push her straight away. Better to give her a week or two to come to terms with the loss before introducing her to the real him. But damn! If only he could just help it a little. He stood and headed for the street, watching as Cara ushered the blonde woman, his mate, to the car.

"And now it begins."

Once Cara and James left, Simone sat in her tiny house alone. Anger fled, leaving her with a hollow feeling in her gut.

Everywhere she glanced there were reminders of Nathan.

The sofa where they'd spent nights laughing, kissing and even making love. She ran her hands over the nubby cloth, closing her eyes as memory after memory assailed her.

On the counter in the kitchen sat the tea he preferred and she gave in to the fury and loss, catching up the box then throwing it in the bin before she could change her mind. She clenched her fists, feeling the bite of nails.

The mug she'd bought him at a market jeered silently. She stood, gazing at the visage of some mythical being, noting the berry-brown grinning face, as if it were mocking her. She nearly threw it too, before she stilled herself. "No. You need to get rid of his things."

The box of items she'd brought home from the office sat in the corner of the lounge. Carefully, she emptied it, laying everything on the floor ready to be dealt with once she had finished packing up Nathan's belongings. The photos in the frames were of both of them and her family. Slowly she picked them up, removed the backs and tugged the pictures out. "I don't want them anymore."

Each image represented a happy time and tears threatened as she dropped the photographic reminders into the box. Next she placed his mug into the package.

In the bedroom she tugged jackets and pants, shirts and underwear from hangers and drawers and carefully folded them. Each item was placed into the cardboard receptacle. There wasn't much now, and she realized that he'd taken a lot of his belongings home in the last few weeks.

In the bathroom she scooped up brush, comb and razor. She swiped her finger across the blade accidentally. "Oww!" She dropped the items into the sink and stared at the welling blood. "Damn."

As with all razor cuts, it stung like the devil. With a loud hiss she wrapped her hand around it. "One more cut, you bastard!" She dropped her head, breathed carefully in and out. She sought her inner strength as she raised her gaze to the mirror. "I won't let this destroy me. I'm stronger than that."

She quickly washed away the blood and anything that may have contaminated the shallow slice, wrapped it with a bandage before carefully gathering up his things. They joined everything else in the box. Discs filled with music and movies went on top, then she stopped. *Where to deliver them?*

She flopped onto the couch, carefully relaxing every muscle. For the first time since she'd arrived home, she was still.

Silent.

It felt surreal.

"This is what it's like to not have a plan for the future." Doubts crashed down on her. What would she do next? How would she manage without an income?

*Knock. Knock.* She sprang up, wondering who it could be? She wasn't usually home at this time of the day…

Simone peered through the small spyglass. There was something familiar about the round man with brown eyes. She sighed as she noted the postal uniform.

"Can I help…?" She flung the door open and the man smiled.

His eyes twinkled.

"I have a parcel for you." He held out the box, long and white.

"But who...?"

The man before her thrust the parcel into her hands. "It's an express delivery. Only came in a few minutes ago."

He turned and walked away as she stood dumbfounded, hoping her tired brain would finally churn into gear. *Maybe it was Nathan...? No. He hates flowers, remember? He's allergic to pollen. It wouldn't be from Nathan.*

Stepping back into the house, she used her leg to kick the door shut. Nathan had always hated when she'd done that in the past. Simone allowed herself a smile. It wasn't a problem anymore.

As she slid the box onto the table, she saw the clear cellophane window and the red and yellow within. "Oh my." Simone eased the lid off and the fragrance wafted around her. "I love roses."

A card was nestled firmly in between the long stems.

*Things can only get better. Think on the positives.*

*Someone who cares.*

*Who...?* Simone didn't have a clue, but right now, this beautiful bouquet had brightened her day.

# CHAPTER 7

On Saturday, Simone scoured the papers, looking for suitable jobs. There weren't many, and she worried her lip, searching the page. One job caught her eye. It was local, it paid well and they wanted someone available for an immediate start. With shaking fingers she dialed the number. Her stomach dipped as she waited for someone to answer. These firms never worked on a Saturday, so requesting applicants to call today, well... They obviously needed someone in a hurry. She curled her hands around the receiver, gripping hard.

"Good morning, this is Jackson and Associates. How may I help you?" The voice on the other end was modulated and confident. It settled Simone's nerves.

"I'd like to apply for the position you advertised in today's paper." She wound the fingers of her free hand in her long hair and gave a tiny tug.

"Sure, let me get some details and we can get back to you if we require further information." Her nerves jangled and Simone sucked in a deep breath.

Then she gave her name and waited for the woman to take her particulars. Within minutes she was staring at the handset in the cradle, knowing that she'd possibly taken the first step on a new path. "Well, that was easier than expected."

The woman had been non-committal enough that Simone couldn't tell if she'd be offered an interview. She could sit around waiting, or get busy.

*Which is the better choice?*

*Will they call me back?*

In that instant she made up her mind.

She looked around the house, seeing the items she'd brought home sitting on the floor and the box filled with Nathan's belongings. She could deliver them now, but what if they called? Instead she carried the box out to the car and placed it in the boot, then set about cleaning her house and re-homing the returned goods.

Just as she was popping the washing on, the phone chimed. Her heart stuttered, then she scurried to the lounge and scooped it up. "Simone Carter speaking."

"This is Kylie from Jackson and Associates. Mr. Jackson has short-listed you to attend an interview tomorrow at ten a.m.. Are you available?"

*Tomorrow? A Sunday?* But instead of blurting out her question, she wisely nodded. "Miss Carter?" the voice prodded and she started.

"Absolutely! Let me note down the address first." She scrabbled for paper and pencil, scratching down the necessary data.

"Excellent." Kylie reiterated the time and place, and for a moment Simone was struck dumb. *I haven't even updated my résumé!* As quickly as the thought had come, she banished it. She had a computer and a printer. Time was on her side.

She sprang into action. Her movements resembled a whirlwind as she booted up the computer and looked critically at the document. Her fingers flew over the keyboard, adding the requisite information.

Finally happy, she printed a copy and checked it for errors, then set the printer to make a final high quality run. Simone tugged a folder from her filing drawers at the bottom of her desk.

Her glance settled on the envelope he'd thrust into her hands. A reference... Would it be worth the paper it was printed on? For a moment the pain from her heart almost swamped her. "No. Not now. Businesslike. Professional." She gulped, settling the queasiness that rose. "A job. I need a job."

She carefully slit the top of the envelope, and pulled out the contents. The check fell onto the desk and her eyes widened at the amount. It was way more than she'd expected and a lump formed in her belly.

The folded paper beckoned, though, and she unfolded it. Read it through. It was a standard reference in her estimation. *Excellent staff member. Highly motivated. Capable.*

"Oh, Nathan. It's a great reference, for all it ended badly." Even as she spoke, she knew she'd use it. Otherwise, they'd have to contact him. She wasn't sure that right now that would be a good thing.

Sunday morning Simone pulled on her suit, made sure her hair was fastened up and back and every strand carefully restrained. She checked to ensure her makeup was flawless. She picked up her folder. "Here we go now."

Driving to the offices took a scant five minutes and she marveled at the idea of a short commute. The interview passed quickly and she was sure that with the references and referees, the documentation and the short exercises they'd set, she'd proved her skills.

Mr. Jackson had been an older gentleman, with shaggy white hair and the requisite black suit with white shirt. His office smelled of paper and ink, no doubt from the legions of titles that sat behind his heavy wooden desk, their gilt-work sparkling in the subdued lighting. He spoke slowly, with deliberation, and she was sure he'd be an exacting taskmaster. She looked forward to the challenge.

"We'll be making a determination this afternoon, Miss Carter, and will contact you to apprise you of the outcome."

When the phone jangled several hours later it was Mr. Jackson on the line. "Miss Carter, I was greatly impressed by your interview. If you are interested, I'd like to offer you the position of secretary. How soon can you start?"

With a grin she pulled out her diary. "I can start Tuesday if that is convenient. I have some business to attend to tomorrow."

"Fine. I'll see you at eight a.m. then."

With a tired yet happy grin she hung up. "One more step on the path."

J ake hated the necessity of the day-to-day lifestyle the humans seemed to somehow thrive on. At home, he would have been able to assume his true persona. Out in the open he'd had to hide it. "Until now." He straightened up, casting a glance at himself in the mirror. The face he saw was the one he'd hidden for as long as he'd been banished here on Earth. The face was bronzed, yet nothing like the berry brown most people assumed was the color of a brownie. In reality he was tall, redheaded and bearded. Trim and taut and well dressed. It was the look he was happy to assume.

This morning there were papers to sign, the first step in creating the dual existence that he would offer his bride.

*That is, if she'll have me, once she knows the truth.*

It had taken him several weeks since the delivery of flowers to Simone to formulate a way to circle back into her sphere. He'd been at the wedding of Cara and James, and he'd watched her play the part of chief bridesmaid. It had given him no opportunity to engage her.

Today... Ah, today he could start his wooing of her in earnest. Giddiness and anticipation flowed hot and thick through his veins.

The first step meant Jake Kendrick was about to buy a house. He ran the comb over his hair one last time.

He gathered up the file of documentation and swept out of the tiny unit he'd been living in. *I'll be glad to be away from here.* Jake let his magic cloak him so people would see only what they expected.

Mrs. Jennings on the third floor called out a happy greeting as he passed. "Hello, Jacob. Will you be at bingo tomorrow night?"

As always, the urge to respond negatively bloomed, but he shook his head slowly. Mrs. Jennings saw the octogenarian, widowed and white-haired man, the one she had a *thing* for as she regularly told Mrs. Duffy on the eighth floor. Cathy McBride on the first floor stopped and stared. "James McDougal, where is that lovely young blonde I last saw you with?"

"Ah, Niamh and I decided we wouldn't suit." His thirty-something persona intoned sadly.

She smiled and patted his hand. "Well, never mind. There are more fish in the sea."

He'd be pleased when he left here and could just be Jake. Not the multitude of assumed personalities and the juggling of who knew which personality. The subterfuge wore a bit thin sometimes.

Once he'd arrived at the basement car park he located and climbed into his car. As he rolled out of his parking space, he reflected that in only a few more weeks he'd be free of this existence. He drove slowly, at odds with his racing pulse. It urged him to go faster. To get to where he was going.

The red brick building with the discreet gold lettering proclaiming *Jackson and Associates* loomed. He sought and found a parking space before climbing out of his vehicle. Two beeps indicated that the central locking had worked and he stepped quickly towards the front door.

He pushed at the glass and wood, dimly noting the way it eased open without a sound. A young woman—she had to be about twenty-one or two—manned the reception desk. He gave his name and she buzzed through to someone—likely Simone—while he waited, then the dark-haired girl, Kylie, indicated to a seat with a murmured, "Mr. Jackson will see you in a minute."

The chair was plush and comfortable but frustration ate at him. He'd see Simone again soon. He had to stop his knee from jiggling up and down as excitement built.

"Mr. Kendrick? Could you come through please? Mr. Jackson is ready to see you."

He glanced up and soaked up the vision of beauty before him. The long, lean lines, the curve of her jaw and the silky strands of hair. Her full pouting lips. His body reacted instinctively as he drank in the sight of his intended. He stood, his brain sending the signals to the rest of his body. He followed her directions to the office out the back.

Simone smiled at him while she held the door open. As it shut behind him, all he could think was that she was a siren and he'd better be quick before someone else snapped her up.

~

er head spun even as she stumbled back to her desk. The red-haired man? Jake Kendrick? *I'm sure he could burn me with a single smoldering look.* She stopped midway down into her seat as another thought crowded in. Could she really afford any kind of attraction right now? And to a client? Hadn't she learned anything from the Nathan scenario? The man who'd just gone into Mr. Jackson's office left her breathless. Red hair had never attracted her before. She dropped with an oomph into the padded chair.

"That was one very yummy piece of eye candy." She jumped as Kylie's voice echoed behind her.

"Oh, I didn't really notice. Did you have something for me?" She turned her head and smiled blandly at the young woman. There was a glint in her eyes as if she doubted Simone's words.

She wouldn't jeopardize her job for a man again. She'd been there and done that. It wasn't a mistake to repeat, she told herself firmly.

"Yeah. Here's the mail." Kylie handed over the pile of envelopes and Simone accepted them with a smile.

"Well, I'll get these opened and entered into the system, then I'll take my break."

Kylie trailed away while Simone battled with herself. In her mind, she knew she was hedging. He'd be out while she was working and she'd catch another glimpse. Try as she might, though, she couldn't dampen her curiosity over the man. She hoped he would return her interest then she shook her head. No, she told her heart.

*There'd been a spark in his eye.*

*Never get involved with clients or your boss.*

Instead she focused on the task, opening and sorting, stamping and entering data onto the screen. When the door creaked open, she was ready for the shock to her system.

It wasn't anywhere near enough preparation. "This way Mr. Kendrick."

She guided him to the door and as he turned to thank her, he pressed a card into her shaking hands. "Would you be...? Would you go out with me?"

For a full minute she couldn't think how to respond. Then reality reared its ugly head. "It's against the rules." She heard the breathlessness in her voice.

He smiled at the mumbled words then turned, headed through the doorway. As it shut, she watched him walk away from the building. Only then did she look down at the card in her hand. *Jake Kendrick— Professional Matchmaker.*

# CHAPTER 8

On Monday, he phoned the office on the pretext of checking whether they had the deposit for the legal work. The young woman on reception—Kylie, he thought her name was—handled that and it left him with a sense of dissatisfaction.

Tuesday arrived. He had papers that needed signing. Who better than someone at the law firm to witness them? Even as Simone emerged from her office to escort him from the door, she exuded a do-not-touch aura. Her pale face and pink-rimmed eyes worried him.

Fire burned in his chest as the pain in her gaze tugged at his soul. "Miss Carter, is there anything I can do for you?"

Her lips thinned and the watery sheen in her eyes increased. "No, thank you. Everything is fine." She moved away in silence. Only a few steps but it widened the chasm between them.

It stung, like a stake to his heart.

Jake knew she was wary—he expected that and so much more. Some of it was because he refused to give up and the rest he could attribute to her no-good ex-boyfriend. He had to push the connection. She was his predestined partner. The love of his long-lived life—at least, he *thought* so.

Without her... His future loomed: Long. Empty. *Cold.*

Anguish emanated from her in waves. The misery and pain tore at his chest and scored his soul.

"Miss Carter... Simone. You're upset. Let me help you." Without thought, he reached out and touched her, wanting only to give her support. He'd never been this close before but as his fingers touched her skin—a flash of electricity screamed through his body. *All it took was just one touch.*

"You can't—" She backed away, breaking the connection and averting her eyes.

"Surely someone can help you." He looked around seeking anyone else. The door to Mr. Jackson's office was closed. The receptionist was missing. "Sit." He bustled her to the chair and for some undefined reason she followed his gentle urging.

"Tell me. Whatever it is. Let me help you."

She hiccupped once, raising her shaking hands to her lips. "They're..." She stopped as if the words were choking her. "He asked her... He asked her to marry him."

*Who asked?* Confusion filled him for a brief instant, then he knew. *Nathan.* He clenched his hands together. He couldn't let on that he knew who she meant. Otherwise it might seem odd, like he was involved in the lie. Instead he leaned forward, inhaling her light scent, and pasted on the most confused look he could manage. "Who?"

"Nathan. My ex." Her voice was low and broken. It was clear how much the news hurt her.

Now what did he say? In the past he would have brushed it off with a little divine help, a hint of magic here and there. But today, now... For the first time in his existence he didn't know what to do. He was forbidden from using his magic where she was concerned and that left him helpless.

Jake squatted down beside her chair, clutching her hand while she sniffled and dabbed at her eyes. As she calmed, he felt the gulf between them.

"I'm so sorry... I shouldn't have fallen apart like that." She laughed and inhaled deeply. "It was totally unprofessional."

"You're human, though. It's okay to feel—"

"Like a total fool? Oh dear, it's a good thing Mr. Jackson isn't here today and Kylie is out attending to the mail." She tugged her hand free of his grip. "So... What did you need Mr.... Uhh... Mr.—"

"Kendrick. I need some papers witnessed."

Simone frowned, her eyes still watery and pink, but he could see that the crying jag was done for now.

"I don't know that I can... Let's see what they are." She took the papers and flicked through them. "You don't need a solicitor so yes, I can witness these." She laid them out, handed him a pen and indicated a couple of spots. As he signed them he felt that he'd achieved something momentous and the bubble of excitement grew in his chest. Then she swung the papers in her direction and gripped the pen. He noted the way her long fingers grasped it firmly.

Her signature was bold and sharp—slashing lines and quick, sharp curves. As she reorganized the papers he decided to try again. "Would you join me for dinner?"

She cocked an eye. "I really can't. It's against company rules."

"Okay then, how about drinks?"

Simone laughed... It might have been wet sounding but there was a hint of mirth below the surface. "You're persistent, aren't you?"

Jake nodded.

"Look... If this gets out, I'll be in so much trouble, but coffee... We could meet for a coffee."

"That would be marvelous. Here's my card, in case you misplaced the last one. I'll let you pick the date, place and time." Jake knew he was taking a chance. She'd suggested it but it didn't mean she'd go ahead. *She'll ring.* He'd already seen that Simone was a woman of her word.

He left the offices with his papers and a jaunty step.

~

Simone showered quickly, washing her hair all the while she considered the situation with Mr. Kendrick. To be honest his invitation was tempting. "But he's a client," she reminded herself fiercely.

Her hair caught up in a towel, she made herself comfortable for an evening in front of the television, but nothing caught her attention. Finally, she turned it off and stood. "Go to bed. Forget him. Forget all men."

It took a while for sleep to claim her.

The interior of Coffee and Co was strangely empty. "Where is everyone?" Two coffees sat on the side, names penciled on the side. Jake and Simone. "How...?"

With a shrug, Simone reached for the one with her name and settled at a table in the back of the room.

The jangle of a door cut through the silence and she looked up. Jake Kendrick entered, his eyes glinting in the light. He caught sight of her and shared an intimate grin. Her stomach clenched as she watched him reach for his drink.

With long, unhurried strides he made his way towards her. "May I join you?"

Desire zinged through her and she could only nod.

Jake settled himself beside her. "It's quiet in here today. Just you... And me."

"Uh... Yes."

"That's excellent, Simone, because that allows me to talk to you. Here I can tell you all the things I want to share with you."

Heat suffused her as she caught his meaning. "Like... Like what?"

"I want to make love with you. I want to run my hands all over your body, Simone. Suck your breasts and bury myself deep within you."

Her breath caught at his carnal speech. She gripped the coffee cup tightly. The lid popped and hot liquid spurted all over her pristine white blouse. "Oh geez! I'm such a clutz."

His wolfish grin had her squirming as she tugged at the hot, wet cloth. "Let me help you there."

Jake reached across and carefully grasped one button, releasing it before continuing down her blouse.

Simone watched, frozen in shock as he stripped her blouse away, baring her white bra. It had also been bathed with hot coffee. "We should get rid of that too. Stand up and let me help you."

"But... What if someone—?"

"No one will interrupt us, Simone. It's a dream. We can do whatever we want here."

She gulped and stood, her legs unsteady. The fire that had ignited in her belly rose, licking at her insides while he unclasped the hooks of her bra. Her breasts released from their confines swung and he reached out, cupping them.

"Beautiful. But I want to see the rest of you."

"Only if you..."

He gazed at her and she felt unsteady and unprepared. "Take your clothes off too." The words wobbled and he grinned.

"Soon. Before I do that, get naked, Simone. I need to see your body. I'm burning for that view. My cock is hard and ready. Can you tell?"

She glanced down towards his pants and noted the bulge there. "You're sure...?"

"No one will interrupt us." He sealed the words with a kiss. Hot and wet, he devoured her. The world spun a little further away and he kneaded her breasts, toyed with her nipples, so they were hard points of hunger by the time he stepped back.

She licked her lips, the desire and emptiness clawing at her. In a split second, Simone made a decision and reached for the buttons on her dark blue skirt. It fluttered to the floor as she stood there, white lace panties and matching garter-belt all that remained of her carefully chosen outfit.

Jake caught the hook closure of the belt, bending to free her from its confines, and the brush of his fingers over exposed skin left her trembling. Once it had dropped away, he reached down, hooked his fingers under the elastic of her underwear and slid them down her legs.

"Step out..." His voice was gruff and the whisper of his breath fluttered over her mound.

*Simone kicked away her shoes and let him tug the fine material from her feet.*

*"The table. Lie down."*

*His panted words matched the uncertain rhythm of her own breathing. Without question she followed his direction. The cool table top beneath her nude body was shocking and she hissed.*

*"I want to see you." Gently he reached for her, parting her legs so that she was exposed to his view. "Beautiful. Pink and wet."*

*He moved closer, his mouth now even with her sex, while his fingers toyed with the folds, never quite dipping within, and she squirmed.*

*"Jake?"*

*"Soon."*

*He settled his mouth over her and she arched up, unable to deny the pleasure that streaked through her body like lightning. He lapped at her, tracing the tip of his tongue over her exposed flesh until she writhed in an agony of desire, heart pounding as she cried out. "Jake!"*

*He speared her with his fingers, sliding in and out, his thumb pressing firmly on her clitoris.*

*She shattered, her mind blanking.*

S imone woke with a start, her body wound tight. "Oh God!" She ached and the emptiness inside her bore down. "Geez…" The panting was finally subsiding even though her body still felt hungry and unfulfilled. "Wow. That was some dream."

She wondered if her psyche wasn't telling her she should do something more about Jake. "Not happening. He's a client."

She gave a vicious tug of her quilt and rolled over. Sleep took a long time to return.

# CHAPTER 9

*S*aturday morning, Simone cursed the emotions swirling in her chest. She kept glancing at the phone as if he'd magically find and ring her number. Magic? It didn't exist in her world. No, for Simone Carter there were years of loneliness interspersed with bright patches of happiness. She usually attributed those latter occasions to her best friend Cara—lunches at the Wait-A-While diner and going to the movies. Now Cara was married, she guessed that had changed, just like the mood at the diner. It didn't feel the same anymore since the regular waitress had left.

She exhaled, watching as the petals on the flower on her dining table fluttered. She could call him. She should. After all, she'd promised.

The tiny business card drew her gaze again. The promise had been made days ago. The steady thumping of her heart reminded her of the passing time as did the tick-tock of the clock on the wall. "Oh, why did I agree?" She clutched her hands together and dropped her head onto them, where they sat on the table.

Because he'd been kind.

Considerate.

Handsome.

He'd made her feel better—good even—in miserable circum-stances. With a quick movement she lifted her head. "Ring him now." Simone grabbed the card before rifling through her bag for her mobile phone.

She pressed the number into the keypad and waited as the phone rang. *Will he answer? Will he remember?* "Oh God…"

After several insistent rings he answered, just as she was about to cancel the call, the curling of butterfly wings filling her stomach. "Hello?"

*What the hell am I doing?* She looked to the ceiling, but there was no inspiration there. "Uh, hi. It's Simone Carter here… From Mr. Jack-son's office." *I feel like an idiot!*

"Simone! Great! I'm so pleased you called. Name the date and place. I'm all yours."

Her mouth dried as the memory of his face, with chiseled jaw line and piercing green eyes rose in her mind. *All mine.*

"Uh, Mr. Kendrick…"

"Jake, please." Over the phone the sensual and satiny voice heated her from within and she closed her eyes as a million sensations—most of them delightfully erotic—rose.

"Great. Thanks, Jake. I was thinking tomorrow if you're free? We could meet at Coffee and Co. It's near the office."

"Sounds great. What time?"

Her mind blanked. *Time?* She hadn't even considered that. "Uh, say eleven?" Sunday morning. She didn't want to upset his routine too much, but a need and yearning urged her to seek this connection.

"Perfect, I'll be there," he whispered over the line and for a crazy instant she was sure there was more to his promise. Her stomach dipped and wove.

"Awesome. I'll see you there then." He hung up—she heard the disconnect tone in her ear.

She opened her eyes, ended the call from her side then flipped through the contacts, seeing Cara's number. For a moment her finger hovered then she rang.

The call went through to voicemail.

∽

J ake couldn't believe his luck. Here he was sitting outside Nathan's office, investigating the nagging feeling that had irritated him weeks ago and the phone rang, just as he was ready to give up. The night had finally drawn in and the weather was starting to turn cool. "Damn." On the back seat sat his black leather jacket. He reached for it, shrugging it on while he dug in the pocket for the device.

Before he'd even answered, he'd known it was Simone. He hadn't given this number to anyone else. He'd wanted to be prepared whenever she'd chosen to call.

His body had hardened on hearing her voice, just as it always seemed to. For a moment his psyche wondered why it hadn't been a factor before—before he'd started to think of her as his. He'd studied her face and form endlessly. His heart stuttered as he allowed honesty to rise. He'd just taken great pains to ignore the reactions before now.

By the time the conversation was done, he was happily looking forward to their coffee date. While he would have preferred something far more intimate and immediate, it would have to do. "For now, anyway."

The car wasn't comfortable but he had other things to attend to. His cover as a gardener was gone, so he'd have to be someone else, someone who watched carefully from a distance. The whole set-up with the woman and Nathan felt odd. He damned his over-extended sense of responsibility. He'd felt a worrying presentiment last time he was here.

Jake knew he could have ignored his concerns—experience had told him to trust his instincts. He sat up just as the door cracked open, then everything stopped. Stilled.

The windscreen turned white as mystic fog rolled away. He could see his father, sitting upon his wooden throne. "Your aunt has been keeping me informed of your progress. I'm pleased to see that at last you've found your destiny. A nice human girl."

Surprise warred with humiliation as he stared at his father.

"So, Diocail, what are you going to do about it?"

Jake wanted to swear but instead clenched his fists tightly as he controlled the instinctive outburst. "Father, she's…" *How can I tell him it's not his business? That his interfering could mess everything up? That she's been hurt before?* His father was the great god Lugh. He couldn't just tell Lugh to butt out.

"Bosh! You might think she's damaged, yet I've a suspicion she's far more tenacious than you give her credit for." His father leaned forward, grabbing the arm of his throne. "Women like her, they have an inner strength."

"What? What have you done, Father? Swear to me now that you aren't spying on me and Simone." His heart raced as his mouth dried. Surely Lugh didn't plan to involve himself in this?

His father's face filled with mirth. "Now, would I do something like that? Unless I'm concerned that my son is making his usual mistakes, cozying up to women with no morals who won't be able to be his helpmate…?"

Jake studied Lugh, knowing his father was dangling him like a fish on a line. They weren't close, but then this man was a god. He'd never met anyone who could get close to a god.

As his father had reminded him again and again, he was a mere brownie whose role was to bring couples together. Until now Lugh had never interfered. This time he wasn't just interfering—he was playing a dangerous game. "It's none of your business."

His father cocked an eyebrow. "Diocail, you are no mere human. You are charged with the protection of love and relationships. That means your attitude towards them must also be right. After all, how can you do your job if your life is in tatters? Remember after your fling with Senuna?"

Jake winced. That hadn't ended well, after her temple had been overrun and destroyed by rampaging villagers. The memory of her wild accusations and hysterical outbursts still left him horrified. "Sir, that wasn't—"

"Perhaps it wasn't your fault. You walked wide circles around women for centuries after. It was pitiful to watch. Then there was your liaison with Armemetia. She sat in her grove for a century after the two of you decided that there was no future. Remember?"

"It was complicated." *How on earth can I bring this conversation to an end?*

"Do the right thing this time, Diocail. Simone has a part to play in your future, and should it go wrong, the consequences could prove more far-reaching than we can foresee. Bring her home and make her happy. That's all I ask." For the first time there was no hint of the stern god. Rather there was a softness to his father's face. "Do what I never could. Make a family, my son."

The clouds closed in before they receded. Was his father right? Was that all there was to it? Make her happy?

As he reflected on his father's words, traffic sounds intruded. Shaking himself, he cast his eyes back to the building, feeling the sense of something being out of balance. He'd been too lost and only caught sight of the vehicle driving off.

Jake sighed heavily. Certainly, something strange was afoot, but he wasn't going to find out what it was now. That opportunity had passed.

He fastened his buckle of his seatbelt and started the car.

Tomorrow was looming and he wanted to be prepared.

# CHAPTER 10

*T*he phone buzzed just as Simone was preparing to sit down to her solitary meal. "Simone here."

"Oh, sweetie, you'll never guess what James has done?" Cara, her best friend in the world, chortled and for a moment Simone's spirits rose at the sheer joy in her best friend's tone.

"I probably won't, so hurry up and tell me, then I can share your good news." Simone glanced down at the toasted sandwich on her plate. Since she'd been alone, she hadn't had much of an appetite. She looked at the soggy mass and pushed the plate away. "Tell me everything."

"He's arranging a party for us. And you're invited. In fact, he's been through all his friends and he's going to find a partner for you." In her mind, Simone could imagine Cara bouncing up and down with excitement. She wanted to groan. Since she'd broken up with Nathan, Simone had been waiting for Cara to set her up. *Isn't that the way of newly married people?*

"Well, that… That's nice, but…" She let the words hang, unsure how to tell Cara that she'd met someone—a man who interested her.

"Hey, this is me, remember? Is everything okay? Do you need me?"

Simone closed her eyes at the concern in Cara's voice. "I'm fine…

Well, I've agreed to a coffee date for tomorrow." The silence drew out and Simone laid a hand on her churning belly. "Cara? Talk to me."

"Well... I have to say you could have knocked me over with a feather. I thought it was going to be harder to get you to a place where Nathan wasn't a... I mean, he wasn't the best catch ever." Cara's words ended on a squeak.

"You said that before. I'm...not sure... I mean, after Nathan, I don't want to jeopardize my career again. I worked too hard. When I left Veha Industries I swore I was going to climb the ladder, but with the breakup that nearly went sour."

"Nathan was more of a side trip than a stepping stone." Cara turned silent.

Simone stood up, phone snuggled under one ear while she lifted the stodgy mass on her plate. She didn't really want it. With a sigh she lifted the plate and tipped the food into the bin.

"Simone? It's a matter of when you're ready. Don't let anyone tell you what's right or wrong for you, okay? Now tell me about your coffee date."

Simone chortled. "Well, you know, it's only coffee. Not a wedding."

"Only coffee. Are you mad? It's your first date. Now tell me about him. What's his name and what does he do? Where did you meet him?"

"His name is Jake Kendrick. I met him at the office. He came in with some conveyancing. He's asked me more than once. When I lost it the other day—"

"You what? You didn't say anything before this. What happened?" Cara demanded.

"Well, it was kind of hard to. You were on your honeymoon. Nathan asked that woman..." The clawing sensation in her chest started again and she had to gulp it down. "He asked her to marry him. For god's sake, she isn't even divorced yet!"

"Hold it right there. What do you mean he asked her? I thought he said he'd never marry again." Cara's voice was steely and Simone found herself nodding.

"So did I... Apparently he only had to meet the *right* woman." The bitterness in her voice cut the air.

"Look, you need to forget him. Find a man who will appreciate you for you. Nathan's old news and Jake is the flavor of the month." The earnestness in Cara's voice reached through the line, soothing the anguish she felt.

"Cara? I'm... I'm confused. I mean, what if I'm using him? Trying to get over Nathan and just don't realize it? I don't want to be like that. I don't want to take advantage."

"Honey, if you have to ask that, then you know that you're aware. You're not a user. Even when you were younger and caring for your father in that grotty caravan, you'd have given the shirt off your back before taking something for yourself. Trust yourself. I do and so does James."

Simone ached. For Cara it was so simple. "Oh, Cara, what would I do without you?"

"You'd be sad and lonely, that's what. Now tell me about this hunk of yours. What does he look like?"

By the time she'd hung up, Simone felt better about her decision to move forward. Far more assured than at the beginning of the conversation. Excitement bubbled through her veins. Tomorrow she was seeing Jake Kendrick.

It felt good.

It felt right.

The tiny coffee shop was crowded when he arrived. When a table for two by the window became available Jake quickly sat down and waited for Simone, tapping his fingers on the polished wood top. He watched the throngs of people passing the shop, hurrying about the usual weekend routine.

Within minutes, he caught sight of her blonde hair, shining in the light. She'd teamed a frilly white blouse with black, skin-tight denim jeans and boots that stretched to her knees. His attention zeroed in on her just as he noticed a number of other men did as well.

She scanned the shop. Jake took a moment to just drink in the sight of her, then she saw him and the smile she gave him warmed him.

"Hi, Jake." She lowered herself onto the seat in front of him. "Have you ordered yet?" She laid her handbag on the table and smoothed non-existent wrinkles from her pants.

"Hi. No, but tell me what you want, and I'll grab it."

She shook her head and he was entranced by the way the light shone from her tresses, some silky strands escaping the tight bun at the back of her head. "I don't expect you—"

"I know you don't, but I want to. Now you'd like…?"

She worried her lip with perfect white teeth. "I'm partial to a Café Americano."

"Then a Café Americano it will be. I'll be back before you know it."

Heading for the counter he had the suspicion someone was watching him. He tried to ignore it, yet the itch at the nape of his neck was compelling.

He placed the order and took the cups when they were offered before he wound his way back to the table. Simone met him with a shy smile. "Hi again." Jake placed the two cups on the wood top as he lowered himself to the metal chair.

"So, have you had a busy weekend?" He leaned forward, wanting to know about her routine. Usually he would have had no compunctions about *peeking* at her mind. But this was Simone. Using magic was forbidden, yet on another level Jake found it intriguing to learn more about her like this.

Simone chatted away, about cleaning house, the latest book she was reading and her friend's wedding. He watched her while she spoke, her movements restrained yet he noted that her hands moved all the time. As she drew a deep and shaky breath he was amused and intrigued by the blush that crept over her high cheekbones. "Am I talking too much?"

He laughed, hearing the pleasurable sound echo in the busy coffee house. "Not at all. In fact, I like listening to you and watching your face. You intrigue me."

The way she dipped her head and spoke quickly—"You do too"—gave him pause.

"I'd like to get to know you better." The words were bold. Honest.

Her gaze met his. Alarm bloomed as her nostrils flared. For a moment he compared her to a doe readying to flee. "I'd... I'd like to, but..."

"Let's get out of here." He knew what she was about to say. He'd heard it once before. *I can't, it's not allowed.* Jake wasn't prepared to take that answer. Not now when their combined future loomed so close.

Simone stood and he placed his hand at the small of her back, elated at the sensations the simple action evoked.

Once outside he stopped, wondering what he could suggest next. It was coming up on lunchtime, and he didn't want to do something pedestrian. There was nothing meek or mild-mannered about the way he felt right now.

"Would you like to join me for a picnic lunch? There's a band in the park today." He said the words in a rush and they filled him with surprise.

"I'd love to."

"Your car?" He glanced at her.

"I got a taxi."

"Well then, Simone, my car is just around the corner and I'd love to squire you for the day." He loved the way she giggled girlishly at his old-fashioned words. "Allow me to escort you to our carriage."

That the coffee date would extend to lunch was a surprise. A picnic and great company were the best way to spend a Sunday, she reflected.

"This is so nice."

Simone half curled on the mat they'd found in the picnic basket, while Jake lounged against a tree stump. "I can't think of a more pleasant way to spend my day, or anyone better to pass it with."

Her belly fluttered at the words. With each moment she spent with him, the need inside her grew—along with the yearning for an emotional connection.

Simone checked her watch and started. "It's four o'clock already." Surely he'd want to go home soon.

"The day isn't over yet. What do you say we go for a walk?"

She rose slowly. "I really need..." Simone indicated in the direction of the bathrooms.

"I'll sort this out and drop it in the car. Then I'll come back for you."

Simone nodded. She needed time—space. Before desire took control and she did something impulsive.

Once in the public convenience Simone sighed. She mulled over their interlude, even as she hurried to freshen her makeup. Jake had surprised her, picking up a gourmet picnic basket. Wasn't he every woman's dream? If she hadn't seen him ring the number, she would have thought that it had all been planned. He'd driven around to Picnic Place and collected their order, and she'd been bemused.

"Is this too good to be true?" No one answered her. Under normal circumstances she might have said yes, but he seemed genuine.

There was a definite connection between them, something she couldn't possibly ignore; felt it in the way her body hummed and vibrated in his vicinity. *How far am I prepared to let today go?* Her body was warm and relaxed, aroused by his nearness and gentle touches. He hadn't kissed her. Not yet. But if—when—he did, she knew she'd be unable to resist his charms.

Her mind warned her that it was too much far too soon.

Simone swiped a final coating of lip gloss on and stood straight. "Maybe this time, I should just let nature take its course?" Deep inside her gut, she worried about ramifications. Last time had ended in disaster. Could she cope with that again? Could she scramble back from a world falling apart because of a man?

Unwilling to question herself further, she thrust the lipstick tube deep into her bag and strode out.

Jake waited in the sun, the dark red of his hair standing out amid the blond and dark-haired people who lazed in the Sunday afternoon heat. "Where to now?"

Biting her lip, she thought rapidly. What else could they do at this time? "Let's just walk down the path. I love the gardens at this time of year. I rarely get out, though."

He tucked her hand into the crook of his arm. It was a charming old world gesture. "Then walk we shall."

They traversed the tracks stopping every short while to admire a piece of sculpture or a building. At the Lady Clarke rotunda he stopped her. A wedding was taking place, the bride dressed in radiant white making her way up the steps. The intense emotions in the scene captured Simone's imagination.

"Oh look! Can we watch a while?"

She turned in Jake's direction, to see his face soften in the dappled sunlight. He tugged her into his arms. Her body wanted to melt at his touch. His eyes sparkled and the immediate pull began to drug her senses. Instead of giving in to temptation, Simone slid around in his embrace and faced the front. It felt right to be nestled against his body, as if they were made to fit together.

"Don't they look happy?" His lips were inches from her ear and she wanted to shiver as sensations of arousal crawled along every nerve ending. A small crowd had gathered around, a teenager in fresh green, her gown the same color as the greenery in the bride's bouquet. The groom turned and lifted the bride's veil and Simone gasped.

"Oh! I know her. She used to work at the diner my friend and I went to."

"Let's watch then. Imagine how they must feel, out here, proclaiming their love, where anyone can see. Unashamed of each other." His words sank into her mind, reinforcing a concept that had been taking root for days.

Nathan hadn't loved her enough to want that. Certainly he hadn't loved her the way she had imagined she'd loved him. He'd taken pains to hide their relationship, instead of sharing it with the world. The knot that had lodged in her chest when he'd told her to go loosened a little more.

This time, when Simone swiveled in Jake's embrace, it was with the knowledge that she wanted the physical connection between them. Her belly fluttered a little as she considered what she was about to ask for. Her gaze captured his. "Jake, will you kiss me please?"

His eyes darkened as he half smiled at her. "You have no idea how much I'd like to do that." The timbre of his voice was low and rich with promise. He dipped his head toward her.

C losing his arms around her slight frame, Jake inhaled her scent. It was rich and heady.

He savored her proximity, hoping that this meant she'd stepped over the metaphoric block which had kept her from him. Placing his lips against hers, Jake was sure that sparks of pure energy suffused him, making him feel lighter and more alive than ever before. He curled his hands over her shoulders holding her close. She vibrated with obvious pleasure given her moans of delight.

When she opened to him, he slid his tongue within her mouth, and he shuddered. Knowing that Simone was welcoming this next step was enough of a drug to intoxicate him.

She tugged away, a tiny smile on her lips as she fanned her fingers in front of her face. "Well... My... That was—"

"Absolutely amazing. I would agree." He loved the way her cheeks pinked under his searching gaze. "You are okay with that, aren't you?"

Simone nodded slowly. "Can we, maybe, get out of here?"

Jake slid his arm around her shoulders, while casting a final look back. He hadn't expected to see either Jane or Davis on their wedding day and pride suffused him. He'd been instrumental in making that happen.

They strode forward, back in the direction of the car.

Once they'd climbed inside the sedan, he turned in her direction. "So where to?"

"I… Uh, we could go to my place?"

Her hesitant words stopped him. "We can?" He spoke slowly, giving her the opportunity to change her mind.

"Let's go then." He glanced at her white knuckles and knew she had doubts.

"We could grab dinner on the way…?"

"No. Take me home and I'll cook for you."

Jake asked for directions and as the sun started to set on the horizon, he pulled into the driveway. "What a lovely house." It was a low, single-story white house, with green trim. He looked around at the small patch of grass that was neatly trimmed and the small metal fence. It wasn't big but it was clearly loved.

"I like it." They climbed out of the car and he followed her up the three shallow steps to the door.

"It's mine, you know? Somewhere I can be myself." Her simple words spoke volumes about belonging. He could understand that.

"One day, I'll have you come around to see my home."

Simone stopped. "Yes, your house. Settlement is—"

"Settlement is less than two weeks away, and I'm really excited. Shall we go in?" He indicated to the half-open door.

"Yeah, sure. Come on in."

She fluttered around the room, and Jake was amazed at how tidy and compact the space was. She'd infused her personality into every nook and cranny. Everything had its place. From the placement of the two-seater sofa to the arrangement of glasses in the small glass-fronted kitchen cabinet. "It's great."

It was quite simply an intimate look inside her mind, because he'd swear she brought very few people here. She was too contained in herself for that.

"What would you like to drink? I have coffee, tea and some wine."

"Wine would be fantastic, and tell me what I can do to help you."

She worried her lip with her teeth. "Well, I can do some chicken breasts with salad… Or if you prefer, I could throw together a quick stir-fry?"

"The stir-fry sounds great."

"Then, Jake, if you pour the wine I'll get the dinner started. Wine's in the fridge, glasses in that cupboard there." She pointed and he followed with his gaze. With a nod he set to work.

# CHAPTER 11

*I*n the close confines of her tiny kitchen, her awareness of Jake grew. The small square table in the compact space kept them constantly rotating in the proximity of one another. Running into each other was impossible to avoid—each pass sent another sensation of arousal rocketing through Simone's body.

There was a brush here, and a glancing touch there as they reached for utensils and drinks. Each touch heated the blood flowing through her veins. Her belly quivered. The scent of him intoxicated her so that by the time she served the dinner, she could barely look at him, for fear he would see the hunger in her face. A hunger that wasn't for food.

During dinner she concentrated on not spilling anything while silently counting her chewing. Anything, she told herself, to keep herself from launching over the table and into his lap.

Arousal curled through the air—thick and heady.

"You know, I could just go."

She glanced up at him. "What do you mean?" Her voice sounded so breathless.

He grinned. "Well, you've been so focused on your dinner that you haven't spoken for a good twenty minutes. And in the kitchen, you shied away every time—"

"Oh God…" She closed her eyes. "I'm, uh… I'm…" *How the hell do I say this?* "I, uh, I want you, Jake. My body's on fire."

The impression of heat and warmth filled her. She felt his hand on her shoulder. Simone hadn't even heard him leave the table or move behind her. She nuzzled in closer, his scent filling her senses.

A deep breath intoxicated her and she opened her eyes. The fork fell to the plate with a clatter and she rose, her chest heaving for oxygen that was laced with his tantalizing essence.

As they came together, their lips moving hungrily, all rational thought fled leaving behind scorching passion. Nerve endings quivered as he feathered kisses over her jaw line and down the curve of her neck. She called out, already incoherent with need. At the sweet spot behind her ear, reason momentarily raised its head. She stepped away, noting that his arms were still by his side.

"Jake? We should…"

"Take this to the bedroom." His words brought her back to reality.

"Uh…" *Am I ready for this?* She gently tugged out of his arms. "If we do this… You understand that, for me, it's serious? I don't…" Her scrambled mind sought the best way to explain. "I want a relationship. That means monogamy and seeing where this takes us."

Simone's breath caught. Her whole body tensed as she silently anticipated his answer to her bold declaration.

"You're an amazing woman, Simone. To be clear, I *want* this and I *want* you. I'm looking for forever." His lips curved upwards and his eyes twinkled. "And I do mean, forever."

He closed the gap between them, stepping close and sliding his arms around her waist.

"You smell so good." Her voice wobbled and he laughed, a deep throaty sound that reverberated in the room.

"Thanks, I think." His eyes darkened and she had the uncanny feeling that he was zeroing in on her lips. They dried under his gaze and she gulped. "Now stop talking."

He kissed her. It was flaming hot. His mouth worked its magic, while he splayed his hands, his hungry caresses firing her body. Every touch was sure and confident, sliding over her belly and around to grip her butt. A low moan filled the air and she hung on, digging her nails into his shoulders, needing stability as she trembled.

The hot whisper of his breath on her collarbone told her that he'd stripped the shirt from her. Then he drew his fingers down over her shoulders, the roughness of his palms a rasp. "God, Jake!"

Simone thrust her hands upright stilling his actions, then she tugged him towards the darkened bedroom beyond.

To her surprise, Jake didn't follow. Instead he quirked an eyebrow at her and the red-tinged cheekbones together with the over-bright eyes caught her attention. "I don't know…"

For the first time since she'd met him, he seemed ill at ease with the frantic pace of their relationship. "Jake? Is something wrong?"

He turned away and it felt like a lump had settled in her belly. "I don't know. I'm not so sure that either of us is ready for this."

*He's stopping? Calling a halt?* "Jake, I want this. I want us to—" She stopped, feeling the tide of the blush crawling over her now heated cheeks. What if she'd read the signals wrong? He'd said… Confusion filled her.

He raised a hand, and softly laid it against her cheek. "I do too. I just don't want *you* to wake up and regret this." He brushed his thumb against her cheek and she couldn't stop the reaction of leaning into his caress.

In that instant, the lump melted away, and she raised her hand to cover his, clasping it lightly. "I won't. This…*us* feels right."

She laid her lips against his and kissed him.

At the foot of the bed he watched her as she carefully dropped her jeans into an untidy pile at her feet. She didn't gyrate or say a word as piece by piece of clothing silently pooled in the most erotic striptease he'd ever seen.

She was gorgeous—all pale flesh and smooth skin. Jake reached out and caressed her shoulder when she stood in front of him in bra and panties. "Beautiful."

Reaching for his shirt, he stilled when she touched his hands. "Let me." The breathy whisper carried a magical charge he couldn't ignore. "I can help."

She shook her head, and the action destroyed him with a flash that was both smoky and innocent at the same time.

Her fingers trembled on the buttons, and she fumbled a little. Simone gave a nervous giggle and his heart filled to bursting point, knowing that she was pushing her own boundaries to be with him.

Finally, he was naked, bathed in the moonlight that peeked through the curtains. Her gaze raked over him and he could have sworn there was a physical connection that followed her scrutiny. His skin goose bumped as she laid her hand against his chest, and slid her fingers through the hairs that curled there.

The sight of her pale skin against his crinkly red hair stole what little oxygen remained in his lungs. "Simone, don't stop."

She exhaled, and the action set the strands dancing. He groaned. A beguiling grin settled on her face. "You like that?"

Unable to speak, he nodded. She slipped her fingers down his naked skin—the soft pads tracing a fiery trail over his abdomen, and he groaned. "Don't... Don't stop." The membranes in his mouth dried as she gripped the head of his cock and gave a squeeze.

"You're so soft." He heard the wonder in his voice and he barely restrained the need to tear the remaining coverings from her body. Instead he choked down the desire to tell her just how hard it was, feeling her circling him.

"You're... You're going to have to let me go if we plan to—"

"Going to what?" Even as she spoke, she dropped to her knees and he shut his eyes—closing them tight—against the pleasure he knew would soon call.

The hot wet glove of her mouth enveloped him. Jake stiffened further, desperately tugging on the last threads of sanity. He tangled his hand deep into her hair, twining the strands around, and tugged. A wet popping sound filled the air and he gulped down the oxygen his lungs screamed for.

"Didn't you like...?" Her face reddened beneath his scrutiny.

"I like it far too much."

He pulled her up against his body, the soft cotton of her bra catching on his skin and lightly abrading it. He closed his eyes, hoping to ward off the sensory overload, the scent and feel of her that was in his mind, eroding what small bit of control he had.

He reached behind, unsnapped her bra, and he felt the give as it released her tightly confined breasts. With a single fluid motion he ran his hands up the straps, then tugged them off her shoulders. The garment now hung loose. "You have such beautiful breasts." She did. Pale globes of flesh tipped with raspberry shaded nipples.

"I'm just ordinary."

He stared at her. "Nothing about you is ordinary, Simone. You're exquisite." He bent his head so his gaze was level with those tips, brushed them lightly with his lips and she moaned. "Everything about you is extraordinary."

Suckling on her distended flesh her nails stabbed into the back of his head as she arched backward, giving him better access. She tasted like heaven. His cock was hard and hungry. Ready to plunge deep within her body. He had to pull back.

"Take. Them. Off." He gritted his teeth against the urgent hunger that ravaged him, knew his face was a tight mask, and he needed her. Needed to be inside her.

"Ahhh..." Simone groped for her underwear, pushing at the cotton.

For a moment the spearing pleasure arrowed all the way down his body. They were naked and here, together. His heart pounded like a freight train, but he had to slow down.

He let her go. He stepped back and gazed upon her. She was rosy and soft as the languor of sexual arousal suffused her.

"What...?"

"Are you sure, Simone? Because all I want right now is to be buried deep inside your body. Answer me, honestly."

"I want you, Jake. I want to be with you. Please?"

Then he kissed her.

The touch of his hand on her was exhilarating. It made her feel more alive than ever before. His kisses were drugging. Her body heated and firmed and she needed him to fill the emptiness of her core.

As she thrust her tongue against his, she tested his readiness—the head of his erection was damp and she rubbed her thumb over it. He reared back, his eyes were glassy with arousal.

"Let's take this to the bed."

She pulled him against her, feeling the way their legs tangled until the edge of the bed was behind her knees. The old wooden bedframe creaked as they fell upon it, the springs squeaking as they laughingly landed together in a knotted mass of body parts. Pillows bounced and toppled from the mattress, making her giggle.

Laughter fled as he insinuated his hand between them, as if feeling the weight of her breast in his cupped hand.

"Ohmygod..." She pulled her legs together, as streaks of lightning coursed through her.

They kissed and she devoured him, hungry for every possible caress. As he slipped his fingers between her thighs, she gave an incoherent gasp.

"Open for me, princess. Let me find the secrets you hide." His questing fingers rubbed over her moist cleft, finding her slick and warm. Ready.

He set a rhythm as she gripped his shoulders, urging him on. "Please. Jake, please."

Instead he continued the sensual torture, pressing on her clit while she writhed beneath him, until a spike of pure pleasure arced through her. "Jake?"

"Let go." His crooning words and masterful strokes were enough to push her over the edge. Her back bowed off the bed as her orgasm splintered her body and soul.

When her senses reasserted themselves she looked down into his face where he rested on her belly. "I... You didn't..."

"We aren't finished yet. Now then, let me see." He dipped his head between her legs and arousal spiked anew. "Jake! But—"

"Never done this before?" She dimly noted the satisfaction on his features. *I've never experienced an orgasm, let alone like this!* Her head spun with the heady knowledge that this man could...

She wound her fingers into the coverlet as he tongued her, his hand skating over the sensitized skin between her spread thighs. "Ahhhhh... God, that feels so good! Mmmm..."

When he raised his head this time, his lips were swollen and damp —coated with her juices. The kiss they shared after he crawled up her body was redolent with her own scent—musky and tangy.

He positioned himself so that the blunt tip of his erection nudged at her and he slid slowly within. His arms bracketed her while Simone's muscles relaxed and welcomed Jake's intrusion.

Fully seated, he waited. She wanted to squirm and move in time to their wordless rhythm, but his hands kept her in one place. "Not. Yet." His voice was low and dark, sending shivers of expectation rocketing through her veins.

"Jake?"

"If you move it'll all be over before we begin. Just... Just give me a minute." So she waited while his chest heaved until she *had* to move. Her body demanded the satisfaction only he could bring.

It started slow, like a refined dance, before they sped up. Their bodies sliding and glancing, gripping and thrusting in an increasing tempo while senses soared.

The coil of pressure deep inside her belly wound tighter and tighter until finally she was on the precipice. She sucked in an unsteady breath and plunged into the maw. He followed, body straining against hers as he jetted deep within her.

Exhaustion stole her senses and she cuddled up in his embrace.

E ven as he lay there, gazing at the ceiling, he wondered when he could share who he was. It was so much a part of him, yet he'd only just come to terms with his life... Now he felt the consuming need to share it with her.

The only accompaniment to his thoughts was the quiet ticking of the bedside clock.

Simone had nestled down in the bed, her breathing evening out after their vigorous exercise. He tossed the sheets and bedspread over them and settled back as the door opened.

A glimmer of soft white light lit the room and his heart nearly stopped as he recognized his aunt hovering in the doorway, her plain white shift dress glowing. This time, though, she wasn't grinning. Instead, a grave look had him clutching the sheet tightly.

"Well, I can see you have got so far—" Her pleasant words belied the concern on her face.

"Aunt Cailleach, what are you doing here?" Jake glanced down, afraid that Simone would wake, but everything had stopped, he noticed. The ticking of the clock had ceased between two clicking sounds. "You can't just—"

"Jake, I understand something about courting humans. They don't take well to interruptions in the bedroom... Something is afoot. I fear your passage to eternal romance isn't meant to be easy. While I don't yet have all the information, I know someone has a grudge against you." She smiled, and the gleam in her eyes was chilling.

This was the aunt that frightened people. "You are my favorite nephew. The only one with the *gumption* to stand up to me. But you..." She waved a graceful hand in the air. "You have a reputation, and I fear it's coming home to haunt you. Be wary."

His stomach knotted. "What do you know?"

"I have heard...whispers. Tales of those with a grudge finally having an opportunity. Guard her well, Jake." She speared him with a sharp look and he nodded.

Cailleach spun on her heel and retreated through the door, the glow gradually dimming before fading away.

"My reputation…" His father had recently made a comment about that too.

For the last several hundred years he'd been on a path that had had no definition. Nothing to make him stop and consider the consequences of his actions. Looking for a relationship and connection, he now knew. Since realizing that Simone was his other half, he'd come to terms with the need to settle down. He hoped that he could be what she needed. He wanted to support her and, if all went to plan, they would welcome their own family, in time.

Thinking over how much damage he may have wrought with his careless attitude to existence was frustrating. Yet, right now, there wasn't much he could do, so he gave a tiny shrug and burrowed down beside Simone

His thoughts didn't go away—they nagged at him even as he drifted into a troubled sleep.

# CHAPTER 12

*D*aylight extended its long fingers through her curtains as the alarm trilled. Simone swung her legs over the side of the bed, wincing a little as muscles groaned and pulled. She grinned. Jake had been a tender and caring lover, and after the first flush of heat had passed, he'd woken her several times during the night. He'd only left before the first streaks of dawn stretched across the sky, with a promise to contact her later.

She glanced at the clock, noting that she still had plenty of time to prepare for the day ahead, while wishing it was already over. She wanted to be with him again—now. A deep breath expanded her lungs and she caught the faint scent of him. The two of them together seemed right.

Though her body ached from the night of passion, she was wide awake. "A shower is what I need."

By seven thirty she was washed, made up and dressed, so she scooped up her keys and headed for the car, knowing she'd arrive early to work. Traffic at this end of town was light so she was at the office in no time, easing the door open. In the quiet she breathed deeply, cleared her mind, then focused on her work day.

Caffeine, in the form of a deep, rich coffee, added to her general feeling of well-being and by the time the others arrived, she was hard at work, letters typed and stacked in neat piles. The others gave her assessing glances as the day progressed, and she knew that her productivity had to be at an all-time high.

As lunch came around, she nearly rang Jake, even though she knew he would call tonight. The need to hear his voice bubbled inside her like fizzy lemonade. At the small café she ordered a coffee and healthy salad. She sat down at a table in the corner.

"Is this seat taken?" Simone grimaced when a woman, dark-haired and somehow familiar, sidled up beside her. She had a long, thin face and when she smiled she flashed bright white, square teeth at Simone. She silently cursed as she realized there went any chance of calling Jake.

"Uh no." She focused on her salad as the woman pulled out her phone.

"Hey, Rhiannon, you'll never guess—I have a date!" Simone tried to turn a deaf ear to the woman's ramblings into her phone. "He's so cute! He's a redhead called Jake."

Simone's heart stopped as a lump formed. She clutched her fingers together. *Surely it's a coincidence? Lots of guys are called Jake.* She leaned forward, hoping to hear more even while alarm bells sounded loudly in her mind.

"I met Jake at the real estate agents a couple of weeks ago. He's buying this big family house, even though he hasn't got kids and isn't married."

The conversation wound on and Simone chewed on the lettuce. Not that she wanted to, but the need to know if it was Jake Kendrick drove her to listen more carefully.

"Gosh... He did mention his last name. Let me think, Kendall? Kendicks? Oh, hang on! Kendrick. Jake Kendrick. What a cool name. Just think, I could be a Mrs. Kendrick." She chortled and Simone wanted to shrivel up in the chair right where she sat.

Simone couldn't face food anymore. The little she'd eaten settled in her stomach like a heavy brick and the first waves of nausea assailed her. With stiff legs she pushed away from the table. Her hopes for the future scattered to the winds.

She didn't look at the woman. How could she? The last of her dreams were little more than ashes in her chest. Tears burned but she refused to let them fall. *Damn you, Jake! You had me in the palm of your hand and I was ready to give you everything.*

Pain slashed her in long, jagged strokes and even as she stumbled out of the eatery she wondered what there was left.

"Work. Work always helps."

She tottered back to work and wordlessly started organizing herself, shutting out everyone except the clients and Mr. Jackson. She'd get over this in a century or two, she told herself grimly. "Been there before, don't need to do it again."

The staff eyed her suspiciously as if they had guessed what ailed her. They didn't say a word, though, which suited her well enough.

J ake felt good. He'd been amazed at how responsive Simone was, and she'd agreed that it was a long-term relationship she was looking for. He'd crept back to the apartment wearing one of his many personas, though thankfully no one had intercepted him.

He showered and shaved, unable to wipe the man in love expression from his face. "You know, Diocail, if this goes to plan, you'll be able to take her home for Christmas." It felt right to say the words in the emptiness of the bathroom.

"That might be wishful thinking, Jake. You have a problem."

Not for the first time he hated that his aunt could pop in when and wherever she chose. At least he was wearing his boxers this time. He suppressed his frustration. *Twice in twenty-four hours? What bad luck is that?*

Then her words bloomed in his mind. "What do you mean?" He glanced into the mirror, watching Cailleach's reflection.

She appeared strained, as if laboring under a huge problem. "Well, I might have..."

A seed of disquiet took root. "You might have what?" He gripped the edge of the sink almost afraid to hear the answer.

"Well, she's just so... I got frustrated with Senuna the other day and I might have let slip that..." She worried her full red lips with perfect teeth, her fingers clenched.

Jake turned slowly in the direction of the blonde beauty. "You might have what?" His quiet words carried a deadly sting.

"Well, she was carrying on about how none of them in the last few hundred years has found their mate, as if it were all *my* fault. Anyway, I mentioned that you had been given an ultimatum before you could return." She held out her hands beseechingly towards him, but blazing anger now gripped him.

"You what? You know Senuna hasn't been together in her head since the episode with her temple. Why would you do that?" He advanced once step, intending only to reinforce his rage, then Cailleach held out her hand and he stilled although he didn't want to.

"It wasn't on purpose. Anyway, the whispers I've heard? They've grown louder... I just received word that she's... She's planning on making you pay. Honestly, Jake, I don't know what she can do. I feel bad about this."

"You feel bad? What...?"

"Simone... Your mate."

She dropped her hand and he stalked past her, palming his phone, before concluding that he couldn't ring her. Not now—she'd be at work. And what could he even say to her? How could he even possibly explain?

*By the way, one of my crazy ex-girlfriends, who just happens to be a goddess, is planning on making me pay?* Yeah, she'd buy that. He hadn't had the opportunity to explain what he was to her. And as for the goddess part? He remembered Cailleach's words from before.

The sense of being powerless alarmed him. "Surely there's been too little time...?" He couldn't finish the words. Simone was safe at work for now, but the truth was, time worked at a different speed for them and he had no doubt Senuna had already devised some devious way to make him pay for his supposed sins. Her issues had been one of the reasons he'd broken things off with her. That and the fact she'd scared him with talk of forever.

"I'm sure you have time, Jake. Just go get her." Cailleach had no understanding of how this world worked. She didn't realize that employment was a necessity that one needed to be able to pay for food and housing. He closed his eyes, his hand wrapped around the phone.

"She's at work. I can't disturb her." His voice rasped and he heard a peal of laughter.

"I can make all this... I can make this easier for you." She touched his face. "I can make all of this so much easier for you by making it so she—"

"No! Don't interfere. You've already—" Jake sucked in an unsteady breath. "I can handle this."

Cailleach scanned his face before she gave a small nod. "All right. I'll go if you're sure, then? You know where to—"

"Yeah, I know how to contact you."

Then she was gone and as Jake looked up at the clock, he felt alarm suffuse him. How long had passed while they'd been talking? It was already well after five in the afternoon. He could call her...

His fingers shook as he dialed. "Simone here."

She sounded tired and more than a little down. Jake frowned, concerned. "Simone. It's Jake. Are you okay?" A long silence had him tensing.

"I, uhhh... Thanks for last night. I... I don't think... Look, don't ring me again."

"What!" he bellowed down the phone, hearing the distance in her voice, and feeling the searing wave of pain that followed.

"I just... I think we both want something very different, and I don't... I have to go. Don't ring me. Please." Her voice broke on the last words and he was already cursing as she disconnected the phone.

*Damn!* Senuna had already wreaked her havoc.

~

Simone's hand shook as she disconnected the call. *How could he call me now?* Of course, she doubted he even knew that she was aware of his actions. The thought splintered her heart.

"I was ready to give him everything." *It's like Nathan again, only intensified, which is silly because it's what? One day? A day and a night?* Inside her chest was a balloon of pain that kept growing, stealing more and more of her breath. "I should have known better." The words echoed through the nearly silent house, battering her with the truth she'd wanted to ignore.

"What am I supposed to do?" She gazed across the empty room. Was this how she was meant to be? Forever alone? Her existence seemed wasted if this was all she had to look forward to.

A single tear quivered on her lash and she dashed at it, hating the weakness yet unable to stem the tide as they rolled over her cold cheeks.

The phone rang and for one short moment she contemplated picking it up and throwing it against the wall, anger burning deep in her gut. She reached out, then snatched her hand away.

*It could be Cara and James.*

Her gut told her it wasn't. If it was him, the pain would be worse. Even just seeing his name on the display would be more than she could bear right now, Simone was sure. Thinking about him was excruciating enough.

She clenched her fingers tightly as the ringing stopped.

On unsteady legs she tottered to the lounge, wondering how she could have made this kind of mistake. *Again.*

"Because you were horny." The cold hateful words didn't make her feel better. A voice whispered inside her head that it had been so much more, on her part. She'd wanted forever. She gave a hiccupping sniff. *Clearly that isn't on my horizon.*

She spied a bottle on a shelf.

Vodka.

She'd bought it on a holiday with Cara years before. Since buying it, there'd rarely been a need for it. With no glass in sight, she debated how to drink it. A shrug of the shoulders and "down the hatch" seemed appropriate. The sip of the clear, fiery liquid burned a path and the noxious scent invaded her senses.

The phone pealed again, and this time she ignored it, taking another cautious sip. Gripping the neck of the bottle, she slowly made for the two-seater in front of the television. She turned on the twenty-four-hour news and took another, deeper swig. Simone gasped at the burn before coughing and spluttering loudly.

"No more men. Not ever." Her words sounded loud to her ears. "Funny, this is supposed to take away the pain." She glared at the bottle. It didn't. Nothing could, she was sure, but she continued to carefully sip the vodka.

*Maybe I should get a cat or a dog. Or just leave here altogether and start somewhere new.* Using both hands, she slid the bottle to the coffee table, feeling her brain drift. "Leave here. Go somewhere else. Never come back." She rested her head on the arm of the chair, promising to watch the television and lose herself in it.

In the distance the phone rang again and she kept her eyes firmly on what was in front of her until it blurred and wavered. Then, finally, she drifted away.

Jake paced and cursed while he waited for the first streaks of light across the sky, before he scooped up his jacket and headed out. He'd had most of the night to steam over the damage Senuna's interference had caused. He wasn't entirely sure what she'd done, but he knew that unchecked it would fester. As Simone hadn't answered his calls he had no idea what the other woman had done to cause mischief.

Jake made his way down the stairs, his agitation growing. Each clattering clank might wake those he wished studiously to avoid. Even one such encounter might make it too late to catch her before work.

"Right now, when I most need my magic, I can't use it." He clambered into his car, muttering angrily, then waited as the engine started. Pulling into traffic annoyed him and he grumbled the whole way. By the time he'd reached Simone's house, his concern and frustration were running at an all-time high.

He noted that her car was still in the driveway. It looked like she'd parked in a hurry. He bounded up the stairs and knocked, the imperious summons leaving him wincing.

From inside he caught the sound of voices and groans.

His stomach dipped. "Simone? Are you in there, Simone? Open up!"

Using the flat of his hand, he thudded again. "Urrgghh..." The groaning sound left him deciding that action was the best course. *She could be in trouble.*

"Open the door, Simone, or I'll knock it down!"

"Wait..." He heard the sounds of movement and her weak response from within. Tension and concern billowed from him in waves.

When she pulled open the door she appeared ill and he pushed past her. "What's wrong?" He placed the back of his hand against her forehead, confused to find her skin was cool, though slightly clammy.

"Go away." She clapped her hands over her stomach and he was sure she was taking on a green tinge around her mouth.

"What's wrong?"

She scowled at him. "I don't want you here."

"That's too bad, because I need to talk to you." He stalked closer, noting with dismay that she paled further, her lips now tightly compressed white lines.

"I have to—" Then she was off, running past him to the bedroom.

He stopped at the doorway as he heard her in the bathroom. She wouldn't thank him for barging in right now, he was sure. The sound of her illness echoed, but once she'd rounded the door—albeit queasy looking— he guided her to the bed. "What did you do?"

She shook her head slightly. "I really don't want to talk about it, and not with you." She closed her eyes, no doubt lying as still as possible. "Hand me the phone and leave, please."

Jake had no intention of letting her off that easily. He needed to explain to her. Instead he stalked from the room, taking the opportunity to think over in his mind how the hell he could explain this to her. He spied the vodka bottle on the table and smiled.

Simone was hung-over, it seemed. The knowledge eased his mind. As he reached the dining room, where he'd seen her sling her bag last time he'd been there, magic fluttered around him.

"Jake, my son. I take it there is a problem." *Great, now my father has to get involved.* Instead of appearing in his usual fashion—glowing white—his father stood on the other side of the table.

"You could say that."

"Humph. I did tell you before that your involvement with those women was not in your best interests." Lugh had never been backwards in sharing his thoughts on his relationships in the past. For the first time, Jake could only nod.

"You were right, mostly. I need you to lift your ban on magic. I have to explain everything to Simone, otherwise she's not going to believe much of what I say."

His father nodded. "I can understand what you are saying, my son. If I allow you this, then you must pay a boon."

Even as he tensed, he wondered what his father would request.

"You will remain on Earth longer." For a moment he considered the cost, then nodded. He'd do whatever was required to care for Simone. "I will lift your ban temporarily so you may bring your mate with you when you come home. Only for a day—long enough to show her what and who you are."

"I accept." He felt his lips turning up in a smile, until his father raised a hand. Jake should have known better. Nothing with the gods was as easy as it seemed at first glance.

"Not so fast. You only have today, in human terms, to use your magic. When the sun sets, your time is done. If you can't overcome this problem in that time, your ban on returning home will become indefinite." Lugh frowned. "I wish you luck." With a wave he disappeared from view.

For a moment, disorientation filled Jake's mind, before he realized that time was slipping away. He needed to make the most of it. With a swift motion Jake found Simone's bag, slipped out her phone and made his way back to the bedroom. "Here—who do you want me to call?"

Simone frowned. "I need to call work and let them know I won't be in." Then she rolled on her side, dismissing him.

# CHAPTER 13

Simone rang the office. "Hey. I'm... I'm really sick and can't get in today. I should be there tomorrow." She felt bad, knowing that she was dodging work for a hangover of all things. That had never before happened to her.

"Sure. I hope it's only a twenty-four-hour bug, though. Tomorrow will be busy, as Mr. Jackson has client interviews." Kylie's voice was earnest and Simone felt even worse than before.

"I think it is. Just leave anything urgent on my desk for me to attend to tomorrow. And thanks, Kylie, for doing this."

"No worries. Mr. Jackson understands these things happen. He might be a little old-fashioned, but he's a great boss like that. Hopefully, we'll see you tomorrow."

Simone hung up as Jake returned. If she hadn't felt so ill, she'd likely yell at him for ruining her life. Deep down, though, she knew that was unfair.

"Drink this. It'll make you feel better." He handed her a glass of blue liquid.

"What's in it?" She was doubtful about drinking anything she wasn't sure of.

When he nodded silently she sighed. As awful as she felt, if it relieved the roiling of her stomach... It gave another uncertain lurch and she gripped the glass. "Thanks."

Taking one cautious sip she waited for her stomach to rebel. When it didn't she swallowed a little more of the sweet berry flavored liquid.

This time Simone drank deeply, feeling the fogginess in her mind clear after and her stomach settle. Energy flowed through her, leaving her tingly and aware.

"What was in that? You could bottle it."

Jake grinned. "I'll explain in a minute. First, come to the kitchen."

*The kitchen?* She wasn't sure food was going to work. Instead of dwelling on her fears, however, she sat up and slid her legs off the side of the bed and followed him out of the bedroom.

"I'm not really hungry—"

"That wasn't why I brought you here, Simone. Take a seat and listen to what I have to say." For the first time in their reasonably short acquaintance, Jake seemed unsure of himself. It was more than a little disconcerting. In all her dealings with him, he'd been so confident.

She sat down and waited.

"I need to share a little about who and what I am. Before you get excited, no matter how far-fetched any of this may sound... Just wait until I'm finished, okay?"

"Why would I think it far-fetched?"

He blushed at her words and she frowned. *He really believes whatever he's about to tell me.*

"I'll start with something easy. My real name is Diocail, which is Celtic. It's hard to pronounce so most people know me as Jake Kendrick." Simone nodded and waited. "I'm not a matchmaker as I have explained. I'm Cupid. Well, sort of..."

She felt the pull of muscles as she opened her eyes wide and couldn't hold in the snort. "Oh, that's stupid! You expect me to believe—?"

He raised a hand, and blushed a deep red. "You promised to listen to me."

"I didn't expect you to talk rubbish, though. You must think I'm an idiot." Anger churned in her belly, hot and caustic. While she'd give him an E for effort, his story was so fanciful that she'd have to have no brains to believe anything else that came out of his mouth.

"Damn it, Simone. I need to tell you all this so you…" He shook his head.

"You can't honestly expect—"

"No, I don't expect you to believe me without proof. I can show you."

She opened then closed her mouth soundlessly. *He can show me?*

"Aunt Cailleach? Can you come here?"

A glow started in the center of the room, growing brighter, until Simone saw a woman, one she'd seen from time to time in the diner. The woman who materialized in front of Simone was tall and lithe, with immaculate blonde hair. "Well, Diocail, your father informed me—"

"Not now, Aunt. Would you explain to Simone who you are and what I am?"

Simone stared at them, sure that her eyes must be as big and round as saucers. "But that was—"

"That was magic, my dear. I'm a goddess and what my poor, deluded nephew Diocail has been trying to explain is that he's a magic being. He's actually a brownie." Simone's eyes grew rounder. "Because his father is so important in our pantheon he was given a more senior role. He is our version of Cupid, though he's nothing like that geeky-looking, buck-toothed—"

"Thank you, Aunt." Jake was shaking his head, cutting off the beauty in front of them from continuing her diatribe while Simone watched open-mouthed. "Maybe you should leave the rest to me."

Before Simone's eyes the glow intensified and finally flashed outwards, leaving just the two of them inside her kitchen. She scanned the counter tops with her gaze, searching for some high-tech equipment that would have caused her to see what wasn't really there.

"My hangover must be causing hallucinations." She put her hands over her eyes and shook her head. Her stomach wasn't queasy and her thinking seemed clear.

"Okay, so it's a dream and I'll wake up in a minute." She nodded, closing her eyes beneath her palms while she searched for a modicum of reality in this weird conversation.

"Simone, this isn't a dream. It's all true." Jake must have rounded the table, because the warm touch of his hands was doing all kinds of odd things to her. Her tummy tingled and her body felt more alive than it had since he'd left.

"Magic doesn't exist." *Or does it?*

"Stand up."

She opened her eyes and stared at him. "What?"

"Stand up."

Without another word, Simone followed his direction and when he held out his hand, she took it, feeling like Alice falling down the rabbit hole as the world turned black.

Home.

For the first time he didn't feel the sense of coming home at the sight of the house. After asking many times to be allowed to return since his father had banished him, the feeling was odd. Off-putting, even. The house was just that—an empty dwelling, not a home—a delineation he'd never before made.

Scanning the view in front of him, he felt little connection to the large white building surrounded by lush green grass and bushes on top of the small hillock. In truth it was only a place he'd existed in. It would probably never be home again, he realized with surprise. "Simone, this is where I live."

She looked scared and lost, and the trembling of her fingers was almost more than he could bear. "Where…? Where are we?"

"Well, technically, it's a small island off the coast of Scotland. We have relied on magic to keep it hidden from humans. The high gods live in the otherworld, but for those of us who are more forward-thinking… Many of us have homes on similar islands."

Her eyes widened as she took a step back. "No. This is a dream. It has to be." A thin edge of panic wove itself into her voice and he winced. She looked around as if expecting something to attack her.

"It's okay. We can go any time you say." He had hoped to soothe her, but she became even more agitated.

"I want... I want to go home, now." He saw her battle with panic and nodded. It was too much for her now.

"Sure. I guess you don't want to see inside..."

Simone shook her head, her long strands of hair whipping to and fro. "Take me home, Jake."

He sighed and with a thought they moved into the blackness of between, where the air was pleasantly warm and spicy, and the convulsive clutch of fingers warned him that the next move would have to be in the human fashion.

Once they rematerialized in her kitchen he scanned her white face. Simone tottered to a chair, before slumping down with an oomph. "What...? What else can you do?"

Jake knew he'd have to tell her all, so he took the seat opposite. "Many things. I can change shape, become anyone so I can blend in and carry out my job."

"Your job? You said you were..." Her words trailed away as if it were just too much to believe.

"Rather like Cupid, my job is to ensure that human couples find their predestined mate. Love." He clarified for her when she exhibited a blank look. "Everyone is supposed to find someone to love. That's how the universe works. Anyway, even gods and goddesses are given—"

Simone held up a hand. "Hang on. By *predestined* you mean no will? We have no choice?" Her voice raised and he sighed heavily.

"It's not so much a matter of choice. It's more the opportunity to meet in the right circumstances. Not everyone makes a successful pairing. We just set the stage. Then it's up to the humans to get it right."

His stomach flipped and flopped at her frown. "I'm not so sure I like the sound of that. There must be more than a little coercion on your side."

"None." Jake leaned forward. "Such actions are strictly forbidden and should we be caught…" He shook his head. "Rest assured, though, that as the most senior brownie—"

"Hang on. I thought you said you were Cupid? And if that's the case, where is your bow and arrow?" The sarcasm in her voice wasn't lost on him.

"Damn it, Simone, I know I made a mistake not explaining any of this to you, but…" Jake reached out and gripped her hands. "For pity's sake—you weren't ready and neither was I. You don't need to be so angry with me. I didn't cheat on you, if that's what you've been told."

Simone blushed.

"I meant every word I spoke the other night. I want to be with you. Only you."

Simone turned her head and he felt hollow, as if he'd lost his only chance at a future with a woman he would adore until the end of time.

"It hurt, Jake."

Even without knowing exactly what Senuna had said, he was well aware she was capable of hurting someone. The knowledge that she'd upset Simone infuriated him. He banked the welling rage. *Later.* He would deal with her later. Right now, his priority was Simone.The silence in the room grew thick. She wanted to scream at him or throw things. She wanted to react in ways that weren't normally her style—or hadn't been until she'd met Jake. She remembered the odd need to throw the phone before tackling the vodka.

"Let me see if I have this straight. Your name is Joe-kay something or other but you're known as Jake. You're a brownie who moonlights as Cupid and you have an aunt who is a goddess and your home is on some island in the middle of nowhere?" She raised a shaking hand to her brow. "And now, for some reason, you've set your sights on me and because of that…?" She pierced him with a direct gaze.

"One of my ex-lovers, Senuna, somehow got wind of it and did... whatever she did."

"Hmm. 'Cause, you know, that's what ex-lovers do, don't they?" She couldn't hide the bitterness in her voice. "You dragged me into the middle of this. You had sex with me—"

"We made love!"

"Excuse me? Ahh, okay, so we *made love.*" Simone bracketed the words in the air and he winced again. "Fine, but we did *it* without a condom and since I have no idea where any of this is going, what happens now?"

His face turned granite-like and for a moment Simone knew fear. *What if I've pushed him too far? I have no idea what he is capable of.*

"So we did." He smiled. It was small but it left her stomach bottoming out.

"Hmm?" She leant forward. "What diseases should I expect?"

His laugh boomed out, filling the room. "None. We don't have any." Jake's face softened. "You are my mate. The only one for me."

"*What?*" Simone pushed away from the table in a single convulsive action. "No. Uh-uh! Don't go there, boy-o. I have no interest in—"

Jake was around the table in an instant, dragging her into his embrace. She felt the solid wall of his chest and her treacherous body wanted to melt as it absorbed his heat. "Simone, you are the only woman for me. Let me show you."

She tugged and pulled. He held her tight and heaven help her she wanted to believe him, desperately. She'd been emotionally alone for so long, and couldn't be sure he wasn't just toying with her.

"I'm not like Nathan. I promise." The hot whisper of his breath fanned her face. "Let me show you."

"She said..." The words escaped before she could stop them and she closed her eyes. She sounded so damned needy!

"Tell me what she said, sweetheart. Let me fix this."

How she wanted to let Jake fix this. Her pride raised its head. *I'm no shrinking violet who needs a man to make me better.* "It's not that simple. I mean, I have to trust me before I can trust you. Don't you see?"

"Sure, but Simone? If I can show you the truth, then perhaps it's the first step in healing yourself. Let me do this."

Her heart squeezed. "Okay. She was on the phone. The woman was on the phone to someone called Rhiannon and described you and how you'd met. That she was going out on a date with you."

"That was the reason you ended it between us?" His voice was soft.

"After Nathan… I'm used to having someone around all the time, and he was always there. I don't know, we kind of fell into the relationship and it was comfortable. When he called it off because of that woman, I suppose it reinforced to me that you can't rely on anyone else. Before you, Cara was the one person who could get close to me. Even that took her a long time." She shook her head, feeling more than a little foolish. "I never meant to hurt you, Jake."

"That's how she works, in sly and devious ways."

Regret filled Simone. She'd made him pay without gathering all the information. Without testing its veracity. "She did her work well." Simone reached out and Jake took her hand as if he understood what her words had cost. Now she needed to know the truth, instead of taking some unknown woman at her word. Or at least at the words she'd overheard.

"Rhiannon is actually one of Senuna's closest friends, if you could call them that. After her temple was destroyed, at the end of our relationship, Senuna changed, or at least her mind did. I had nothing to do with it. She blamed me ending it for what happened. She threatened revenge, but I was sure she was hysterical. After all these years, I thought she'd got over it. I never would have expected this."

"Why would she do this? I mean, it doesn't make a whole lot of sense. How did she know about me?"

He let go of her hands and fidgeted. "Well, that's probably because they— The rest of the pantheon usually know before we do who our mates are. It's like an in-built radar, which lets us know that someone is spoken for, in simple terms. She must have found out, then put her plan into action."

Simone sighed. "Okay, so that explains a lot. There was something familiar about her. With her long brown hair and those teeth." She frowned as the memory rose in her mind. The size and shape telling her she'd seen the woman somewhere else before.

"Teeth?" Jake tensed, his face turning hard under her scrutiny. "What do you mean by teeth?"

The impression that this was important somehow flickered through Simone. "Well, she has these sort of square and solid teeth. A long face..."

"Oh damn. She played us both like bloody violins." Jake's eruption of anger startled Simone, who watched him with an open mouth. Who was he talking about?

"Nathan's new client? The woman he asked to marry him? That's Senuna."

Simone clutched her stomach. "No, I've met— The bitch!" It fell into place. M.A., the horsey woman. The way Nathan had just brushed her off. The quick changes of situation with the engagement. Now she knew how she'd been played, fury coursed.

"Wait till I—"

"No. We'll deal with her, later. You know I didn't cheat on you, right?"

Simone nodded. "Yeah, you're as innocent as me."

When Jake smiled at her this time, there was a banked heat in his gaze and it dried her mouth. "So... Now you forgive me and all is right with the world. While we are on the subject of innocence..." The grin turned wolfish and her body warmed through again.

Her eyes darkened and he felt a ribbon of arousal thread through him. "I really don't think we should, you know, do anything until this matter is sorted out." Her voice sounded hoarse and he felt the grin creep across his face. It was clear that she was laboring under the same sensual spell as him.

"We could cuddle and see where this goes." Jake winked, his private yet playful manner emerging.

She coughed and spluttered. "You're walking sex on a stick and you expect me to believe you'd be happy cuddling?" Her words stopped him in his tracks. That she would see it from that angle shouldn't have surprised him, but it did. He took a moment to regroup.

"Yeah, I do. I'd do anything for you, sweetheart, and if you say no, then I'm happy to abide by that. At least until you understand I mean everything I say. You are my forever, and I won't jeopardize that for a quick tickle in the sack."

She searched his face and he had the uncanny thought that she was searching for the truth. "Okay. I'm sorry, I guess I'm just not exactly the most trusting woman at the moment." She glanced away and he slid a finger under her chin, turning her back toward him.

Jake gazed into her eyes, seeing the uncertainty and doubt there. Another man had damaged her trust, or at least bruised it. He'd need to prove to her that he was reliable and dependable.

"Simone, I know what Nathan did hurt you. I promise you now, I won't do anything like that. If all you need is to cuddle, then that is what I'll give you. Above all, I won't cheat and I won't lie."

She nodded. "I know I'm making this harder for us…" A small blush crested her cheeks and he groaned silently, as his body reacted to her nearness.

"Let's get out of here. Do something where I won't be tempted to kiss you until you're breathless and pink."

Simone's giggle, which sounded so carefree and told him he'd made the right decision. "Okay." She snagged up her bag as he led her to the door. Outside the sun had reached its zenith.

"I love summer and being outside. It's the best part about living here." She grinned at his words.

"I don't get outside as much as I'd like. My job is pretty much inside all the time."

He'd take her to see his home, the one he hoped she'd soon share with him, but as he pulled up outside the estate agents, Simone was frowning again. "Why are we stopping here?"

"I'm taking you to see my house. Or it will be in a few more days." His words didn't banish the look of hurt that reappeared on her face. "Why?"

"Because *she* works here, or at least, that's what she said. I sound like an idiot, don't I?"

"Well, if she's there then we can bring this to a close. If she isn't then we'll just go see the house." He turned off the car and waited for her reply. When she remained silent he reached over and took her hand in one of his. "We'll get there. Just have a little faith."

She smiled up at him and his chest expanded with pride. *My woman.*

They climbed out of the car and at the door of the estate agents, he held it open. His reward was a charming smile and heat bloomed inside him. The young redhead on the counter remembered him. "Mr. Kendrick! Is there something—?"

"I'd like to show my girlfriend the house. Is that possible?" He smiled, oozing just enough charm that the woman smiled back.

"Of course. Since the house has been empty for a while, there's no problem. Would you like me to—?"

"No thanks, Tanaya, I'll drive her over and back." He watched as she opened a drawer and pulled up an envelope containing the keys to his soon-to-be home. "So long as you don't get in trouble?"

"Oh, not at all. When you bring them back, we can arrange how you'll take delivery of all the keys on settlement day." Tanaya's bright words dimly registered as Simone took his hand, and she moved her thumb over the mound at the base of his thumb. It was highly erotic.

By the time they were back in the car, he was glad to be sitting down and, as discreetly as possible, adjusted himself. A glance in Simone's direction told him that she'd noticed his actions.

"To the house." Her words were sultry, causing his heart rate to increase'.

"I thought you said…?" His dry mouth made speaking hard.

"I was wrong. About a lot of things. Take me to your house, Jake."

The car handled easily, and he was thankful for that as his concentration was less than stellar. By the time they pulled into the driveway, Simone was rubbing his leg with one hand, and the muscles in his thigh, not to mention elsewhere, tensed with each pass.

"Just a moment." He was out of the car as her laughter tinkled.

The old screen on the house squeaked as he opened it then unlocked the door and he turned to find Simone behind him. "Come on, Jake. Show me your new home." As she brushed past him, her hand fluttered over the placket of his pants and he tensed, as his erection pulsed harder than ever before. He locked the door behind him then followed her up the hall, watching the enticing sway of her hips.

She slowly made her way down the hall, opening and peering inside each room as she passed the doors. "I love the wood floors and the colors are so cooling. And right now my skin is so hot!" She pulled at the loose top she wore, a sneaky grin on her face.

# CHAPTER 14

*I*n her mind, Simone finally understood that Jake was innocent. It was no one single action that had made her believe in him, more like the realities having coalesced. She'd all but jumped on him since arriving at the house and he'd yet to do anything about it. Simone grinned. It was time to take another step.

Each new relationship, no matter how simple, felt like throwing herself over a hurdle. Yet Jake *felt* right, all the way to her bones. It was time to show him that she was ready to take that chance with him. At the kitchen she tugged her camisole away from her skin. "I love the wood floors and the colors are so cooling. And right now my skin is so hot!"

Jake had stopped in the hallway, his eyes hooded and dark. She noted the stiffness about him, the ruddy glow on his cheeks and the compressed white look of his knuckles. "Simone?"

Her breath caught, and she knew this was what she wanted with him. And here, in what would be his home, would be the perfect place to start afresh. With a yank, she caught the edges of the cami and pulled it over her head. Beneath it was a pale bra, decorated with lacy panels. She could tell the instant he understood what she was doing.

"We can't… You need time." He stepped back and she let her fingers stray to the button of her jeans. They sagged as she released the clasp and she ruthlessly slipped them over her hips. The warm air whispered over her almost nude body and made her shivered in response.

"I don't need any more time, Jake. I only need you." She hoped he'd understand the message contained in the words, because she meant them. Every word. "I want everything you have to offer me."

He surged forward, jerking off his clothing, and she laughed, while she reached for the clasp of her bra then rolled her panties down her legs.

Finally, they were naked and breathless. He ran his hands over her body and she responded in kind. Their skin dampened with sweat as they kissed, each one a deep and drugging caress that stole her senses, and she struggled to keep her eyes open. Simone gave in, glorying in the senses that sparked and jumped under his ministrations.

He dug his fingers into her sides as he lifted her to the kitchen counter. The granite was cold against her heated body and she moaned.

"God, you have no idea how much I want you." He muttered against the inside of her leg as he dipped down.

The scalding touch of his breath against her inner flesh had her clenching, she quivered with need. A warm wet brush—she knew it was his tongue—lapped at her.

Simone arched back as he sucked at her. "Jake. More!"

When the first orgasm rolled through her she cried out. He didn't stop the sensual torture. He buried a finger deep within and the intrusion wound her sensitized body up again.

"You— Oh God, Jake, inside me!"

He laughed, the rumble toying with the small nub of nerve endings between her legs.

"Anything for you, sweetheart." He moved away even as she reached out, needing to touch him, to run her hands over his muscular chest.

"Let me touch you." She caught her breath, held it while he shook his head.

"Not this time, I'm too close."

He pushed her back to the dark counter top and caught her hips with his hands. The feel of his erection nudged and ignited the rampaging fire and slowly he filled her. Tears leaked from between her tightly clenched eyes as emotions welled deep in her chest. This is more than sex, her beleaguered mind realized. This was more like bonding her soul to his. Everything about it was deep and rich. *Powerful.*

"I need to fill you. I need to plant myself deep inside you. I want us to create life. I want to watch it grow. Say you want that too."

Her chest tightened at his words. "I do. Please..." She broke off, unable to form a coherent thought, and let the sensations take over.

The coil in her belly left flickering trails of electricity that sparked deep inside her, the erotic thrust of his cock...

She splintered. "Jake!"

His pounding stopped as he tugged her hips to him, spilling his seed deep.

"Well now, isn't this a pretty picture?" The voice was a vicious snarl breaking the communion between Jake and Simone.

He knew that voice, his mind cried as he pulled Simone into his arms. "What do you want, Senuna?"

"I want what was always mine! You!" She stalked forward and Jake knew a moment of real fear. Not for himself but for Simone.

"I was never yours, Senuna. What we had was sexual, that's true. It was a long time ago, though, and I never made promises to you. You knew that." Her face, once beautiful with high cheekbones and lustrous eyes, now seemed dull and empty. "What you've done to Simone— That was unconscionable."

"Ha! She's nothing more than a pawn. She brought me you." She held out a hand and a short bolt of light arced between them. Simone stiffened, cried out in pain as the bolt of power connected with her chest.

He tugged her tighter against him, while his mind tossed over what he could do to save her.

"Let her go and I'll make it easy for her. The pain won't last long." Senuna's face took on a feral expression, her eyes gleaming. This time they contained madness.

She meant to kill Simone.

He wouldn't let that happen.

"She's innocent in this. Let her go."

Simone was panting and crying and his chest burned watching the woman he loved fight for her very breath.

"I don't see much innocence about what she was doing with you."

Even as she spoke, twin globes of light shone over her shoulder, splitting his concentration. "No, don't interfere!" He should have known that his father and aunt would insinuate themselves into the confrontation.

Senuna laughed and Simone slumped bonelessly in Jake's arms. He lowered her to the floor. He wanted to whisper an apology but he didn't dare. Not with the madness he saw in Senuna's face. He moved forward. "Let her go and I'll come with you."

"Jake, no…"

Simone's broken words cracked his heart and the pain of the looming separation grew. He ignored the wrenching sensation in his chest, reaching out to the woman in front of him. Now he had to do whatever it took to make her leave Simone alone. It pushed his rage to incandescence that Senuna would imply that he'd lied and promised her something that was never meant for her.

She'd wreaked so much damage and potentially destroyed the fragile connection between him and his mate. He would do anything for Simone. Take any step necessary to protect her. He opened his mouth to speak, and his father raised a hand.

"Son, this is not your choice anymore." He felt clothing wrap around him as his father and aunt took positions on either side of Senuna. She finally registered their presence and screamed in rage.

"He's mine! He was always mine! Now he has to pay for his betrayal."

"Senuna, he was never yours. He never promised anything. Child, come with me." Cailleach held out her arms and Senuna dodged, flinging her hand in Simone's direction.

Jake knew what she was about to do. He'd seen her do it to followers in the past who'd infuriated her. He refused to let Simone face such an end.

Without thought, he dove in front of her just as a bolt of power erupted from the tips of Senuna's fingers.

It hit him in the center of his chest and he cried out to Simone, "I love you!" His body jerked as the raw power raced through his system and the world turned black.

# CHAPTER 15

"Jake!" Simone screamed as she pushed herself from the floor shakily. "No, don't leave me! I love you, so you can't die on me!" She scrabbled across the tiles.

The tableau being enacted in front of her held no interest as the one called Senuna shrieked and the two others who'd materialized grabbed at the struggling woman. She knew that one was his aunt. She'd seen her in the kitchen at her home.

Right now, all Simone could focus on was Jake. The way his body quivered and shuddered in front of her. Her stomach clenched and she prayed to any possible deity who may have existed. *Don't take him. Leave him here with me. I'll do anything you ask, just don't let him die.*

She reached him, tears blurring her gaze. "Don't leave me, Jake." She touched his chest. She didn't know what to do, except that on some primal level the need to touch him overwhelmed her. She gave in, sliding her hand along his heavily muscled arm.

A final scream rent the air then disappeared abruptly. She felt a soft touch and raised her head. "I don't know what to do."

The woman before her smiled kindly. "You're here for him. That is all you need to do. Wait. This will pass soon."

The sudden movements Jake had been making ceased and Simone was sure he was dead.

Her heart ached and tears streamed.

When he opened his eyes she threw herself at him. "You're alive? I thought you were going to die!"

A coughing laugh impinged on her consciousness. "Father, if you could help Simone up?" Jake's voice was weak, yet it was the most amazing sound she'd ever heard.

She let the man Jake had called Father help her to her feet, amazed as a light robe covered her body, then turned immediately back to Jake as he stood. Even as she wrapped her arms around him, he felt more alive than ever before. "I love you, but if you ever do that again…"

Jake cupped her face. "I hope never ever to do that again." Then he kissed her, as if pouring his whole soul into the embrace. She burrowed into his grasp as he pulled back gently. "Uhh, you better meet my family, or at least some of them." He gave a nervous laugh while his father harrumphed and his aunt giggled.

# CHAPTER 16

$S$imone knew that today would be momentous. Their first full day in their new home. Together. They'd put off moving day until they'd gathered the right furniture for the house, with some pieces from her own home.

She rolled over, feeling energized. She rubbed her body up against his back and giggled as he grunted. "Jake?"

"What?" His words slurred sleepily.

"Wake up, Jake." The secret she'd been keeping had chewed at her for days. "Jake?"

He didn't move, just gave a gentle snore and rolled over. Simone sighed as she pushed away the covers.

Fishing in her bag, she hunted for and found the tiny box, the bright pink text declaring *Accurate At Ten Days*. "Better now than never." The mutter didn't calm the fighting butterflies inside her belly. 'What if it's negative?' warred with 'It's just got to be.'

She shivered a little in the cool air as she made her way to the bathroom. "Should have grabbed a shirt."

Her breasts had been achy and full for days and her stomach uncertain from time to time. She'd put that down to something she'd eaten, but when it hadn't dissipated, knowledge had settled in her mind. Checking her diary, she realized that she was already late, by nearly two weeks. A fact she'd somehow missed.

With the door closed, she tore open the box, dragged out the information sheet and the tiny plastic device.

Ten minutes later, she put the indicator down on the vanity unit. "Holy Moley!"

The door to the bathroom opened and she looked up, catching sight of Jake. "Everything okay in here?"

"Ah... Well, yes. Jake?" She had to stop her hand from dropping instinctively to her belly as she palmed the evidence and turned. "You do want babies, right?"

He frowned. "You know I do."

She gulped in a deep breath. "Well, that's a good thing." Simone shoved the plastic into his hands and she watched as he glanced down. Blinked.

"What ...?" He surged forward, capturing her against him. The instant their bodies touched, the flame that never abated roared to life. Her body all but melted as it prepared itself for what she needed. Him. Filling her.

She gripped his jaw in her hands and dragged him closer. "You're going to be a daddy."

They kissed—passion flared, weaving its spell around them. His mouth felt cool as he devoured her, using lips, tongue and even gently biting. "Jake? I need to touch you."

Simone slid her hands down, capturing his long length. She caressed his cock, from the firm round head to the sac at its base. He hissed. "I can't wait. I need you."

Suddenly neither could she. Her body was on fire. "Don't wait. Fill me now."

Jake gripped her hips, and swung her up, setting her on the cold marble vanity. Her hot skin made contact and she gasped as he slid between her thighs. "Now, Jake. Now."

The grip loosened and he trailed his hands down to her pussy, sliding gentle fingers over the lips and separating them. "So wet and hot. Ripe for me." One finger sliding deep nearly tore her senses apart.

She arched, hunger roaring through her veins. "I…"

"Not yet." His touch slowed, letting her drop back just enough to calm the edges of her desire.

"Jake… Don't… Don't tease— Geez."

He kissed her again, branding her with his lips and tongue. He pressed his thumb over her clit and she wanted to explode.

"Liked that, didn't you?" She barely knew his voice, deep and gravelly. His face was a mask of carnal hunger.

"Jake?"

"Now." He spread her legs farther, making room for his hips as he tugged her to the edge of the vanity. "Now I'll fill you." His words and actions, as Jake fitted himself against her, left her senses reeling. Then he thrust deep and she moaned.

They climaxed together and she clung to him, her fingers biting deep into his skin as she cried out her release, his grunt of exultation coming at the same time as his orgasm.

Simone opened her eyes and gave a tiny shiver. "That was some show, god-boy, but can we go back to bed? I'm cold."

He laughed, his chest moving. "Anything for my lady."

# EPILOGUE

Simone smiled and laid a hand across her heavily pregnant belly. "I really think I would have preferred the nursery to be mint colored, but I like this too." She chewed on her bottom lip as she surveyed the room, the tiny prints of Scotland and fairy tale locations fought teddy bears and rabbits for space.

"Simone, you have to be joking. Jake just finished painting it that pale violet." Cara's voice was full of humor.

"Oh, I'm not going to change it now. I just think I might need the linens to break up the color a little."

Jake winked at her. It was their secret that he'd conned some of his brownie friends into doing the work, leaving him time to put together the furniture.

Simone had promised to make them dinner—and to their surprise the other brownies had all accepted with alacrity.

"Whatever my sweetheart wants, she gets. Now, Cara, James was sending the car for you right about...now!" A honk from the street sounded as he spoke and Simone had to smother a laugh.

"I don't know how you do that. It's just spooky, like you can do some kind of magic." Cara leaned in and gave Simone a kiss on the cheek, their bellies touching, one stomach jostling the other.

It seemed appropriate that they were due within days of each other. And if what she'd seen at the park today was correct, so was Jane. When she'd mentioned it to Jake, he'd just got a broad grin on his face and said how much he loved his job.

Cara moved away, rubbing her hand over her belly. "Only three weeks to go." With a sigh she bent over and picked up her bag from the rocking chair. "Okay, well, James will be a mess until I get home, so I'd best go."

Jake followed Cara as she waddled in the direction of the door while Simone waited for his return. As the front door closed out the world she leaned against the wall. "You know, after everything, this still feels more like a dream than reality."

Even as he strode towards her, the heady thrill of being with this man forever filled her.

"If it's a dream, I never intend waking up. Now come on, Cailleach and Father are due here any moment for dinner and I want you off your feet."

Simone followed him down the hall.

If someone had told her a year ago that not only would she see Cara settled and married to James, but that she would also meet and fall for her very own Cupid and would be expecting their first child, she'd have laughed. "You know, this time last year, you and me... We were here..."

"Under very different circumstances. You don't regret anything, do you?"

Simone shook her head. "No. With you I'll never have regrets. I love you, Jake. I always will." She cupped his cheek with her hand, thinking over the time that had passed.

Senuna was now under the care of a talented healer. One day, Lugh had told her, she'd be well again. Until then, she'd receive whatever help and attention she required.

Simone settled herself on the seat he'd pulled out for her.

She'd married Jake. Twice. Once in a formal human ceremony and once in front of his family at his island house, before he'd relinquished it to the mists, telling her that he now had a true home. Her stomach jittered and she rubbed it, looking down. Cailleach and Lugh had also entrusted her with the gift of immortality, so that she and Jake would never be parted.

Her hand fastened around the glass Jake pushed at her. "Now drink up and take your vitamins. You need to be ready for the day we welcome our baby."

A light flared in the gathering gloom of evening. Simone looked up, ready to welcome the rest of her new family home.

**If you enjoyed this book by Imogene Nix why not check out some more of her titles by scrolling through to the following pages?**

# INHERITANCE OF THE BLOOD BY IMOGENE NIX

*In the darkness evil waits...*

As a young bride Kira was whisked away from everything and everyone she knew, including her new husband and became Christina, an operative of the Displaced Persons Unit.

As the danger grows she sees an opportunity to save her husband Vasya and sister Serina. But nothing is the same. Serina is grown up—married and pregnant.

Vasya too is older and darkly forbidding. Trusting Christina doesn't come easily until a catastrophic event takes place. Now, knowing the truth everything he thought he knew is changed. But at a very high cost.

The four must work together to defeat the Demon, Zuor and the stakes are higher than they imagined and all could be lost.

---

*The burning at the back of her neck warned she was being watched. A quick glance didn't clarify it. Instead, she turned around in time to see her mother's face, pale. "Mama?"*

*She took a step forward, but her grandfather snatched her wrist.*

*The grip was painful, and Kira stilled. "Let your parents talk."*

*She didn't know what the topic of conversation was, but it couldn't be good.*

*The dappled sunlight seemed cooler than before.*

*Her father crooked his forefinger at her grandfather while they stood there. For a moment she wished Vasya had come with them, but he had to work. Just the thought of her new husband warmed Kira.*

*She only had a few minutes to contemplate her newly defined status as a married woman, when her grandfather pulled at her hand. "Come with me." He tugged and, confused, Kira allowed herself to be towed away.*

*A glance at her parents' faces stole any feeling of well-being.*

*"Grandfather?"*

*"Shh, my love. You must go." His grip was implacable and his face stern, but he shivered.*

*"What are you doing? Where are you taking me, Grandfather?"*

*They moved rapidly through the village they'd visited to sell their wares just that morning, and for the first time since they'd arrived in the market place she felt fear. What was wrong? Was it something to do with Vasya?*

*"You are in danger. We must send you away." The words confused her further. Send her away? Danger?*

*"Where is Vasya?" She stumbled over a stone, but he kept tugging her onwards.*

*With a quick glance around, he hauled her into a dirty laneway between the buildings. Kira gasped, trying to drag air into her starving lungs. "There's no time. We must get you away."*

*A nondescript shopfront lay ahead, and he pushed on the door. It rattled and opened with a loud groan. "Andre? Andre, are you here?"*

*An older man shuffled into the room, bent nearly double from the weight of the load on his back. "Marat? What do you want?"*

*"My granddaughter. They are coming for her and us. Get her away. Take her now, while you can."*

*The man's face clouded over. "Are you sure?"*

*"Grandfather, where is Vasya?" Fright had the blood in her veins pounding.*

*"Hush, my precious. Andre will see you well." He turned. "Whatever it takes, Andre. Take her now." With surprising speed, her grandfather whirled and was gone.*

*The man, Andre, eyed her. "Come this way, child. There is no time to be lost."*

*Eleven years later*

The tattoo of her heart and cry of terror woke her, as they usually did. Once again, as she had since that rapid flight from those who sought her, she found herself in a lonely bed. Hundreds of miles away from everything she'd dreamed of, in a house she'd built for them to share. As always, it left her wishing that Vasya had fled with her.

Instead, here she was, exiled without her husband. With a sob, she rolled over and let the tears fall.

Available from Beachwalk Press
**books2read.com/IOTB**

Direct Autographed Copy

http://bit.ly/2w6g4K6

# HERO OF HEARTBREAK HALL

*Second chances can be a killer...*

When Connor meets Kelly it's clear that she's been hurt before and the reason she fights the growing attraction between them.

When her past raises its ugly head, the question becomes: can the outback town of Heartbreak Hill—and Connor—heal her broken heart?

---

The sound of a car slowly inching up the road had her turning and the fear that she'd been so sure she'd thrown off swamped her. The car inching into her driveway was a white four wheel drive. *Connor.*

He would understand if she told him she didn't feel up to tonight. Cowardly though the thought was, she did, for just a moment, considered shutting him out.

He closed the car door and advanced towards her, his long strides eating up the gravelled path and he carried two bottles of wine—a joking reminder of their first unofficial outing together.

When he caught sight of her face, his tightened, gaze narrowed and lips thinned. "What's wrong?"

She struggled to find the words, but the hot sting of tears burned. "I... I need to tell you about me, Connor. There's so much I haven't..."

Finding the words proved difficult, but he carefully stood the wine bottles on the small outdoor table and took her hands in his. The warmth of his palms scorched her frozen fingers and Kelly realised that in the time since the call, she'd chilled.

"Kelly, let me help you."

He would. He'd do everything in his power to keep her nightmares at bay she realised. The last six months of outings and dates had been marred by her inability to share her history with him. It was past time to rectify that.

"Connor, come sit down." She patted the chair beside the one she was perched in.

Available from Beachwalk Press
**books2read.com/HeartbreakHillHero**

Direct Autographed Copy

http://bit.ly/2UeC90V

# BIOCYBE BY IMOGENE NIX

*Can a cyber-enhanced warrior and a ship's captain find love together?*

Levia Endrado never wanted to be a warrior, but at seventeen she was deemed suitable for battle. After intense training and multiple enhancements, which gave her superior strength and healing ability, she was sent off to defeat the enemy—a killing machine with a mission.

When the war was over, she had to find a new life. At twenty-seven she's a washed-up veteran without a future. Or she was, until she met Sandon Daria.

Serving as a pilot aboard Sandon's spaceship the *Golden Echo* makes Levia long for a different and gentler life. But old hurts and even older enemies aren't so easily forgotten. Particularly when they come back for her.

Sandon is determined to show Levia that she's more than just a BioCybe...she's the woman who completes him. Getting close is just the first step, keeping her alive is an even bigger challenge, but one he's willing to take because the prize is their combined future.

--------------------------------

Levia scanned the long line of other hopefuls entering the chamber. The large building in the center of town was cold, and she dragged her wrap around her body, even as she craned her head, looking to the high ceiling. She'd never before had an occasion to enter the testing complex, yet she'd seen the lines of teenagers every time they passed the building.

Once she'd asked her parents why the teens were lined up and her mother's face had shuttered. Her stepfather had just shaken his head and growled. They'd stopped her questions with a carefully uttered, "You'll know soon enough, Levia." The pain in her mother's eyes had been enough to shush her questions. For endless months afterward, her parents had traveled different routes to the educational facility she attended and Levia lost interest in the puzzle of that building.

Now, as she looked around, remembering that long ago spring day, it was her opportunity to find out. But she felt a surge of concern at what lay ahead. She likely wasn't the only one, given that there were probably two to three hundred seventeen-year-olds gathered in the one place. Ahead of her, she caught sight of a couple of girls, their arms linked together and wide smiles on their faces. Scanning the crowd, she became aware that, by far, a majority of those gathered displayed both fear and trepidation.

"All female subjects will enter through doors three, six, and seven. All male subjects will enter through gates four, eight, and ten." The speaker above her was loud, and she jumped before checking the numbers etched on the black metal sign over her head.

The massive doors beside her swung open, and now an uncertain silence reigned. Many of the youngsters hung back, clearly discomforted by whatever testing regime lay ahead. This was where they'd been told their futures would be determined.

"Oh gosh, I hope they only have an aptitude and psych eval. I don't think..." Levia turned to see the white face of the girl behind her. The girl had uttered what many must silently be thinking.

Levia dragged an unsteady breath in, her hand resting flat against the plane of her belly as she looked around. No one had entered yet. It was clear many were on the verge of taking the step, but still they hung back.

She straightened her shoulders. "I'm not afraid." It was always wiser to approach things head-on, she believed. When her biological father had died, she'd been one of the few to view his capsule before it was sent into the massive gray structure built to accommodate those who'd moved onto the next life realm.

Her legs shook as she wobbled toward the entrance. Beyond the doorway, she spied sealed cubicles and her heart stuttered. Why cubicles? Usually testing—med and psych—were in eval-units, hidden only by billowing white curtains. She glanced back, noting that others had taken the first step.

"Move along, subjects." Once again, the androgynous voice of the address system blared.

Of course, given it was her seventeenth anniversary of birth, she was technically considered an adult now.

She thought longingly of baby Rald and her half-sister, Elda, waiting at home for her to return, and the celebrations to be held that night. That made her smile. She would need to make them proud of her.

She entered a row and the tall Educational Specialist, the edu-specs as her peers laughingly called them, stopped her. "Present your credentials to the scanner."

She'd done this many times since the tiny implant had been slipped below the dermal layer of her skin at birth. The small unit in her wrist heated as her details were checked.

"Enter the first cubicle, Levia Endrado, and follow the instructions to complete your assessment."

Thus dismissed, Levia moved to the first unit, laid her palm against the scanner, and the door slid open soundlessly.

"Welcome, Levia Endrado. Take your place in the eval-unit." The soft contralto of the voice echoed after the door closed silently behind her.

"What are you evaluating?" Her voice was breathy, and she peered around.

"Your skills—physical and psychological. Your emotional and medical status. Your educational attainment levels."

It was an answer that shed little insight into the many things she was hungry to know. "Why do all seventeen year olds—"

"Take a seat, Levia. Then we may begin your testing."

If she'd expected an answer, she was sadly mistaken, she considered sourly. She dropped into the seat, the soft leather-like surface molding to her body.

"Levia Endrado, you are required to remove all non-specified apparel."

She jolted in the chair. "It's cold."

"The temperature will be amended. Remove the non-specified apparel."

Her misgivings grew as she dragged off the light wrap she'd brought with her, and then threw it to the floor at the side of the unit.

"We will begin, Levia Endrado. At any time, should you experience any malfunctions of the unit, simply depress the red button." It glowed and she grimaced.

Levia reclined against the chair and waited for the testing to begin.

The first examination was based on her understanding of the

political system, where she saw herself, and her knowledge of the rights and responsibilities accorded through citizenship of both her planet and the commonwealth.

The second test was mathematical and scientific proficiency. It felt like hours had passed by the time she'd finished, and she lay limp on the seat, exhausted.

"Levia Endrado, you may rise. The sanitary unit will emerge once you trigger the yellow button at the door. Should you require refreshment, press the blue button and a restorative will be made available."

"Can I leave?"

"Negative, Levia Endrado. Your needs will be catered for in this capsule."

"Why?" Her voice hitched and true fear rose for the first time. Why did they keep her in the alcove?

"All will be revealed at the end of the testing cycle."

Levia looked at the now empty screen before hurling a curse word. It was met with silence.

The urgent throb of her bladder reminded her that she needed to use the facilities, so, with

a sigh, she rose and clambered from the seat. After attending to the needs of her body, she walked around the unit, peering at the door, but it was obviously programmed remotely. She poked and prodded, but it made no difference. With a huff, she headed back to the chair.

The moment she'd settled in, the viewing screen shone bright. "Welcome back, Levia. The next sequence will evaluate your psychological reflexes, then that will be followed up with the general knowledge portion of the evaluation."

"When can I leave?" It seemed better to ask bluntly, she told herself.

"Once the examination is completed. After the next set of evaluations, you will be subjected to the physical aspect."

"Then I can go home?"

"Levia Endrado, you will now complete the psychological test. This will be undertaken by one of the center's personal evaluators."

She frowned. Personal evaluators? She bit her lip, and the sting reminded her that this wasn't something to joke about. In her seventeen years, she'd only heard of personal evaluators being brought in once before, and that was when one of the girls at her academy had been in a serious accident. Both legs were amputated and her body's ability to keep her alive had been gravely compromised. Her peers had been informed that the girl had requested the assessment before she could request her support systems be disconnected.

"Levia Endrado, are you ready to recommence processing?" The emotionless voice echoed once more and she gulped.

"Yes."

Available from Beachwalk Press
http://www.beachwalkpress.com

Direct Autographed Books
http://bit.ly/BioCybe

# ALSO BY IMOGENE NIX

**Warriors of the Elector**

- Star of Ishtar
- Starline
- Starfire
- Star of the Fleet
- Starburst
- The Star of Eternity

The Star of Ishtar & Starline - Print

Starfire & Star of the Fleet - Print

Starburst & The Star of Eternity - Print

**Blood Secrets (Re-releasing 2020)**

- The Blood Bride
- The Illuminated Witch
- The Sorcerer's Touch

**The Search Duology**

- Miss Elspeth's Desire
- Miss Isabelle's Craving (Not Yet Released)

**Reunion Trilogy**

- War's End
- The Assassin
- Executing Justice

The Reunion Trilogy in Paperback

### Sex Love & Aliens

- Tangled Webs
- False Webs
- Covert Webs

### 21st Testing Protocol

- Cyborg: Redux (Not Yet Released)
- Children Of A Greater Evil (Not Yet Released)
- When Evil Came To Stay (Not Yet Released)
- Finis: The War To End All Wars (Not Yet Released)

### Celtic Cupid Trilogy

- Blame The Wine
- A Stranger's Embrace
- Revenge On Cupid

The Celtic Cupid Trilogy in Paperback

### Zombieology

- The Reset (2018)

### Single Titles

The Chocolate Affair

A Sapphire for Karina

BioCybe

Hesparia's Tears

Tomorrow's Promise

A Bar In Paris

Inheritance Of The Blood

The Plan

Loving Memories

Hero of Heartbreak Hill

Raspberry Dreams (Not Yet Released)

## Non Fiction

Self Publishing: Absolute Beginners Guide (With Suzi Love)

## Written as Ciara Cave

25 Curated Ways To Get Rid Of Telemarketers

Book Signings for Absolute Beginners

# ABOUT THE AUTHOR

Imogene is published in a range of romance genres including Paranormal, Science Fiction and Contemporary. She is mainly published in the UK and USA.

In 2010, Imogene Nix (the pen name not Imogene herself) was born. Imogene sat down and worked tirelessly for 3 months culminating in the book Starline, which became the first in a trilogy titled, "Warriors of the Elector." Since then she's had over 30 titles published and is now focusing on hybridising herself - with a mixture of traditionally published and self-published works.

In fact, she's taking control of many of her back catalogue books, which are slowly re-releasing as self-published titles.

Imogene is a member of a range of professional organisations world wide, and believes in the mantra of mentoring and paying it forward and is actively involved in mentorship (through NaNoWrimo and her vlog: In The Chair With Imogene Nix) and tutoring of new and upcoming authors.

In her spare time she loves to drink coffee, wine & eat chocolate and is parenting 2 spoiled dogs and a ferocious cat along with her husband and 2 human daughters and looks forward to weekends away with her husband in their caravan "The Seven Year Hitch!" Do look forward to her caravan romance at some point!

*To Contact Imogene*

www.imogenenix.net
imogene@imogenenix.net

facebook.com/ImogeneNix

twitter.com/ImogeneNix

instagram.com/ImogeneNix

www.ingramcontent.com/pod-product-compliance
Lightning Source LLC
Chambersburg PA
CBHW071459110726
47908CB00003B/663